S0-AAB-085

Post-High School
Reality Quest

A CALIFORNIA COLDBLOOD BOOK
RARE BIRD BOOKS

LOS ANGELES, CALIF.

High School Quest

**A TEXT ADVENTURE
FOR YOUNG ADULT READERS**

BY MEG EDEN

Set in Minion
Cover design by Leonard Philbrick. Credits: Pribanovalenka.
Meme illustrations by Stefano Terry.
Printed in the United States
Distributed by Publishers Group West

Publisher's Cataloging-in-Publication data

Names: Eden, Meg, author.

Title: Post–High School Reality Quest / by Meg Eden.

Description: Los Angeles, CA: California Coldblood Books, 2017.

Identifiers: ISBN 978-1945572234

Subjects: LCSH Human-computer interaction—Fiction. | Computer games—Fiction.

| Teenage girls—Fiction. | Mental illness—Fiction. | Science fiction. | BISAC YOUNG

ADULT FICTION / Science Fiction / General.

Classification: LCC PZ7.E221 Po 2017 | DDC [Fic]—dc23

For Vince, and all those walks and pep talks that kept me writing.

Hello, World:
May 25, 2010

YOU ARE IN A PSYCHIATRIST'S office.

> No, I'm not.

I'm sorry, I don't understand "no, I'm not." Who do you think they're going to believe? The narrator, or the character who is here because she was found living in a telephone booth on the other side of town, talking to herself?

> This is a *doctor's* office. It's a safe space. Psychiatrist sounds so…

Judgmental?

> Yes. Exactly.

Well, I'm sorry to break it to you but you *are* in a psychiatrist's office. You're here because yesterday your father found you in the last existing telephone booth in your town, after driving around for days. You were sitting on the floor, stuffed up against the phone, telling someone you wanted them to stop following you, that you were tired of being *hacked into*. When your father finally wrestled you out of the telephone booth, you accused him of working for *the game* and tried to hit him with the telephone receiver.

> I *did*?

Do you remember any of this? Your mother brought you in first thing this morning, says she's been worried about you for a while. That you've never been very social.

> What do I have to do to get rid of you?

Don't rage quit, Buffy. It's unbecoming.

You look down at your wrists. They're locked into the chair you're sitting in. Man, they must really think you're crazy.

You know your mother means well. She just wants to make sure you feel like there's a way for you to talk about what you've been experiencing recently—

> What's there to talk about? If you'd just leave me alone, then there'd be no telephone booths, no problem!

Isn't that oversimplifying a little? What exactly does a player do without a game?

> You make it sound like I want to be playing a game in the first place.

Well, you are the one that started it, so yes—it sort of seems to be a given that you would *want* to be playing a game. Just maybe not the one that this turned out to be.

You sigh and lean back in your chair. You hit the headrest. You hit it over and over, into what might almost be a consoling rhythm.

You wonder: Is that something a normal person does? Or only a crazy person? Or maybe just any kind of person, when they're fed up with everything not going the way they planned?

The door opens.

"Hello, Elizabeth."

"Buffy."

"Sorry, Buffy. I'm Dr. Moritz, I'm here to check in and see what's going on. I hear that something's been bothering you. Could you tell me what's been going on?"

"I'm not crazy. I didn't mean to do anything—I just wanted to get away."

"Your mother says that before you ran away, you asked to stop living on campus. Could you tell me if something happened to lead up to yesterday's incident?"

Where to start? *"It was getting hard to be around people."*

"Your mother mentioned that your father heard you talking to yourself, that you talked about trying to 'cut it out.' Do you know what that was referring to?"

"The game. There's a game stuck inside of me."

"A game? Well, that's a first for me. But I suppose stress can manifest itself in all sorts of ways. Do you think this 'game' could be like that, a way to handle stress?"

A shrug.

"I see. So, when was the first time you started 'playing' this game?"

Graduation:
May 12, 2009

Y OU ARE IN THE CAFETERIA. There is a high school graduation happening. Mason, the valedictorian, is giving her farewell to the class. It takes a long time.

In your pocket, there is a letter. It's crumpled and smeared from you reaching in and touching it so many times, to make sure it's still there.

Exits are: out, back, and stage.

Tristan was almost valedictorian. He was about .002 points away from it. And he makes sure to not let any of you forget. Not that you'd ever forget a single word he's ever said.

> Back.

You get up from your chair and go to the back of the room. There is a piano. You look longingly at it.

> Examine piano.

You go over the piano. You run your fingers over the keys but are too shy to actually play anything. That's what everyone says about you: that you want to do something but never actually do it. That's why you wear gothic Lolita dresses only at home, curl your hair once a month, and paint on the weekends. Anything else might be too much.

> Exit out.

You are now in the main hallway. It is very long. There are lots of doors.

You wonder if you hide in one of them long enough you can avoid growing up. Everyone says that after today, everything that you do actually matters. That every decision you make will invariably have consequences on your existence and wellbeing. The only consequences you're used to are not saving before entering the water temple in *Ocarina of Time*, or using up your master ball before encountering Mewtwo in *Pokémon-Red*.

Exits are: cafeteria, door, another door, bathroom, main office, and out.

> Door?

You go into one of the doors. It's not very exciting.

> Out.

You are now in the main hallway. It is very—

You go into the bathroom. There is an acidic smell you can't quite place coming from the stalls. Sephora is in front of the mirror, fluffing her insignificant breasts. No one believes her birth name is actually Sephora but no one has any proof to say otherwise. She doesn't look like a make-up model but you keep that kind of commentary to yourself.

Exits are: bathroom stall and out.

"You dying out there too?" Sephora asks, pressing her hands on her stomach. "It's so humid in that small room."

You nod. "Yeah, it's really hot." You feel sweat run through your hair, down your scalp.

"When there's a whole twenty people graduating, you'd think it'd be shorter than this. But they still find a way to make us miserable." Sephora reapplies a layer of lipstick. "And this uniform makes me look even fatter than usual. Ugh."

You just graduated from a religious high school. You say religious because, as hard as it is for you to stomach the concept of a god, words like *transubstantiation* are even less comprehensible to you. And as much as your music class sings about concepts like grace, the signs posted on every door with commandments like: *skirts shorter than your finger-tips are unacceptable* and *earrings should be no larger than a nickel,* have made you eager for the alleged freedom of college.

And not just freedom from rules, but freedom from people like Sephora, who are "your friends" only because of your small school population. Because everyone has to survive somehow, and it's dangerous to go alone.

But you've survived, at least this far. Congratulations.

Sephora sighs, scratching at the dead skin on her cheek. "I can't wait 'til the sun comes out again. I mean, look at my skin! I need to tan again."

Even if you hadn't seen Sephora in size 00 bikinis before, one look at Sephora makes it clear that she has the Scottish pasty skin that never tans. Just like you. Besides your gender and your love of obscure video games, this is all you have in common with her.

"You know, now that summer's coming, I'm thinking about trying something new, just for the kicks." Sephora looks you in the eye. "I'm even thinking about going out with Tristan. Who knows. It might be fun! And I've been seeing him eye me…"

You want to tell Sephora that she's too stupid to date someone as brilliant as Tristan, that he has better taste than that, but you can't seem to get the words out.

> Wrestle Sephora to the ground.

You wrestle the lipstick from her hands and scream, "you whore!" and write mean things on the mirror. Then you stuff her head in the toilet and prevent this horrible story from actually happening.

And by that, you only daydream of wrestling Sephora to the ground.

If you had actually done that, you might've beaten the game in record time. Assuming life's a game and you remembered to save more frequently.

> I don't like this story.

I'm sorry. I don't understand "I don't like this story." You think we get to choose our stories?

> Go into bathroom stall.

You go into a bathroom stall. You pull up your graduation gown, unzip your skinny jeans, and let them fall to your ankles but you don't sit on the toilet. You don't pee. You just stand there and say softly, "Why Tristan?"

What you don't say is that you've loved Tristan for the past three years for reasons that can't be disclosed at this time.

"'Why'? Does there have to be a 'why'?" You hear Sephora smack her lips, like she's testing the durability of her lipstick. "I mean, he's nice. He's cute. He won't cause any drama and I don't have a summer romance planned yet. Plus, I think he might be interested, which always makes things easier."

> Check inventory.

You check your inventory[1]. In your bag, you have:

- two unopened tampons
- Tristan's graduation picture (which you were way too excited to get a hold of; it's creased in the corners)
- your wallet with ten bucks for Merrill's pizza money, even though you don't eat pizza (Merrill is the mafia lord of pizza, after all)
- a fake rose someone gave you for graduating
- a drawing of a narwhal you drew one day during class[2]
- a pack of "emergency" crackers

---

1 In middle school, you nicknamed your backpack "inventory." You thought it was clever. Man, you really are a freak.

2 You've always loved narwhals ever since you saw them in an aquatic animals picture book. The narwhal is always pictured alone, swimming in deep benthic waters. You can relate to him, in a way. You just have to ignore the true meaning of his name: corpse whale.

- a letter from someone you do not know and cannot remember what it says.

Then of course, there's that paper in your pocket that you stuff deeper into the creases of your pants.

"Buffy?" Sephora calls when you don't say anything.

> Attempt to kill myself.

You might wanna rethink that—

You make a noise. It's the sound of drowning.

You stuff your own head in the toilet. It's better this way.

Except that you forgot to save again.

You are now dead. Thank you for playing POST–HIGH SCHOOL REALITY QUEST! Would you like to load a saved game?

YOU ARE IN A CAFETERIA. There is a high school graduation happening. There is a piano in the corner. Mason is finishing her farewell address and, in the audience, Tristan grumbles about not being up there instead.

Exits are: out, back, and stage.

> Stage.

You get up on the stage. Mason is very mad. Everyone else cheers. You feel like you're the hero of an unwritten novel until the principal beats you over the head with his podium. You are now dead. Thank you for playing POST–HIGH SCHOOL REALITY QUEST! Would you like to load a saved game?

> Sorry. I've just always wanted to do that sort of thing.

AFTER THE CEREMONY, EVERYONE GOES outside to talk and take pictures. Your legs shake as you step forward. You touch the paper in your pocket. You're going to make something of your life today.

Outside, Merrill's mom is trying to get a picture of your group.

"Buffy!" She waves. "You got a minute? We're still waiting for Tristan and Sephora, but I'm sure we'll find them soon…"

You feel your chest clench and your mouth suddenly go dry.

> North!

You run past Merrill's mom, between parents taking pictures of their kids. An over-defensive mother calls you out for being rude, but you'll never see most of these people ever again. Maybe you'll never see any of them again.

You feel the blood rush to your head—that's exactly why you need to find Tristan, fast.

You have reached the end of the parking lot to the road. Across the street, there is a church graveyard that no one visits except the goths, art students, and couples that want to make out during lunch break.

> Cross road.

You cross the road. A mini van pulling out of the parking lot honks at you. But you're not dead. Not yet.

> Enter graveyard.

You open the graveyard gate. There are lots of tombstones, but few of them have legible names. One day, you'll have a tombstone somewhere.

> North.

You cross through the graveyard toward the big willow tree at the other end. Your instincts were right, because from the distance you see Sephora and Tristan talking. Sephora's leaning against the tree, tucking her hair behind her ear over and over. Her mannerisms are so contrived that you want to go up and vomit into her hair.

> Hide behind farthest tombstone.

There's only so close you can get without being obvious. From your tombstone shelter, you see Tristan reach for Sephora with his awkward thin fingers, holding her upper arms and slowly approaching her. Even from the distance, you can see Sephora's smile as he brings his head close, bends over, and leans his forehead on hers. As far as you know, Tristan's never dated anyone, let alone kissed before. Maybe he was just waiting for someone, anyone to show interest in him.

Your hand reaches for the paper in your pocket.

> Examine paper.

You pull out the paper and ball it in your fist. You throw it over the tombstone and walk back to the parking lot.

You are in the graveyard, and you are in a cafeteria, simultaneously. There is a high school graduation happening. You reach over the rows, hand Tristan the paper. Merrill sees it. Sephora sees it. Tristan unfolds the paper, reads it, smiles, folds the paper, puts it in his pocket. He never mentions it— never acknowledges the letter that says you love him, that you don't want graduation to be the last time you see the only people that matter to you, that you're afraid of losing his friendship when college starts.

You are in the graveyard, leaving the graveyard, in the road. Maybe the letter was too heavy-handed. You've never been good at expressing your thoughts and feelings. Does it really matter? Sephora and Tristan won't last long. You are about to enter college; there will be so many other people. So many other friends. You might fall in love with someone else, someone better than Tristan. Heck—you might never see Tristan again anyway.

But what gets you is that feeling that something has just ended. You've never reached the end of anything before. All of the cartridges and discs in your room, you've never finished any of those games, never won any of them before.

> I will win something, eventually.

"I guess that's the first time I heard it. But it didn't seem so weird at the time. I mean like, before graduation, when I was applying for schools, trying to figure out where to go, and getting all the letters for the scholarships I didn't win, I'd make these brief jokes to myself like: 'you are in a room. Exits are: community college, state school, out of state, working at Kmart.' It was never anything serious, though, nothing that lasted longer than a minute. In fact, it was funny—it made me feel like I had some control over my situation. Or maybe even better, distance from it. Like it wasn't my life that was falling apart, but someone in a game's, and I was just playing through it all, and just as easily I could walk away and start over at any point in time…But then at graduation, it was like I couldn't get out of my own joke. Like I was stuck in my own game."

AT NIGHT, YOU TRY TO wrestle with the philosophical question of why Tristan would willingly choose someone like Sephora instead of you. You've begun compiling a list of obvious reasons:

You forget to shave your legs, unlike Sephora who has bragging rights over having knock-out skinny, clean legs.

When you're friends with a guy too long, it's like they forget you're actually female/dateable.

Tristan likes brunettes. You've gone over this already.

Tristan's mostly oblivious to everything.

You've done nothing to make it known to him that you're even an option.

Before you fall asleep, you imagine going to the store and buying some brunette

hair dye.

You are in Merrill's house. I really don't know why you come here. But you come every Saturday to do nothing. It smells like his mom's cigarettes and dusty crocheted dolls. If you think about it for too long it becomes unsettling, how the antique smell of the room can transfer onto you, so that when you go home and change your clothes, they smell like Merrill. There are some things that aren't so easy to get rid of.

Exits are: upstairs and out.

> Out.

You go out the back door. Merrill asks where you're going. He says they all have just started a new game he insists is cool this time. There's only one cookie left on the plate his mom left down here, but you don't take it.

What *are* you doing?

You are outside of Merrill's house. There's no house number on the mailbox but you know the house number is 404. Sometimes, it's like the house doesn't exist.

Sometimes you all shoot fireworks from this yard. But that's illegal in this state.

Exits are: window, woods, street, backdoor.

> Window?

You climb in through the window. For a moment, it makes you the star of the show. You fall from the ceiling straight onto the couch, where Tristan is sitting.

> SAVE.

You save. Good job.

Everyone looks at you like you're a misplaced angel or a piece of falling dry wall. Tristan doesn't push you off, but neither does he embrace you the way you dream he would. But his warm lap is enough to keep you motivated for the next month.

Sephora turns her head toward you. With just her eyebrow movement, she conveys a desire to eat you whole and never let you see the light of day again.

> SAVE.

You save. You have used all your save slots.

Merrill doesn't look. Merrill has already given up on his tabletop strategy game and turned on the Xbox. He's playing *Halo Live* against someone named DELMAR. You think of the Delmarva Peninsula, and how polluted the water is.

Exits are: off Tristan's lap.

> Why would I *do* that?

"Buffy—we're almost done making our characters," Tristan says, as if the fact you are on his lap has no significance. He points to a blank paper on the coffee table that's meant for you. His legs are so long that it makes you feel small.

> Get off Tristan's lap.

You get off Tristan's lap, your movements slow and disjointed. Tristan smiles awkwardly at you in a way that's complicated to translate.

He hands you the paper, sending a glare to Merrill. "We *were* making characters, until Merrill decided that's too hard. Said at least *Halo*'s already got the characters made, and you can still shoot things."

"Yup," Merrill shouts from across the room, his curly dark hair pressed to the back of his head from too many days of not showering.

He says, "If you fill out your character profile, we might convince Merrill to play. He'll be outnumbered, see?"

> Examine room.

You look around the room. It is full of very bored looking people. These are your friends.

Do they have to be your friends?

> What kind of question is that?

Post-High-School Reality Quest

Sorry. Right. It's a personal choice, who you choose to associate with.

Tristan sighs. What sort of character did Tristan make, anyway? He's not exactly known for his creativity. That's why his Xbox Live screen name is: tristan_watson, and his email is tristan_watson@gmail.com.

The character sheets stay on the coffee table. They are stained with pizza grease after sitting around too long.

> "Steal" empty character sheet.

You put your empty character sheet into your inventory.

Merrill says, "We got pizza, Buffy. We got cheese for you."

You are vegan.

You thank Merrill for his effort but don't move. You don't like the way Sephora's glancing at Tristan, and it's not at his face. She's never glanced at him like that before.

> Try to do something productive.

You ask, "So...are we gonna do something?"

Merrill shrugs. Sephora starts dancing in her seat, and you notice Tristan's eyes glancing to the edge of her rising skirt.

This sort of situation should be considered normal by now; every time you come over, nothing really happens. But today, you want a revolution, before everyone is in college and gone. You look at Tristan, wanting him to notice you, but it's clear nothing will happen—Tristan will not fall in love with you today, the group will never get focused on playing a game together, and Sephora will always be the bane of your existence.

Exits are: bathroom, out, up, window.

> Get out of this place.

Your head feels a little light. You say you need to go home, that you're not feeling too good tonight.

No one looks up. Merrill turns quickly from the screen, scratching his head and saying, "See ya."

With that, you leave. No one follows you.

YOU ARE OUTSIDE MERRILL'S HOUSE. There is a tree you never noticed before. It is very dark out here.

Exits are: right, left, woods.

> Turn right.

You turn right down the street. Down to your own house, if you can remember where it is.

Is that where you're trying to go?

Do you even remember?

A DARK ROOM. SOMEONE'S JUST TURNED on the lights—they're so small, fiber optics. From the table, they look like stars embedded in the ceiling.

"Now, we're gonna see if we can figure out what exactly's going on in that head of yours…"

The white paper gown rustles against the table.

In the dim light, he looks oddly like Tristan's dad—with the sandy blond hair, rough shadow of a beard, and this inexplicable way that he holds his fists that makes him convincingly like an alligator wrestler.

"Are you from…Australia?"

He laughs. "That's a funny question." He holds out earplugs. "Now I need you to just lean back until your head rests into this frame on the bed."

How many of my questions are "funny"?

"I'm actually from Auckland, oddly enough." He takes a plastic helmet in his hands. "That's in New Zealand, you know. Now I'm about to put this helmet over your face—it will snap into the frame underneath your head."

The helmet has two holes for eyes, but besides that, my body is encapsulated.

"I might have claustrophobic tendencies…"

"Ah, you'll do fine." The man presses a button on the panel beside you, raising the bed. "It's only a quick scan. You can even take a nap during it— won't even remember you're in there. Now I'm about to move the table in. You ready?"

I feel like I might vomit but I bite my lip and tell him yes. The table speeds into a tunnel, and I feel like I'm in some capsule spaceship, about to fly across the universe. But instead, someone's about to see what's going on inside my brain. Somehow, that seems like a much more frightening frontier.

I T'S ABOUT FOUR WEEKS BEFORE school starts and there's a feeling like you're counting the days until your funeral. As much as you dislike your current life at home, at least it's familiar. You've heard stories of what happens to people in college: they get shot, mugged, wasted, and charged absurdly high fees for parking tickets.

Merrill texts you about the other night. "Are you feeling okay?" he asks. "You left kinda early, even for you."

It's not like Merrill to text you about your feelings. You wonder what he really means, if anything.

> Maintain a state of normalcy.

"I'm okay," you lie. "I was just tired."

He doesn't ask if it was about Tristan, but you wonder if he already knows.

YOU ARE AT BED BATH and Beyond with your mom, buying things for your new dorm room. You don't understand why this is necessary—don't you already have sheets, clothes, and an alarm clock? What else do you need?

Your mom says that this is supposed to be a "special treat" for you, an opportunity for you to pick out what you really want. She says she doesn't want you "to feel stuck with what you have right now," wants you to feel like "you can start with something fresh and new." It's like she knows that you're coping with loss and need a restart. That, or she sincerely thinks that your life revolves around what your bedding looks like.

"Are you excited?" your mom asks. "It's less than a month away now."

Excited isn't exactly the word that comes to mind. But out of courtesy, you nod.

"I had so much fun in college," your mom says. "You get to really find yourself. It's not like high school where they tell you what to take; you get to do what you want to."

You're not sure if that sounds invigorating or troubling, having to make even more decisions.

"Plus, you're not stuck with the same groups of people—and where you're going, there are *so* many students. You'll get to find the friends *you* want to hang out with. I mean—not that your friends aren't nice..."

You stop walking. "What's that supposed to mean?"

She laughs, adjusting her earring. "It's just—I understand what it must be like, being in a small school, being stuck with lots of people you'd rather not be with. Things get easier in a way, when you get to choose who to spend your time with. It might cheer you up a bit, being with different people—"

"I don't need cheering up," you say, your arms folding over your chest.

> It's because the A/C's cold in here.

"I didn't say you did!" Your mom puts her hands up in defense. She totally thinks you need cheering up. "I just see you with your friends—and well…"

"My friends are *fine*. I *love* my friends."

> Do I?

"All I'm saying is who knows? In college, you find the people who are there for the rest of your life, your best friends, people who stick beside you through thick and thin. You might even find a special someone…"

Your mom has been making pointed conversations toward dating since sophomore year of high school. It's something you've almost gotten used to, except that you haven't.

There is nothing wrong in your world. Everything is absolutely perfect. *Everything*.

YOU ARE WITH YOUR MOM in the middle of Bed Bath and Beyond. Everything is absurdly overpriced, and whenever you think about how much the things in your shopping cart cost, it makes you want to bend over and vomit. But as you look through the electronics aisle, you see something that makes you want to vomit even more: at the end of the aisle, you see Tristan and Sephora, holding each other's faces. They start kissing, and it's clear that Tristan knows nothing about kissing. They make all sorts of weird sounds, but Sephora seems forgiving of it all. You wish you could be the one forgiving him.

> Follow them.

You run past the electronics and As Seen on TV merchandise, down to the kitchenware, hoping to come up behind them. In the process, though, you are confronted by box after box emblazoned with Billy Mays' smiling face. May he rest in peace.

"Beth?" your mom calls, trying to catch up to you with the cart. "Where are you going?"

> Save.

You've saved over your own graduation.

In that moment, something feels irrevocably lost.

You get behind a Tervis tumbler stand and start throwing tumblers at the back of Sephora's head. She makes this whimpering noise and turns around. All she sees is a stand of tumblers.

Tristan asks if she's okay, and she nods. They return to kissing.

> So much for that.

You turn to the wall shelves, where there are stacks of heavy ceramic tableware.

> Take a box of plates.

You take a box of plates from the bottom. You think about opening the box, taking each plate one by one, and throwing them at Sephora's head.

Wow. You have a sick, twisted mind, Buffy.

> And who's fault is that, do you think?

You look at the box of plates in your hands. *Plates are so delicate,* you think to yourself. Unfortunately for you, the remaining plates stack is unsettled, and a series of boxes falls on top of you. Before you die, you catch a glimpse of what looks like Tristan's head. His nice dark hair. And you think about how much you love him and want him.

You are now dead. Thank you for playing POST–HIGH SCHOOL REALITY QUEST! Would you like to load a saved game?

You ARE WITH YOUR MOM in the middle of Bed Bath and Beyond. There is—

> Strangle the text parser.

I'm sorry. I don't understand "strangle the text parser."

> Text parser.

Yes, that's me. It's my job to make your stay as safe and boring as possible.

> Clearly, you're not doing a very good job on the "safe" part. How many times have I died since we've started this—

I'm sorry, I don't understand "Clearly, you're not doing a very good job." Trust me. You need me. Who do you think brings you back every time you die?

You ARE WITH YOUR MOM in the middle of Bed Bath and Beyond. Just an aisle away, Sephora and Tristan are kissing their hearts out. Your mom asks what you're thinking in terms of room design. "You are the artist after all," she says.

Sephora is kissing Tristan. In the fluorescent store light, you notice just how skinny and Barbie-like she looks. How totally not fair it is that some people just look that way naturally, and that you're not one of those people.

You try to imagine what you could possibly do to ruin them, but you have no ideas. Your mind is an empty vault, and all you can do is just stand there, staring blankly at the shelves in the electronics aisles.

> How anticlimactic.

But it's then that you realize—they're already ruining themselves. *They're like a building that's caught on fire,* you think to yourself, *and even trying to extinguish the flames won't save the building underneath.*

That's very poetic, Buffy.

"Beth?" Your mom leans on the shopping cart to face you. "Is everything okay? You seem kind of…out of it today."

Around you, there are shelves and baskets filled with unnecessary things. They make you think of comfort food, the kind of things people condition themselves into thinking they need.

Turning away from your mom, you begin to pick up everything you see: aloe-infused pink socks, a floral Thermos, a Snuggie, several cans of hairspray (which you've never voluntarily used in your life), a box of Mighty Putty with Billy Mays' face on it, and a stuffed animal that becomes a pillow. *This must be how hoarders think,* you say to yourself. *Wanting to get surrounded by needless stuff. It's comforting in a way.*

"Ah, pink," your mom says, "Good choice!"

Forget your mom. Forget Tristan, forget Sephora, forget everyone.

> But that's just it—I can't.

YOU AND YOUR MOM ARE walking through Bed Bath and Beyond toward the check out. The shopping cart is very heavy and hard to push. You've been in this store too long—the air feels thin and it's like the walls are trying to fold in and kill you.

"I think I saw one of your friends earlier," your mom says. "The one that dresses like a harlot."

You laugh. You laugh so hard and fast that you snort. It's good to know that you and your mom agree on at least one thing.

YOU ARE OUT OF THE store. Hallelujah. There is a large parking lot. Someone has left flyers on the cars.

> Examine fliers.

Even though you walked here, you pick up one of the flyers from someone's windshield. It advertises a dating site you've never heard of. It reads:

Lonely? Single? You're not alone!

Find single men and women based on:

career

hobbies

looks

personality

…and more!

> What do I want?

I don't know. What do you want?

You wonder how many guys are like Tristan out there: who can have a nerdy conversation without drowning in it, who has the same lack of interest in sports as you do, who's never dated anyone before[3], who you've known and been able to evaluate for the past four years.

> Lower love standards.

Despite your better judgment, you put the flyer in your inventory. To keep your options open.

As you look it over, you see Tristan and Sephora leave the store. Their fingers are interlocked. You wonder how those kinds of things just happen, if it's like murder: Is there premeditated destructive dating?

Or is it always unintentional?

And when they walk by, it's almost like Sephora looks right into your eyes. Like she can see you from the other side of the car, and see just how badly you want Tristan. Like she feeds off how sad you are.

Maybe your mom's right. Maybe you really do need to make some new friends.

You are in a parking lot. Some of the flyers slip out under the windshields and fly away. Exits are: down the street, inside.

Your mom asks, "Did you have fun?" as she puts the rest of the bags into the car.

"Yes," you say. "I actually did."

Even so, you can't ignore the empty feeling in your chest, as if part of your heart is rotting out.

---

3 An unquestioned dating criteria you've had on your list since fifth grade.

When you get home, you open your inventory. There is the letter you found at graduation.

> Examine.

You examine the letter. So far, you've refused to open it, as if doing so will be like opening Pandora's box, and you will never have Tristan as a possibility ever again. You think about opening it.

But when your mom calls, you leave the letter on your nightstand, next to the dating flyer.

"All right, that seemed like an intense session for you. Could you tell me why? Maybe, is there something about that memory that's particularly meaningful to you?"

"I—I don't know..."

"Maybe here's another way to go: What was it about Tristan that made you want him so much? What did you like about him?"

"Tristan? Well, he was different than the other guys—you know? I'd never had guy friends before high school, and, when I met everyone, Tristan was the only one who—who was a friend. I mean, I felt like...he was safe. Being with him made me feel like I was doing something good, that I was able to help someone. I was able to help Tristan, and he was able to help me. In our own way. And I was scared that after high school, I might never find another guy like him. I guess you could say he was familiar."

"Did you ever wonder if Tristan was worth it? All these things you were doing?"

"I guess I wasn't thinking about that. All I was thinking about was that he was gone, and I might never have him. That time might run out, and it'd be too late. And that was the most terrifying thing I could imagine."

Your Bedroom: August 16, 2009

Y OU WAKE UP IN YOUR bedroom. There are posters of foreign pop stars you wish would love you and drawings that have yet to be finished. There is a black dress hanging over the chair that your mom says looks like funeral garb. If you were overdramatic, you'd say every day is a funeral. A funeral for what could've been a happy life. But you try to have a brighter outlook on life than that.

From the hall, you hear your mom say something like, "It's 10:30 already—aren't you going to do something with your life?"

> Do something with your life.

You lean over to your nightstand and check your cell phone. There are two texts. They're both from Merrill:

Buffy, you wanna come to my place tonight?

Tonight we're having end-of-summer fireworks before everyone leaves for college tomorrow.

Exits are: under bed, hallway.

Something unsettles you about the texts. The second is much more of a Merrill text. It relays only facts. The first one, however, sounds more like a Freudian slip. Like something only Sephora would actually say out loud, but that anyone might think.

> Stop over-thinking.

Not sure how possible that one is.

You reach into your inventory and pull out the flyer for the dating site. You lay it on your desk, alongside that letter from graduation you almost forgot about. It's still in the envelope.

> Rip open envelope.

You rip open the envelope and unfold the letter on your bed. It's typed, but there's no signature at the end. No handwriting to interpret, no clues to who it is. It says:

Roses = #ff0000
Violets = #00aeff

If school.graduate = 1
then You*I = ???

If time.summer > time.school
then You*I = <3 ?

Give me some variables to plug in.

You were totally not expecting that.

For the next ten minutes, you stare at it, hoping something will make sense, until your mom calls for you again. But you don't reply.

> Determine the culprit.

Maybe it's better to not focus on that.

> Determine the culprit.

You make a list of all the men in your life:

- *Tristan*
- *Merrill*
- *That kid who lives by Merrill's who you try to avoid*
- *Lawrence (the one we don't talk about)*
- *Adrian the Hardware Guru*
- *The two people who faithfully reply to your blog posts*

You remind yourself of the only facts you can be certain of:

- *You got this letter at graduation.*
- *You found it on your desk in homeroom.*
- *There was no one else in the room.*

Unless it was one of the four boys in your class that you never talked to, it only seems reasonable that the letter was either from Tristan or Merrill. Maybe Adrian, but that seems unlikely for lots of reasons—mainly because you're not Asian.

For Merrill to send a letter like that would be extremely out of character. You look back at the old text: *Buffy, you wanna come to my place tonight?* Maybe it was just one carelessly sent text, one not meant to hold that kind of implication. But you can't help but wonder.

It's most believable (and desirable) to you that Tristan would send this. But if so, then why did he suddenly go for Sephora? Tristan isn't the player type— one of the many things you like so much about him.

Then it occurs to you: what if Tristan wanted you, but you were too late to respond? What if he went for Sephora because he thought you weren't interested?

Your throat suddenly goes dry and you reach for your phone.

> Hope for the best.

You send Tristan a text. "Tristan—I need to ask you something."

It's probably the most to-the-point thing you've ever said.

You send the text and leave it at that.

As for fireworks, you decide to go, even if you don't really want to.

FIREWORKS ARE ILLEGAL IN THIS state, but that doesn't stop Merrill. You are in Merrill's backyard with Sephora, Tristan, Merrill, someone you don't know, and Chase. There are piles of explosives on the grass. Exits are: inside, driveway.

You've met Chase before, maybe once or twice. You first met him on top of a batting cage at the local park. The second time was when Sephora had a pool party and came out in a skimpy bikini and high wedges and she laughed all the time, holding a water balloon in her top, freaking out about how it was her "third boob."

Chase does things that are physically impossible, and usually discouraged by neurotypical adults. He is cooler than the rest of you combined. Chase is Asian and you envy his tan, not-peeling skin.

Merrill tells you all that he and Chase will be roommates this upcoming year. Whenever his name is mentioned, you notice Sephora look up with attention.

Over the lawn, there is a pile of Pennsylvania fireworks: party poppers, streamer pistols, Roman candles, and lots of kinds you don't know the names of. Every year, Merrill saves to buy hundreds of dollars' worth of fireworks. Sometimes his mom and uncle come out to watch, too. Sometimes the police come to tell you all to stop, but end up watching the show when Merrill offers them some Mountain Dew Code Red. It's become a tradition that you know you can't miss, even if you hate the loud noise.

Tristan goes inside to use the bathroom and, when he disappears, Merrill grabs a pack of streamer pistols and says, "I think we should all ambush him when he comes out."

You're not sure Tristan will appreciate that kind of joke, but Merrill hands you a pistol. You take it and stow it in your inventory.

Merrill hides in a nearby bush, and Sephora leans against the wall like one of Charlie's angels. Merrill's friend you don't know doesn't know what to do with himself, so he just stands next to the door until Merrill tells him to do something. Chase climbs up the siding onto the garage roof, his pistol aimed at the space in front of the doorway. And you hide under the patio at a safe distance.

When the door opens, Merrill shouts, "Semper Tyrranus!" and all the dollar store pistols go off in one big cloud. Somewhere in that cloud, Tristan screams. You don't remember ever hearing Tristan scream before and it makes your chest sting.

Everyone laughs but when the smoke clears, Tristan shouts, "Dumbass! You could've blown my eye out!"

The laughing continues. You are under a porch. Exits are: out.

> Out.

You climb out from under the porch and go over to Tristan. You examine him for any wounds and ask, "Are you okay?" Your fingers accidently glaze his hand. His skin's so soft—probably from being inside at a computer so much.

Merrill snickers. "What're you, his mom? It's just a bunch of toys."

"Even toys have choking hazards," you say, which in hindsight sounds sassy. Someone makes a low whistle sound.

Tristan looks away. You notice his hand's shaking. "I'm fine."

Sephora leans over and kisses him on the cheek. "Lighten up—you take everything so seriously!"

Tristan breaks from her and goes into the basement. No one follows him.

From the garage, Merrill is pulling out boxes of fireworks. "He'll come back out," he says to his friend that you don't know. "He always does. He's just a drama queen."

> Inside.

You tell everyone you're going inside for a soda.

Inside, you find Tristan in the washroom by the fridge, bent over playing his Nintendo DS. He's sitting on the cold tile floor. *Like a boy,* you think. You think it's so cute, how focused he is. You also wonder why he chose the washroom and not the basement couch.

You usually avoid the washroom as much as possible, asking Merrill or even Sephora to get you a drink instead of having to go in there yourself. The dimly lit cement block walls make you think of a prison cell, but right now there's something oddly sensuous about the darkness and the grime by the soda fridge.

> Get a water bottle.

You open the fridge. There must be about a hundred cans of Jolt in there. Last month, Merrill heard rumors about the company going bankrupt and bought as much of it as he could find.

> Take a blue Jolt instead.

You unscrew the can lid and it hisses. You have to admit, the idea of shaping a can like a battery is both innovative and alarming.

"Tristan?" you say. "You're gonna miss the fireworks."

He shrugs. "I never liked fireworks. All that noise."

"Merrill worked really hard to throw this off—"

"Forget Merrill!" Tristan says, louder than you can remember ever hearing him.

You don't know what to say.

Tristan lets out a sigh, turning off his game. "I don't get it—why does Merrill always have to be such a dick to me? I get messing around, but there's a limit." He looks up at you. "Do you get it, Buffy?"

> Offer inspiring advice?

You open your mouth but nothing comes out. Merrill isn't the kind of person who can be explained. You settle with: "If you don't like Merrill, then why do you come here?"

"Maybe I won't anymore. Maybe I'll just leave," he mutters under his breath. He doesn't move off the floor.

> Tell him I want him here, that I come to Merrill's because of him—

Through the window, you can hear everyone outside, chattering away. Especially Sephora.

> Isn't that her job as a girlfriend, to help Tristan when he needs help?

> To at least check on him to see if he's okay?

> I just want to help

> I just want to help him.

You resist the urge to touch his forehead, to brush the bangs off his face.

"You texted me," he says.

You nod, feeling your body tilt like you're riding on a ship.

"What's going on?"

Your hands are shaking.

> Save.

You've saved over falling on Tristan's lap.

A chill of thrill runs through your spine.

Just don't get your hopes up, okay?

"I got this letter at graduation," you say. "But there wasn't a name on it. I thought it was probably someone I know, but I have no clue who it is."

Tristan strokes his chin with his hand. "A letter? What kind of letter?"

Your heart is freaking out inside your chest. "Um…I think it was someone wanting to ask me out."

"Hm. I think I might know who it is, but I don't want to say for sure."

You mean it's not you? You want to blurt out.

"You don't have to tell me if you can't—"

He nods, getting up and opening the fridge for a Jolt. It's incredible that his thin fingers can hold such a large can. You wonder if this is the last time you'll ever get a chance to be alone with Tristan again. You open your mouth to say something when you hear Merrill's voice in the basement—

"What're you doing, you kids? You're missing the action!"

Tristan turns from the washroom and runs over to Merrill. Faithful as always.

Faithful to Merrill.

You look out the door at Merrill, and he returns the look with the hint of a smile pulling on the corner of his mouth. The taste of vomit rises up in yours.

Exits are: out, bathroom, up.

> Bathroom.

You go into the bathroom and lock the door behind you. Whenever you're uncomfortable with one of Merrill's jokes, or the group is watching a show you think is inappropriate, you do this.

There is a toilet. You sit on it, lid down.

You don't want Merrill to love you. You don't like Merrill's jokes and he says mean things and plays all the video games you don't like. It just wouldn't work out. You know that much on your own.

If you were a horrible person like Sephora, maybe you'd think about pretending to date him just to try to get to Tristan. If Tristan would even be tactful enough to notice what you were trying to do.

But you're not a horrible person and you refuse to lead Merrill on. At the same time, you're reluctant to bring up the issue and say no. Merrill doesn't like to hear the word "no" and you don't like to say it. The best solution for now, you decide, is to ignore it and continue life like you never got the letter, like you have no idea who sent the letter.

You vomit into the toilet, and can't stop vomiting. As if it were that easy.

Thank you for playing POST–HIGH SCHOOL REALITY QUEST. Would you like to load a saved game?

YOU ARE IN THE GRIMY washroom with a Jolt in your hand. Tristan is still sitting on the floor. He asks you what's going on. You open your mouth, but what's the point of going through that dialogue again? You tell yourself, this might be the last time you're ever with Tristan alone.

"Tristan…why are you dating Sephora?" you say, slow.

He frowns, studying you. "What'd you mean? She's nice, she's our friend. What's wrong with us dating?"

> Tell him Sephora's a slut.

"I just—I want what's best for you, Tristan. And, I don't know, I'm not sure you two are compatible."

He gets up, reaching in the fridge for a Jolt. "I appreciate your concern, Buffy." He shakes his head. "But to be honest, it's none of your business, what Sephora and I do. We're not in high school anymore, and I'm not going to have some stupid high school drama."

"But that's just it, Tristan—you *are* in a drama. You'll always be in a drama if Sephora's—"

Your mouth hangs open like a fish as you see Sephora's silhouette in the hallway behind Tristan's head. Maybe you expect her to wear a "you are such a bitch" face but instead she walks over, smiling.

"How's it going, you two?" She reaches over and rubs Tristan's shoulder. "Everything okay?"

Tristan nods. You nod.

She reaches into the fridge for a water. "Buffy. I hope you aren't trying to start some drama. Don't you think we're a bit old for that?"

In her mini skirt and handkerchief top, you want to push her into the fridge. Maybe that would make her reconsider her fashion choices or—with any luck—her life choices.

"I just needed to ask Tristan about something," you say, trying to keep your words even and calm. "What makes you think that Tristan talking to someone besides you means drama?"

Sephora laughs. "Calm down, Buffy. I'm not the jealous type."

> She's totally the jealous type.

"I don't freak out when he's around just *anyone*. I just don't like the idea of *you* being alone with him, considering how you feel about him and all."

Tristan looks at you. But it isn't that *hopeful-excited* look that you dreamed about. It's just a downright confused look. "Buffy? You mean you—"

> Restart game.

I'm sorry, I don't understand "restart game." You think it's that easy, to get a fresh start?

You look at Sephora. It's like time has stopped. She smirks at you with this look like she thinks she owns the world. And that's what finally breaks you down, because for a moment, it feels like she does own your world, and that she thrives in the fact that you have permanently lost something.

> Make a fist.

Before you can think or stop yourself, you're hitting Sephora with the side of your clenched fist. You hit her down her back, over and over, and at first she takes it, but then she starts running and you follow her, your hits getting harder, and louder against her skin.

Outside, a firework goes off.

"Buffy! Stop! What're you—" Tristan's voice trails in and out of you. It's like you're no longer in your body, like someone else is inhabiting you. It should be terrifying, but instead all you can think about is how many times Sephora has taken something from you, and how maybe if you hit her enough times, she'll understand to shut up.

Sephora starts crying. She stops in the middle of the carpet of the basement and falls to her knees. You keep hitting—the skin on your hands gets red and tired. Her skin, rough and dry. Tristan doesn't try to pry you off, he just stands there by the doors, watching, like he knows that nothing he does will help.

Outside you hear familiar voices. Merrill says, "Hello, Officers. Hope you're having a good holiday."

A man says, "We've heard some reports of fireworks and disruptive noises... you know the drill."

Merrill chuckles. "Yes, sir—we have one neighbor who's very sensitive to sound. I'm sorry for the trouble, Officers. Can I offer you some soda?"

Tristan turns to the sliding door as the two officers and Merrill walk into the basement only to see you hovered over Sephora, your fist raised in the air, her body bent over, tears streaming down her face.

Your fist opens, and you lower your hand to your side. Everyone is stopped, silent and watching, until Merrill says, "Buffy, what the *fuck*?"

Your head is spinning and you feel like you might vomit all over the tacky maroon carpet. Sephora looks up at you, and with her smeared mascara and wet hair sticking to her face, she looks so pathetic, and you wonder if she has much of anything else in her life besides Tristan. Your lip quivers.

You start crying when an officer puts his hand on your shoulder and asks if you would come with him. For a moment, you wonder if Sephora is the only person close to understanding how you feel.

You ARE IN THE GRIMY washroom with a Jolt in your hand. Tristan walks in. He asks you what's going on. You open your mouth, but promptly close it again. You tell yourself, this might be the last time you're ever with Tristan alone. You say, "Tristan, I hope no matter what happens we'll always be friends."

"Buffy?" He frowns, stepping forward to study you. "Is everything okay?"

> I guess there's nothing to say.

You turn away and nod.

> Exit washroom.

You are in Merrill's basement. The couch is empty. Exits are: out, bathroom, up.

> Out.

You go outside, and Tristan follows. In the time you've been gone, Merrill and Chase have already set up the first batch of fireworks. The guy you don't know has set up lawn chairs, where Merrill's mom is sitting down, cradling a hot mug of coffee.

"There you are!" Merrill says. "We didn't wanna start without you."

It's the first time you feel that your presence has been noticed. You smile, and Chase lights the first batch. There's a loud popping sound and suddenly the sky lights up.

Sephora sighs; Tristan comes up behind her and squeezes her hand, cringing at the fireworks' explosion.

> Attempt to feel less lonely.

You imagine your own romance scene, but it leaves you feeling cold.

Merrill stands next to you, his body stiff like a military officer. Like he thinks you're going to inspect him. His eyes stay rooted on the sky, but his mind is elsewhere. You know him well enough to tell that much.

And then the police come, despite your hopes. They know they're supposed to tell you all to stop, but the words don't come. A written warning is given for good measure, but they camp out in the backyard with the rest of you, watching the fireworks. The whole time they're there, you feel as if you're being inspected.

You watch the sky. Things explode. Things shatter and look beautiful in the process. Inside your chest, it feels like your life is beginning to shatter, and you wonder if the result will also end up being beautiful. Without thinking, your fingers grip your arm and pinch it, like you're afraid that otherwise, it might just come off, rise above you, and burst.

When the police are gone, Merrill shoots one last firework. It barely misses the lining of the trees and dives into a stranger's lawn. You all run for cover in the basement and invent an explanation, in case anyone asks. But no one asks.

WHEN YOU GET HOME, YOU open your email client and compose a new email for insertwittynamehere@gmail.com. You type: *Is this Merrill?*

You know it's not the right thing to type. Despite wanting to know for certain, you already know. And stating the obvious won't help, that is, if you don't love him back.

> Is it possible, that I could love him back?

You delete the email and climb into bed, hoping that'll help you forget. Instead, you lay there for several hours in the dark, staring at the ceiling and thinking. Always thinking.

College:
August 24, 2009

YOUR PARENTS DRIVE YOU TO your new college. Once everything is unloaded from the car, they drive away to prevent anyone from crying in public.

This is supposed to make you feel free, being here, away from authority, but instead, you feel suddenly claustrophobic.

You are standing outside your new dorm room with bags around your feet. Though you've already realized that going to college means you won't see anyone you know for a while and that you have to solve your own problems, now you actually have to confront those realities. At the same time, your chest fills with adrenaline (the good kind), realizing that this is the chance to start over, get new friends, and find someone new to love. Someone who isn't Tristan.

You are standing outside your dorm when a girl with blue-streak dyed hair comes up to you. "What're you doing—regretting life decisions?"

You can't believe how well she's nailed down your situation on first glance, and contemplate the possibility that she's a witch.

"I'm moving in today," you say. Your smile isn't very convincing.

She says her name is Aquitane. You realize she's one of your roommates. Because seriously, how many girls on campus could be named Aquitane?

"Look, I've been where you are. It sucks. But if you wanna drink your sorrows away, Alice and I are going out tonight. We can show you around, introduce you to some new people."

New people. You've never been a very social person, but the possibility for new friends sends a shiver of excitement through you. Maybe someone to fall in love with, who might fall in love with you.

There's not much you know about your new roommates except that they're both art majors, like you. In your "unfailing optimism," you think this means that the three of you will have some umbilical connection. You've never had art buddies before.

Against your better judgment, you say you'll go. For the funsies.

You are in your dorm room. The walls are peeling and give the room a feeling that the whole building should be condemned. Alice and Aquitane have tried to alleviate the bad feelings by covering the walls with Taylor Swift posters. Needless to say, this only makes things worse.

> You aren't very optimistic, are you?

I'm a realist.

Exits are: out, closet.

> Closet.

You stand in the closet, hoping your roommates' fashion sense can rub off on you from proximity.

Alice opens the door and sees you standing in there, and she looks very confused.

"Um…"

> Attempt to defend your strange habits.

"I was just looking for something," you say. But you know if she asks what you were looking for, you wouldn't have an answer.

"You mean the booze?" Alice says, reaching for a skinny green dress next to your head. Her hair is black and bobbed short to her chin. She wears a green headband that shimmers like a vending machine item.

"Um…"

She laughs. "Guess Aquitane already told you about the closet stash." She parts her dresses to show an unholy amount of alcohol. You have no interest in consuming any of it. You've always sworn to never get involved with alcohol, like a good, responsible adult.

"Aren't you coming tonight?" she asks. "Because if so, you should get dressed. We're heading out soon."

"I don't have a dress," you say, though this isn't completely accurate. You have your cosplay $400 gothic Lolita dress, but that's not for parties. At least, not these kind of parties.

"Aquitane?" Alice calls. "She says she doesn't have a dress." Alice unzips her pants and lets them pool at her feet. You've never gotten down to your underwear in front of another human being. You try to focus your eyes on the window, or Taylor Swift with her bedazzled guitar.

"What? I don't believe you." Aquitane puts on blue lipstick that matches the blue streak in her hair. To you she looks like an arctic version of Lady Gaga. "What about that lace dress on your bed? That looks sexy."

Your cosplay habits have been found out!

> Hide under the bed.

There's not enough room under there.

You say, "Oh, that's not really—"

"Not really what? Vintage is all the rage," Alice says as she squirms into her tube top dress like a manufactured worm.

You look at your gothic Lolita dress and try to remember the last time you wore it. It was probably junior year, when all of you went to a local anime convention and dressed up. Merrill got your picture in the yearbook, wearing that. Now, you can't help but wonder if there were other reasons he took those pictures.

"I don't know…" you say.

"Try it on for us!" Alice says.

"Yeah! We'll tell you what we think."

You are in your dorm room. Your roommates are looking at you expectantly. Exits are: out.

> Out.

You grab the dress off your bed and run to the hall for the bathroom.

You ARE IN THE HALLWAY. There is a trashcan. Exits are: dorm room, bathroom, stairs.

> Bathroom.

You go into a bathroom stall and lock the door. You don't trust anyone. Hanging the dress on the door, you examine its detailed lacework.

If anyone vomits on this, you're demanding the money from Aquitane.

You undress and lace yourself into the dress. From your inventory, you grab the fake rose from graduation and put it in your hair. Stepping out of the stall, you examine yourself.

Everything inside you says this is a very bad decision.

> But that's half the reason it's so appealing.

BACK IN THE ROOM, AQUITANE and Alice look you over with artistic scrutiny.

"It's lovely," Alice decides.

Aquitane nods. "Like a real virgin," she says, like it's a horrible, yet desirable, trait. Regardless, you are one, and aren't you proud of it.

> Yes. I'm also not pregnant, and it's great. I hope you didn't mean all that sarcastically—

I'm not programmed to be sarcastic.

Aquitane pulls out a tube of plum lipstick and patters your lips. The presence of color is reassuring.

"Ready?" She asks.

You nod.

THE THREE OF YOU ARE walking down the sidewalk. Even from here, you can hear people having sex in apartment complexes above you. There is a tree with shoes hanging from the top.

YOU FOLLOW AQUITANE, WHO SEEMS to know where she's going. Next to these girls, you feel like the before picture on *Extreme Makeover*. It's only been four hours here but you know you are already something different.

Alice starts talking about a boy she met before, and Aquitane laughs a nasally laugh, tucking her hair behind her ears. You see now that she has five piercings on her right ear alone.

She turns to you, her eyes serious. "If someone hands you something, smell it first. Pour your own drinks. God knows what people put in there."

Alice nods. "Also, stay away from Jeremy. And Delonte. You never know what they'll try to pull next. They know *nothing* about women."

"Nothing," Aquitane agrees.

"And make sure that before you go to the bathroom with a guy, that you already have a condom—"

"*What?*"

"There was one time that I forgot to bring any, and even though I asked, no one had any." Alice shrugs. "The guys never have them. It's not as important for them as it is for you."

"I don't think that's my—"

"You have to be responsible, Elizabeth." Alice digs into her purse and hands you a condom. You have no idea when you'd ever put it to use, but you don't want to offend her, so you put it in your inventory.

You contemplate running back through the dark without them.

Please do it. Please.

AQUITANE TURNS AT THE CORNER and stops in front of a high rise. "We're here. Remember—leaving at one."

"*One?*" Your bedtime has consistently been no later than eleven.

Aquitane squeezes Alice's shoulder. "No matter what. I don't wanna hear any 'I found my true soul mate.'"

"That was only once! I know better than to believe in soul mates now."

> Tell them I want to go home.

"I don't know—" you begin.

Your roommates stare at you in your costume dress for a minute then giggle.

"Poor Elizabeth—it's your first party, isn't it!" Aquitane laughs.

"Cute virgin," Alice coos.

"Don't worry—just stick with us. We'll show you how it's done."

Five minutes upon entering the apartment, your roommates are gone.

YOU ARE AT A PARTY. It smells irrevocably of vomit and sweat. There is a boom box playing Rhianna, which doesn't make anything better. There is a flashlight on the wall. Exits are: out, bathroom, bedroom, kitchen.

> Out.

You open the door to walk out, but then realize you have no idea where you're going. What's more, it's already late and the idea of walking around alone at night on a foreign campus terrifies you.

"Whoa—already cashing out, baby doll?" A boy walks up to you, his head cocked to one side more from the inability to hold it up than anything else.

When you don't say anything, he explains, "Baby doll, because of your dress. Not like—endearment or anything."

"God forbid," you say, rolling your eyes with Merrill-like sarcasm.

> Merrill-like? Really?

Really.

> That's kind of creepy.

Yes. Yes, it is.

"So you didn't answer my question," he says, leaning toward you. "You checkin' out already? The night's only just started, you know."

> Stay at party.

"I...just need some fresh air."

"Oh, I get that." The cup in his hand crumples a little. There's something about the way he looks at you that's attractive, like you're the only person in the room he needs to focus on. "I could go for some air myself—follow me. The name's Jeremy, by the way."

You question whether going on a roof with a semi-drunk person with the same name Alice warned you against is a good idea.

> Try to be nice.

"I'm not sure..."

He puts his hands in front of him as a defense. "That's okay. If you're not into that, I don't mind. We can just stay here, you know."

You nod, fingering the pendant around your neck.

"Oh—is that a cross?" he asks, leaning forward. He grabs it and examines it. You're not sure how to stop his fingers, just above your clavicle. You've never had a boy's hand that close to you. "Are you religious or something? Is that why—"

"Not exactly," you say, pushing his hand away from you. Are you religious? After a pause, you say, "It's complicated."

You say, "Let's go to the roof."

Y<small>OU</small> <small>ARE</small> <small>ON</small> <small>THE</small> <small>ROOF</small>. There is a patio table and chair up here. From here, you can see your dormitory and the English hall. It really isn't that far away, FYI. Exits are: stairs down, off the roof. Literally.

> Off the roof! Off the roof!

You sure?

> Save

You save over falling on Tristan's lap the second time.

> Off the roof.

You step off the roof. Jeremy screams, trying to grab for you, but he's too late. You feel your skirt ride up to your stomach, and the air rush out of your nose. For a moment, you hope that this means the game will finally be over. But it's not.

You are now dead. Thank you for playing POST–HIGH SCHOOL REALITY QUEST! Would you like to load a saved game?

Y<small>OU</small> <small>ARE</small> <small>ON</small> <small>THE</small> <small>ROOF</small>. There is a patio table and chair up here. From here, you can see your dormitory and the English hall. It really isn't that far away, FYI. Exits are: stairs down, off the roof. But you tried that one already.

Jeremy shakes his head and empties the red cup off the edge.

You watch what's left of the alcohol splash against the sky in one long, clear stream. You wonder if some unfortunate pedestrian will get hit below.

"You're not really into this partying shit, are you?" he says, examining you.

You're not sure what the correct answer to this is. "I came with a friend," you say.

He nods. "It's okay—I'm not much into it either."

"You're not? Then why're you here?"

He looks over the edge of the roof. For a moment, you wonder if he could be the kind of person you'd hang out with after this party. Maybe even more than that, over time. He's not bad-looking. Not exactly the kind of guy you would've seen yourself falling for—the whole boy-band blond hair, blue eyes thing—but there's something endearing about him. The way he holds his chin reminds you of Tristan.

> Oh gosh, Tristan...

"Alice was always into this kind of thing," he says, looking away.

"Alice?" You wish you knew your roommate's last name. "You don't mean—"

"Everyone says I should be over her, but it's not that easy." He laughs, but to you, it sounds forced. "Have you ever had that? Someone you can't stop thinking about, even though you know you should?"

> I totally know that feeling, bro.

You nod. "It's horrible, isn't it?"

He laughs, much more freely this time, you think. "And it's so stupid, but you know, I come to these things, hoping to see her again. Isn't that dumb? Why do I do that?"

"If it's any consolation, I do it too," you say before you can stop yourself. "In fact, I hang out with a bunch of people I don't like, just to see him."

He looks you over and smiles. "Thanks. For coming up here and everything. If I'm boring you, we can always go back down."

But the thing is, you don't want to go back down. You want to stay up here, where it's dark and quiet, and get over Tristan. You want to fall in love with this boy, for some reason you can't put into words.

He nods, looking over the edge. "You know, it's not that far down," he says. "Sometimes, I just…"

Your heart stops.

"I always stop on bridges and stuff, and look down. Never have the guts to do it, though. These parties…they can't help but make you feel weird. Like you're missing something."

You totally relate.

"I totally relate," you say. "But that doesn't mean I should jump off a building. It means I need to rethink my decisions." You want to tell him that you jumped off a building once (this same building, in fact), but that you still came back alive, with all the same problems still there.

"But that's because you're pretty and shit. I mean look at you."

You look down at your dress. You're not sure how to take that.

"But sometimes I wonder if I'll ever get over Alice. And if there might only be one way to fix that."

You are on the roof. There is a patio table and chair up here. Exits are: stairs, off the roof.

> Save the day.

You don't know what to do. You grab his arm. "I don't know if I'll ever get over Tristan," you say, "but I hope I will."

He stops and looks down at your hand on his arm. His skin is so warm between your fingers, you don't want to let go. Moving away from the edge, he puts his hand over top of yours. You really aren't sure how things escalated so quickly, on multiple planes.

Exits are: stairs, off the roof.

> Escape horrible pending romance scene.

You let go and lean away, wondering if you can try this over again. But you know you can't. "I really need to find my friends," you say.

"Oh."

"Come down with me, okay?" you ask, only to clear your own conscience.

He nods.

> Stairs.

You go down the stairs. It is very dark. Jeremy reaches for your hand once more. You regret having hands.

You are in a living room. There is a party. It still smells irrevocably of vomit and sweat. There is *still* a flashlight on the wall. Exits are: hallway, bathroom, bedroom, stairs, kitchen.

Jeremy looks away for a second and you wonder if you should escape—before you fall in love or something. Or worse, before he falls in love with you.

But you don't even have to try. The crowd is thick and he vanishes for a moment.

"Wait—" Jeremy calls for you. "Can I have your number? Or anything?"

You try to move away but it isn't working too well. "I don't really use my—"

"I see."

Exits are: hallway, bathroom, bedroom—

A guilt seizes your stomach. You hate disappointing people.

> Give him number.

You recite your number. You know you'll come to regret this, but what else can you say to him?

He fumbles to pull his phone out of his pocket, his fingers shaking. Once he plugs it in, he asks for a picture. "To put on the profile," he says.

You fold your hands in front of your lap and smile. The lace rubs at your legs, and someone's elbow nudges the small of your back.

He smiles and thanks you, like you've saved his life. Probably because you have, in a way. The burden overwhelms you.

"I'm going to find my friends," you say. "Have a good one."

"Have a better one," he replies.

```
> Save.
```

You save over the roof file. You don't want to relive that again.

THE FIRST PERSON YOU FIND is Aquitane, her head thrown back, chugging from a red cup. Only from the distance do you notice just how long and blue her fingernails are. That, and how much she looks like Sephora in silhouette.

"Elizabeth!" she calls, waving her arms around. "Look—I chugged it all!"

You're not sure you want to know what "it" is.

You are in the kitchen. The counter is crowded with half-empty bottles of various alcohols. One of the drawers is open. Exits are: out.

"I think we should leave," you say, your voice low.

"What? I can't hear you."

"I think we should leave," you repeat, not any louder. You lean closer to her ear. "I found Jeremy."

"Jeremy? No way! What'd he do, puke all over you?"

"What? No."

```
> Tell her what happened.
```

You tell her the whole story and see how she responds. She isn't surprised but she agrees that you all should leave.

Aquitane knows where Alice is. She runs to the bathroom and pulls Alice's head out of the toilet. You all leave the party like shadows.

But this would be too easy.

WALKING OUT, YOU GET A text from Jeremy that says, *It's my fault, telling a stranger what I'm feeling. But you looked so trustworthy. Whatever. I'm not blaming you.*

You turn to the apartment and see a shadow plummet from the roof into the ground. Someone looks out the window and screams.

Aquitane screams but Alice is too lost in her own state to understand, or care.

Aquitane starts running down the road and Alice tries to follow, but her stupor makes her run into a light post. Aquitane can't be stopped. You're lost in the dark with a drunk roommate. Exits are: backward, forward.

```
> Forward...?
```

You go forward, only to get mugged by a strange boy. Alice offers to have sex with him for free, but he just shoots her in the head. And when you scream, he shoots you too. And once you're both dead, he takes all your money. And by all your money, I mean the whole of fifty dollars between the two of you.

If only he realized that Alice wasn't kidding. Maybe you wouldn't be dead. Maybe Jeremy wouldn't be dead.

Oh wait, that was your fault.

Thank you for playing POST–HIGH SCHOOL REALITY QUEST! Would you like to load a saved game?

YOU ARE IN A LIVING room. There is a party. It still smells irrevocably of vomit and sweat. There is still a friggin' flashlight on the wall. Exits are: hallway, bathroom, bedroom, stairs, kitchen.

> You browse over the crowd, looking for your roommates. But you know it's not going to be that easy to find them.

In fact, you spend at least fifteen minutes looking for them in this small apartment and find nothing except a girl named Cat who tries to sell you household cleaner chemicals, and a boy named Arnold, who allegedly had an erection at one of Aquitane's pool parties.

Across the room, you see Jeremy. He makes eye contact with you.

Exits are: hallway, bathroom, bedroom, stairs, kitchen.

> Stairs.

On the stairwell, you find what you think is Alice, smoking a hookah with this guy you don't know.

"Elizabeth! You want some? This shit is *soooooo* good." She puts her hands on the hookah the way a boy puts his hands on a woman's hips.

You shake your head. "Isn't it getting late?"

"Fuck if I know," she says.

"Well, we really need to get going."

"What?" She pouts. "C'mon, Elizabeth. That's no fun at all. The night's just started!"

She holds out to you the mouthpiece, but you don't take it.

"Yeah—c'mon, Beth." The guy next to her leans back, his head hitting the edge of the stair.

You check your watch. It's almost one. "Seriously, Alice. It's late and there's drama. We need to go."

Her ears perk at the word drama. "Oh?"

"It's complicated."

"Who was it? Oh my gosh, don't tell me you—"

You shake your head. "No, not like that, it's just—"

"Welcome to the party life, Beth," the guy says.

Alice nudges him. "Shut it, Delonte." She looks up at you like she's examining your face for smudge marks. "You really don't look so good, Elizabeth. We should get you back."

It's the most lucid thing you've ever heard her say. Alice gets up, unsteady in her heels, and you open the door.

Exits are: out.

The girl named Cat starts screaming. When the crowd tells her to shut it, she points out the window to the red and blue flashing lights. The party becomes even more chaotic with panic. You're scared of dying again.

You are in a living room. There are lots of drunk people running into walls screaming. It smells irrevocably of vomit and sweat. There is still a friggin' flashlight on the wall, dang it. Exits are: hallway, bathroom, bedroom, stairs, kitchen.

Alice gets lost in the crowd.

> Seriously?

Seriously.

You don't know what to do, but you notice the flashlight on the wall. Finally.

> Take the flashlight.

Out the window, you see police officers entering the apartment. Some people run out the doors, but they don't get very far. Your thoughts spiral: You think about the police from the fireworks night and wonder if they'll remember you, if you'll get put in prison and never graduate college—

> Out.

You part through the drunk people, armed with a flashlight. A police officer stops you and asks if you were in a party. You say you were accompanying your friend but that you don't do the party thing, your voice shaking as you speak. He asks you to walk in a straight line and pats you down. One look in your inventory and he realizes he's wasting his time. "Go home now," he says. "It's gonna get messy in there."

You nod and turn toward campus.

You try to remember which way your dorm is, and where you saw it from the roof. It's very dark outside, except for the flashing blue and red light behind you.

> Turn on flashlight.

You can see now. There is a sidewalk lined with trees. Exits are: backward, forward.

> Forward.

You walk forward. There is a brick wall. Exits are: forward, backward.

> Climb wall.

You climb the brick wall and rip the edge of your skirt. But you feel like you're on top of the world.

You are on a wall. Exits are: down, forward, backward.

> Forward.

A guy calls out to you from the grass. He says you look nice.

> Pull out your firecracker pistol.

You pull out the firecracker pistol from Merrill's. In the dark it looks almost legit.

"Oh shit, you's one mean bitch!" he says, putting his hands up.

You keep walking and he follows.

"I jus' need ten bucks, lady. Can you help me out?"

> Fire pistol.

You fire the fire cracker pistol and the guy screams, more from surprise than anything else.

> Run.

You run faster than you knew you could. You almost fall off the wall, but you stay up there. It feels safer that way. Ahead, you see familiar street lamps by your dorm. You don't hear the guy calling. And once you step into the light you feel safe for the first time all night.

You swear that's the last time you'll ever go to a party.

OH, IF ONLY YOU FOLLOWED your promises.

IN YOUR ROOM, YOU CAN'T sleep for the next three hours. You don't get any unpacking done except for your bed sheets. The rest sits around in open boxes, waiting for rapture.

You can't sleep because you're scared of Jeremy jumping off the roof, or the policeman asking for an explanation, the couples making out, and your brain automatically photoshopping Tristan's face on top of every guy, your face on every girl, eventually metaphysically morphing into Sephora, because in the end Sephora has Tristan, not you.

You imagine what might have happened if you'd just taken the flashlight and left as soon as you got there: before Jeremy, before the police, before anything could go wrong. Even better—what would've happened if you'd just stayed home?

> Die.

I'm sorry, I don't understand "die."

> Find a knife and cut wrists.

You look around the apartment for something to kill yourself with. But there are no knives.

> Booze.

You go into the booze closet and take a bottle of vodka to your lips. After one sip you start gagging. Why do people pay money to voluntarily drink this stuff?

> Window.

You try to open the window but it's stuck. Even so, you're only a floor up from the ground. The best you'd do is break your leg, and that's no fun.

> Toilet.

You run to the bathroom and enter an empty stall. There are no lights, except for some streetlight coming through the window.

You must be thinking about graduation? When you drowned yourself in a toilet?

> Something like that.

You look into the toilet. The college toilets are somehow dirtier than the ones in high school. What is it with you and your fascination with toilets?

> You got any better suggestions?

I'm sorry, I can't condone suicide.

> So I can die and restart when I make stupid mistakes, but when I actually do something that matters, I can't go back to fix that? What kind of game mechanic is that?

Outside the bathroom window, you see a figure walking in the dark. You can't be sure who it is, but you wonder if it's Jeremy for a moment. Why do you wonder that? Why is he the first person that comes to mind?

> You still haven't answered my question.

I'm sorry, that was a question? Better question—why do you get to restart at all?

It's 4:23 a.m. according to Aquitane's alarm clock. You've never been up this late before, and you've accepted the fact that you're not going to get any sleep for the first night of your life. Unfortunately, it's not the last night you'll have insomnia.

The door opens. You see Alice in the doorway, her top buttoned in the wrong holes. Her eyes are red and you hide your head under the covers, afraid to look at her. Afraid to look at anything. But even from under the covers, you hear her shuffle across the room, sit down at her desk, and sob.

"I don't think it meant badly…the game, I mean. I think it was trying to help me all along. Like it was my conscience or something."

"It's interesting that you say that, Buffy. What makes you think that? And how does that make you feel about the game, as a whole?"

"I don't know. Just some of the things it told me to do…seemed bad at first, but now that I look back on it, maybe it was right. Maybe I was making really bad decisions, and that wasn't the game's fault. I don't know how I feel about that."

"We all make mistakes, Buffy."

"Yeah. But in the game, it feels like I can undo those mistakes. Like I can go back and fix everything."

"But can you, Buffy?"

"No. I guess not."

Campus ESOL Class: September 9, 2009

You are supposed to be preparing your lesson plan right now. But your thoughts are too unsteady for that kind of effort.

Your first week at college and you've already volunteered to teach an ESOL club. Aren't you so thoughtful. You've had your training, but still the idea of standing in front of a class intimidates you. Maybe you thought that volunteering would help you get the initiative you need to survive college: to tell someone if you love them, to make friends, and stop making the same mistakes. Or maybe it's a kind of penance after that party. This is all merely speculation.

> Maybe I just wanted to do something nice for other people. Did that idea ever occur to you?

It's not that you're not a nice person, Buffy. It's just that, well, humans are by nature selfish beings—

> That's a bit of a doctrinal statement, isn't it?

YOU ARE IN AN ESOL classroom. You didn't sleep much last night—you dreamed about Jeremy finding you in a dark alley and kissing you into the wall—but when you looked up, it was suddenly Merrill's face. All day, you've felt like you're living in six months in the past. You think about how, a few weeks after graduation, Merrill bought a box of condoms and gave them to Sephora. It was funny, until Sephora put them into her bag and said, "I'll hold onto them. Just in case."

And how she winked at Tristan. How Tristan shivered, and you couldn't tell if it was from pleasure or terror, or both.

Merrill looked between the two of them right at you. And though you thought it was kinda weird, you tried to not over think it. But in light of everything else, you begin to wonder if there were multiple meanings behind the gift. And multiple meanings behind the look.

Last week, Merrill texted you to say he's got some time this weekend, if you'd like to hang out. You ask who else is coming. Maybe that was mean, you wonder in hindsight, but he replied that the whole group was coming, like it wasn't a big deal. Sometimes, you don't know what to make of Merrill.

The door opens and a boy walks in—he's short, maybe even shorter than you. He studies you for a moment, then realization surfaces. "Buffy?" he asks.

> Interact with a person.

You nod, lifting yourself off the surface of the desk. You don't want to look like a complete bum. "Yes, I'm teaching the ESOL club."

"Great!" He strides over, his hand out in front of him. "My name's Jake, it's great to meet you."

"Jake," you say. "Your English is…really good."

He laughs. "Well, gee, I'd hope so, considering I've lived here my whole life."

The lack of sleep still afflicts you. "Sorry?"

"I'm here to help you with the class. Didn't they tell you during your training? We're going to co-teach. I hope that's all right with you."

It's more than all right—it's the best possible solution in this scenario. "I'd love that," you say.

He smiles and sits next to you. Maybe you expected to feel more excitement, sitting right next to a boy, but it's like he's not even there. He looks over to your laptop and notices your stickers: a giant Pikachu and Tyrande Whisperwind from *World of Warcraft*. "So I see someone plays games here..." he says.

"Oh, yeah..."

"What's your favorite game?"

> Zork.

Seriously? Nothing from—I don't know, this *century*?

"*Zork*," you say.

He frowns. Inwardly you curse yourself. You should've said something mainstream like *Pokémon* or *Halo*, something he might actually know.

"Your favorite game...is a text adventure game?" He studies you. "Wow, well that's definitely not an answer I expected."

"What, people can't like text adventure games anymore, now that there's *graphics* and *3-D rendering?*" You smile. "I see how it is. You're one of those *Call of Duty* people."

He laughs. "Heck no. I appreciate the classics. And I admire your good taste."

Was that a wink? You look to the door, where a girl walks in. Your first student. She looks like she's from Vietnam, but you aren't sure and you don't want to stereotype.

"Welcome!" you say, getting up from the table.

She looks at you with wide eyes and points at the necklace around your neck. You remember you're still wearing a cross. Not the most politically correct icon.

"Jesus!" she says.

You nod, recalling years of middle school theology classes.

> Avoid politically incorrect conversation.

"Yeah..." You finger the necklace. "My mom gave it to me. Here, it's a cultural thing."

She tilts her head, studying you. "Do...you know Jesus then? Because I just met Jesus." Her face lights up, her hands open as if she's carrying something full and incredible. "And you know how I met Jesus?"

When you don't say anything, Jake answers, "How?"

"I had a dream," she says. "And I saw this man, who was covered in light. He motioned for me to follow him, and so I came to him. When I came to him, he smiled, and I felt at peace. Even though I still had hard things in my daily life, I had joy. When I woke up, I knew his name is Jesus. Have you had dreams like this?"

You have had dreams about lots of things, but Jesus is not one of them. You shake your head. "Not really."

She smiles. "Well, I hope one day you do. It's a good feeling."

As other students enter the room, you feel your legs shaking. Why did you volunteer for a job that requires being in front of people? Even if you're not having to say anything yet, you feel weird being in the front of the room, with all those strangers staring at you. If Jake hadn't shown up, you're not sure what you would've done.

Jake starts the class asking everyone to share their favorite English greeting. The room fills with "hello"s, "how are you"s, and even a couple "yo"s and "what's up, homies"s.

You watch that girl sitting in her seat, and she looks so relaxed, as if nothing could ever go wrong enough to make her freak out. You imagine the ability to be forgiven, over and over again, but know you can't even forgive yourself.

> It's a nice thought, though.

It is, Buffy. That it is.

BACK IN YOUR DORM ROOM, you set up your desk and get online. You see that Sephora's commented on Chase's status. Again, and again, and again. In fact, as you scroll down his page, you see that pretty much every time he's so much as typed, Sephora's replied.

> What a stupid whore.

When Alice comes in from class, you ask, "I have a hypothetical situation."

Alice doesn't know what the word hypothetical means, but she's listening. You can tell because she sits down, facing you, and doesn't do anything with her hands.

And you describe the situation with Sephora and Tristan and you and Chase—with changed names, of course. You make sure to note how amazing and brilliant Tristan is, and how he's going to become a famous mathematician—and what a complete whore Sephora is, except not quite in those terms.

> Gain Alice's sympathy.

Once you're done with your story, Alice laughs. She turns to her desk and opens the drawer. There's a pile of opened envelopes in there.

She grabs a pen and closes the drawer. Pointing the pen at you she says, "Elizabeth. The first rule of love is to fuck as many people as you can. Literally, and figuratively. Because you can never be the one left behind. Got it?"

You decide to never go to Alice for love advice ever again.

Treatment II:
June 7, 2010

"YOU CALLED?"

I open my eyes. The room's white; there are no decorations except for a framed picture of a narwhal.

"No. I'm just here. Actually, I don't even remember how I..."

The man smiles, holding up a clipboard. "I guess your mother's in the waiting room?"

Waiting room. What would she be waiting for?

"Great. So, listen…Buffy. That's what you like to be called, right?"

"Yes."

"Not Beth or Elizabeth or Liza…"

"Those are all overused." I smile.

He laughs. "Right, right. I hear ya. So, Buffy. We got the scans back from your fMRI, and I want to show you something."

He holds up the picture of my brain. It looks so unsacred that way, so simple in black and white. I see the black voids in the middle of my forehead and shout, "I have holes in my brain!"

"No, that's normal. Those are your ventricles. They hold the cerebro-spinal fluid—whatever. Everyone has those. But yes, that's exactly what I want you to look at. These are your ventricals, and I'd like you to take a look at this other picture…" He holds up a second scan of a much fatter head, where the ventricles are smaller.

"You see the difference? This first one is you, and the second one is a neurotypical person."

You look away from him, turning to the picture on the wall. The water is so empty there, so flat. Even the narwhal looks so small.

"We often see this difference in patients who have been diagnosed with schizophrenia. Now, usually the ventricles are much larger in patients with these symptoms—in your case, they're just a little larger. In most cases, we'd say that's in a typical range, but with the symptoms you've mentioned, and some other things we saw, it's quite possible that this is the answer to what's been going on in that head of yours recently."

"What...else did you see?"

He pauses, pressing his lips together. "Sometimes in schizophrenia, we see certain areas of the brain have more, and less, activity. You said you sometimes *hear* this game talk, right?"

"...Yes."

"Well, that would make sense with what we saw. We saw some of the areas that deal with auditory processing—the anterior cingulate, the right thalamus, and some of the auditory cortex—were activated. And sometimes, you say the game feels like it's *attacking* you. Do I have that right?"

"Yes. Though I'm not sure if I'd say attacking—it just feels like I'm, well, powerless, and almost—like it knows what's going to happen, and is just messing around with me."

He nods. "We saw some abnormal activity in the amygdala, which deals with emotion, and the medial prefrontal cortex—sorry for all these big names by the way. But this is common in patients with schizophrenia who have positive symptoms—that is, behaviors that are not found in typical experience. For example, hallucinations."

"I'm not hallucinating. It's actually there: the game, the voice, everything. I know it sounds crazy, but—"

"Buffy, I understand that what you're experiencing is confusing. But remember, we're here to help. And we can't help unless you let us."

What's that even supposed to mean? "I appreciate it, but I think I just need rest."

When I get up, he hands me a piece of paper. "Your doctor would really recommend you get this prescription. Just give it a shot—it might change your world."

Haha. Like I haven't already tried to change my world.

Merrill's Driveway: September 26, 2009

SEPHORA HAS A TRADITION OF changing her name whenever she dates a new boy.

Freshman year, when she was dating Jordan, she called herself Angelica. She said it sounded elegant. When they broke up and Jordan decided he was homosexual, Sephora said she was Octavia now. That's when she started chasing after Marcos, the head of the debate club. Half of sophomore year, she said she wanted to be Lynn while she flirted with Adrian (who did not accept). Once she got the hint (and by got the hint, you mean Adrian came by and threatened to get the guidance counselor involved), she said she was never Lynn. She was Marie now. It was only the end of junior year when she changed her name to Sephora and told us she was dating this guy online who was twenty-six. She said she did better with older men. They were more mature, she said. More to her maturity level.

Which is both funny and sad, when you think about it.

But the weird thing is that when she started dating Tristan, she didn't change her name. "That'd make things too complicated," she said when you asked her. And that made you suspicious, Sephora not trying to make things more complicated.

You'RE ABOUT TO GO INTO Merrill's house, but Sephora drove up the same time you did which makes things awkward. As soon as she gets out, you call out to her and she stops. You may feel like an idiot, but you know this may be the only opportunity you get to express your feelings of frustration with her. If you can actually get the guts to talk about your feelings.

You are in Merrill's driveway. There is a wild Sephora coming toward you. Exits are: car, door.

> Examine Sephora.

Sephora looks confused, like she almost didn't expect that you had the ability to speak. She tries to hide a smile.

> What a slut.

"Hey, Buffy," she says. "What's up?"

Sephora's wearing a shirt that's built for a middle school girl. It lifts at her belly button. Her jeans are cut in places you don't like thinking about.

> Talk about your feels.

You open your mouth. You plan on saying *why do you hate me so much?* or *Stop pretending you love Tristan, you whore!* But instead, you begin, "How are—"

But you should've known better. Sephora does the talking. "Oh my gosh, Buffy—I have to tell you what happened the other day."

You listen.

"So I went into Games Workshop because I needed some new dice for our tabletop. And I love going in there because the guys are *so pathetic*. So I was looking through the dice, and this big guy, he comes up and asks if I need any help. And I tell him I'm fine. But he just stands there. He just stands there! Can you believe it? I started feeling uncomfortable so I asked him, 'Do you need any help?' And you know what he said? He said, 'Well, if you'd like to go out sometime, then maybe I do...'" She breaks out laughing her bird-squawk laugh. The one you hate so much.

> Actually say your feels, but in a passive-aggressive way.

You laugh. "You really like attention, don't you?"

Sephora stops laughing.

You realize you just said what you think to Sephora for the first time. You're both terrified and proud of yourself.

Exits are: door, car.

> Run into a bush.

You try to run into a bush but you realize the bushes are too shallow. Instead of hiding you, it covers your ankles.

Sephora says, "You're fucking insane, aren't you?"

"Do you have to use that word?"

Sephora frowns. "You totally have a thing for Tristan. It's really obvious, you know. And it's kinda annoying, since you don't really do anything about it."

"Don't you?"

Her frown vanishes. "Kinda. You know. But I did something about it."

You are highly skeptical of her claims and want citations. "What is it you like about Tristan?"

"He's a good guy. You know that."

"What I mean is—you knew—"

"I read in a blog that girls should date geek guys," Sephora said. "That they don't have much experience, and because of that they're awed by anything with an hourglass. That they treat you good 'cause they don't know any better. And after my last ex, that's just what I want. Someone in awe of me."

You think she meant that to sound much more powerful, but it only came out sounding lonely and pathetic. And very human.

For a moment, you feel bad for her.

"You know what, Buffy—I think I know what'll help you." She puts her hand on your shoulder like you're the one that needs help. Which is funny, but true in a way.

"You need to meet some more guys. Look at the other fish in the sea. Tristan's just one guy, and I think you like him just because he's the only guy who's remotely decent that you've met. But really, Chase is a good catch too. You should count your blessings."

You try to move toward the door but Sephora stops you.

"I think if you looked around, you might be happier."

"About Chase—" You begin, thinking about how many times you've caught Sephora oogling at him. She turns to you and smiles, and there's this undertone in her expression that you can't quite read.

> If you love Chase so much, then why don't you
just date him?

You open your mouth to call her out, but Sephora turns her head away, biting her lip, and you wonder if everything's more complicated than you've made it to be up until now.

YOU ARE IN MERRILL'S BASEMENT. The floor is covered in empty cans of Gamer Fuel. Exits are: out.

> Bathroom.

The door's locked.

> Go upstairs.

You try to go upstairs, but the stairway's covered in old Orson Scott Card paperbacks. Your path is blocked.

"If you wanna go upstairs," Merrill says, "Just go outside and use the front door. It's easier that way."

Merrill's the only one sitting on the couch. The emptiness of the seat next to him seems to be more than a subtle implication. Tristan and Sephora are attempting to share a chair, but you see Sephora's eyes turn to Chase, who's sitting on the floor, attempting to build a hostile weapon out of LEGO pieces and Nerf darts.

"Let's watch a movie and drink our sorrows away," Merrill says, holding up what must be his fifteenth can of Gamer Fuel. He looks at you. "Are you just gonna stand there all day? Sit down."

You want to sit on the floor, but you see Merrill's eyes flicker to the empty seat next to him. You don't like where this is going, but you think there's nothing you can do to stop it.

> Sit on couch.

You sit on the couch next to Merrill. Even from here, you can sense his body tense. Like he's afraid of you. Everyone's already decided on the movie before you came. Tristan tightens his arms around Sephora's waist, like he knows he can't hold onto her much longer. She tries to meet Chase's eyes, but he doesn't look up from his work.

Merrill whispers to you, "We should totally kick Tristan and Sephora outside."

You don't like the feeling of Merrill's lips near your ear. But you imagine he does, since he doesn't move away after he speaks, but hovers with his chin against your hair.

You tilt your head like you're looking at something very far away. Merrill turns the other way, his face flushed red.

Chase leaves his monstrosity on the floor and puts the movie in. You open your mouth to protest, but what's the alternative? Already, you feel aware of Merrill's body heat beside you.

In the corner, Sephora begins work nibbling on Tristan's ear.

And even though none of this has personally happened to you before, you've watched enough movies to predict the progression of the night:

Merrill puts his arm around the back of the couch. The arm's only waiting for the moment to come down over you. Even though it isn't touching you, you feel its presence, which sends the hairs on the back of your neck up, trembling.

Once you get through the first fifteen minutes or so of the movie, he'll assume you've acclimated to his position. He'll gradually lower his arm down. He'll do this in increments to wait for you to get used to it, or, if he's lucky, to get a positively reinforcing body cue.

After a while he'll get impatient and hunker his arm down on your shoulder. You'll try to pretend that nothing's happening, but internally, your heart will try to commit suicide. His hand will gradually lower to grasp the ball of your shoulder and, maybe if he's daring, he'll dig his fingers into your skin. You'll despise every moment of it, but there'll be too many witnesses to openly reject him.

Lucky for you though, you see this coming before it happens. Maybe that means you can make a proactive defense plan.

> Make a proactive defense plan.

You lean toward the armrest, curling your arms around your body in a self-contained hug.

Merrill asks, "You cold?"

"No, I'm fine. I was just—"

Merrill throws a blanket over you, leaning closer. He almost looks worried. "Is that any better?"

You smile and thank him, rolling your body into a protective cocoon. Like a chastity belt.

You wonder if Merrill gets the hint.

Ten minutes into the movie, Sephora and Tristan are kissing so loudly that Merrill sentences them to making out outside for the rest of the time.

"But it's cold out there," Sephora says, rubbing her arms. "It's cold enough in here, anyway."

"Then all the more reason to get close and shit—you're ruining the movie."

"You can't just kick us out," Tristan says.

"Well actually—yeah I can, considering this is my house." Merrill gives Tristan a look that you can't quite read.

Tristan looks at you, and there's this moment of realization on his face, though you're not sure what exactly the realization is.

Without another word, Tristan goes outside, slamming the door.

Sephora calls after him, then looks at Merrill. "Sorry about him—I'll take care of it." She opens the door, putting on her jacket and snow boots as if she's about to go out into Snowpocalypse.

About five minutes later, Chase says he's gotta use it. He goes into the bathroom, but five minutes later he's still in there. You wonder if he's doing okay.

Then it dawns on you what's really happening.

Merrill turns to you in the dark. He opens his mouth to say something but nothing comes out. Which is weird, since Merrill's known for his words.

In fact, you try to remember the last time you saw Merrill speechless.

"Buffy—" he begins. "I don't even know what to say."

You don't know what to say either.

> STRANGER DANGER.

You move to get off the couch, but Merrill puts his hand on your shoulder. It feels large and warm and it catches you off guard.

He leans forward and for a moment, he looks so small. He says, "I really like you, Buffy. I'd really like to kiss you…if you'd let me."

And you know you should have a better answer to that.

But Merrill leans and you can't stop him. He presses his lips to yours and it's like he's eating your entire body. You can't move away, but neither can you actively move your lips against him. So you just sit there like a doll, and let him work against your lips.

And that's when Tristan and Sephora walk in.

You only know because the door closes and Tristan says, "Oh, snap!"

Everything in you wants to die.

Merrill retreats and you regain control over your body. You look over to the door, where Sephora watches with wide, excited eyes. Either she's legitimately happy for you, thinking that you've found true love, or finds it extremely funny to see someone like Merrill being physically affectionate, especially to a girl like you.

When you look at Merrill, his face is drained of color, like he's been caught naked.

Then Sephora starts clapping. Tristan starts clapping, too. A moment later, the backyard door opens and Chase walks in.

"Chase!" you say. "I thought you were in the bathroom!"

"I was," he says, "But then I climbed out the bathroom window. And once I was outside, I just had to climb the gutter drain to get to ground level."

You don't ask how the gutter drain supported his weight.

Merrill regains his composure and laughs. "Never saw that coming, did you?"

Behind you, the movie continues playing. Some things can continue their pace of life regardless.

Sephora shakes her head. "*Never.* But now that I see it, it's kinda cute. You two are total opposites, but you know what they say—opposites attract!"

Tristan brushes noses with Sephora.

> Escape horror.

You excuse yourself to go to the bathroom.

You are in the bathroom. There is a toilet and a cracked-open window.

For a moment, you contemplate Chase's escape and wonder if you can pull it off too, and run somewhere far away.

Instead, you sit on the toilet, lid down. You bury your face in your hands and try to maintain any composure you have left. Once you get a hold of yourself, you take the towel to your lips and try to wash off any presence of Merrill still on them.

You need to make him stop. You know that.

You exit the bathroom. But as you step out, Merrill's there to meet you. Even though the signs keep coming today, they still catch you off guard.

He kicks at the carpet, and you think that translates to, *are you okay?* But you can't be sure.

> Examine Merrill.

His back's arched, almost gently. Merrill's always given you special treatment.

You think about that time at lunch in high school when he said, "Raise your hand if you're going to Hell." People started raising their hands, but then he turned to you and said, "Not you though, Buffy. You go to church and stuff." You wondered then if your eternal destiny should ride on the fact that you go to church and stuff, but maybe you should've put Merrill's feelings together earlier.

His hands are deep in his pockets. He waits for your consent. You know he doesn't mean to break you. Something like fear twitches on his eyebrows, like he already knows you can't love him.

Without a word, he walks back to the living room.

Maybe that was enough, because Merrill tries no more moves on you for the rest of the evening. When you say you have to go, he nods but doesn't look you in the eye. He doesn't ask why or try to make you stay.

When you get home, Chase is online. He confesses to having encouraged Merrill's advancements. "It's weird for Merrill to be like that over a girl," he says, "So I thought it probably meant something. Like that you two should give it a shot."

When you don't say anything, he adds, "And with Tristan hooking up and all, it seemed like you could use someone."

You hate how he's totally right.

"Hello, Buffy? This is Dr. Moritz. I'm just calling to check in and make sure you're doing all right. We've missed you at the office the past couple sessions. Give us a call so we can see if we can reschedule, and make sure everything's going okay. Have a good one."

YOU BELIEVE IN GOD EVEN if you don't like talking about the specifics.
For your thirteenth birthday, your mom got you a cross necklace. For some reason, you don't take it off. If you had to answer why, you wouldn't be able to explain it. Habit, you'd probably say.

Your mom's hung up a picture of Jesus—or what someone thought Jesus looked like—over the kitchen trash can, as if to remember that Jesus made fish and bread multiply, and if he lived now he'd recycle and not contribute to the dump.

All that to say, despite your uncertainties, there are some convictions that are hard to shake off. Like that stealing is wrong, especially stealing a girl's man. Or that you shouldn't make out with someone just for the sake of making out. That you shouldn't lie, even if unrequited feelings are involved.

And above all that, you are convinced that internet dating can only be bad, and be for lonely people. You're certain that somewhere in Leviticus, it reads: *and you shall not seek partnership on the Internet, for this is the most evident form of loneliness. That, and the man pool is very mediocre.* You think about high school Sephora and her alleged twenty-six-year old boyfriend you never met. Why can't people just meet in real life? Wouldn't that make more sense?

> Print current prospects.

- Merrill.
- Jeremy.
- That boy in Psych 101.

You begin to reconsider your convictions.

On your desk you still have that flyer for the internet dating site. You look at it whenever you sit down and imagine all kinds of possibilities. It's horrible, really.

> But the nice thing about the internet is you can back down whenever you want.

Explain.

> You can make a profile, and if things get weird, you can delete it. It might be kind of fun. At least get my confidence back up...

It might be a little more complicated than you're making it out to be.

> Besides, how much harm could it really do?

> Make a profile, despite my better judgment.

> Look through computer to find a good profile picture.

You only have a few pictures of yourself. The first is at graduation, where you managed to pose next to Tristan. You pick that one because you're actually smiling. You crop out your cap and gown, until the box is filled with a pixelated image of your eyes, nose, mouth, and some of your hair. You look like you've pressed your face against a window, waiting for someone to open a door to let you in.

The computer says: *Tell me about yourself.*

Which is creepy. And you don't even know where to begin.

> Tell it about yourself.

You write:

plays well with others

gets an interest and sticks with it

faithful

sometimes too shy

You know how to write this, because it's what your report cards have said throughout your childhood.

You read it again and realize it sounds like you've described a dog. So you add:

loves pretty much all table-top RPGs and MMOs

It asks for your gender, orientation, age, and complexion. These are questions you do know the answers to.

Then it asks a much harder question:

What do you want in a partner?

You sit there and read it over ten, twenty, thirty times.

> Type: "Tristan."

You quickly highlight it to hit delete. But before you hit delete, you wonder for a moment that if you leave it up, will he see it and find you? It's like those women that put messages in bottles and throw them in the ocean and hope that a man will find it and love them for it.

Because women rule out all probability statistics when devising love strategies.

> Type: "NARWHAL."

You type NARWHAL but that doesn't really explain much of anything. When you begin thinking about narwhals, though, it makes sense. You start brainstorming attributes of narwhals, and without having to think too hard, you come up with:

"Narwhals live in benthic cold waters. Their socializing is limited but intense. They're faithful to their group, and creatures of habit. Friendly, unable to be alone. While similar species thrive in captivity, the narwhal can't. There's so much still unknown to science about narwhals—still so much to learn. Narwhals are mysteries of nature. They're utterly fascinating, and scientists might spend a lifetime just to catch a glimpse of one."

You realize that you're no longer writing about narwhals but about Tristan. What does that say about you, or narwhals?

> At least it doesn't say "Tristan."

You're going to get so many replies from otherkin. Just saying.

It doesn't matter to you, though. This is the start of something—

> And besides, it's just *for fun*.

But is it?

Regardless, when you save, you swear to yourself that no one can find out about this profile. It will be your secret life.

The thing is, secret lives never stay secret for very long.

Your Room at Home: September 28, 2009

MERRILL SAYS THIS'LL BE FUNNY a few years from now, but you still have your doubts.

You are in your bed. Next to you, your phone goes off.

It's a text from Merrill, inviting you over to his place today, considering *it's a three-day weekend so we have more time and stuff.*

> Be honest with yourself.

You reply, *I'm not feeling too great.*

Ten minutes later you get a text from Merrill for you to step outside.

You look out your bedroom window and see Merrill's car in your driveway. He steps out of the car in his socks, his hair unbrushed, and looks around. *He looks like a wild animal,* you think to yourself.

And, somewhere in your chest, you feel a heavy weight of pity.

> Open front door.

You go downstairs and open the front door. Merrill looks at the door then looks back in his car.

"I was just heading out," he says. "And wanted to check up...make sure you're okay."

You look at his now-muddy socks. His crinkled T-shirt. You think about all the lies Merrill's teased you with over the years, and how you've believed all of them until now.

"I'm okay," you say. "I just don't really feel like going anywhere."

He nods but doesn't say anything, looking down at his toes.

He's totally waiting for you to invite him in, FYI.

> I know. I just—

You don't want Merrill in your house. Especially when your parents are gone. Or really, especially, ever. You don't like Merrill. Not that way, at least.

> I should just tell him no. Tell him no...

As you open your mouth to speak, Merrill says, "Look—I'm sorry. I don't know what's gotten into me this weekend."

> Speak before thinking.

"You're jealous of Tristan, right?" you say, your voice shaking.

Merrill laughs. You laugh, too.

"I mean it, though—it's only since Tristan was dating that you started hitting on me. Seems a little too...I don't know, well-timed."

"It's not like that, Buffy. I swear, it's not."

But it is. Because you totally feel the same way.

You smile. "What I mean to say is—I don't think it'll help either of us—trying to love different people."

Your body feels weak. Even standing still you feel your body sway. Maybe you really are sick.

"I'm sorry—I never meant to, I don't know—push anything on you."

"It's cool, Merrill. Really."

"You think we can just act like it didn't happen?"

"Sure," you say. Though you know internally it never works like that.

> Don't look back.

You walk inside, but you do turn around for a moment and look through the window. Merrill doesn't follow you. He doesn't call for you to come back. He just stands there in the driveway, trying to hide the fact he's looking at you by brushing his bangs over his eyes. But he's watching you, knowing right now that he's losing something. Like he wants to chase you down and kiss you on the doorstep.

Like maybe he really does love you deep down, or something.

What's hardest to watch, though, is how he gets back in the car and pulls down the driveway, out into town. For a moment, you almost chase him down the street. But you don't. This is the bravest move you've ever made, and it feels beautiful and horrible at the same time.

WELL DONE. I KNOW THAT was hard, but…you did a really good job there.

> Yeah.

If we were keeping track of points, this would be your high score!

> …

You doing okay?

> Yeah.

Would you like a snack?

> No. I'm okay.

Merrill makes no attempts to text you anything that's not a mass group text. He makes sure to keep a distance as if there's a three-foot radius barrier rising out of you. Some damage can't be undone.

But you did the right thing, Buffy. You really did.

AFTER CLASS, IT'S BECOME A ritual to check the status of your online dating profile. Maybe that's because unlike your Etsy, Deviantart, blog, and Facebook accounts, your dating profile is getting followers, comments, and likes. An Amish guy with the beard, hat, and everything sent you a request yesterday saying, *I think it might really work out between us.* And just three days ago, a man who must be in his forties liked your narwhal description. *Very deep and mature,* he said. *Maybe we should give it a shot.* Another reply read: *Am open to any species relationship. I am a caster, though—so I identify as a vampire, just to warn you ;).*

But you think about the other profiles of girls with top-down boob shots, who misspell their description to say, *Brians and Beauty—Im' smart, to.* And you wonder if maybe you should have higher standards for yourself.

All that to say, there's not that much competition of excellence out there. Except for the boobs part.

And despite the mediocre responses, there have been a couple boys in your age range[4] that have shown interest. You've never received this much attention before. Maybe this is what it feels like to be Sephora.

It's only when Aquitane comes in one day that you realize it's an addiction.

"Elizabeth—look at your desk!" she says.

> Look at desk.

You look at your desk. It's covered in old Arby's curly fry boxes and some half-eaten carrot sticks. A cloud of flies has made your desk lamp their breeding ground. Even you think it's grotesque.

"Don't tell me. You're heartbroken, right?"

Are you really this easy to read?

> Hide evidence.

You close your laptop lid. There's a hidden shame in your new hobby.

Aquitane gets closer to your desk. The blue in her hair shines. "Tell me about it, okay? You want some rum?"

You shake your head. She reaches into the closet anyway and opens a bottle. "You know, I'm with you right there. I was in this open relationship with this girl last week, and her girlfriend just came back into town, so it's all cut off for good. Well, I guess unless she breaks up with her girlfriend." She takes a swig of the rum. "It's heartbreaking right now, but I'll get over it in a few days. It was a nice week while it lasted."

You know this is the point where you're supposed to say you totally relate, but you don't. You really don't. So you nod sympathetically.

Aquitane shakes her head. "Enough about my love life. What about you?" She points to the computer. "Don't tell me your doing that eHarmony shit."

You think about all the men who have messaged you, how many of them probably have wives and are trying to be twenty-two again. But you also think about TheDisasterRoom, a boy who you've been messaging with back and forth for a whole week now. Sometimes, he sends you gifts of .gif rose bouquets and pixelated chocolates. It's the thought that counts. He also gives you compliments that he can't possibly verify as true, such as, *when the sun hits your hair, it just glows* and *i love the way you smile* ☺.

All the same, it feels nice to be appreciated. Dangerous, even.

When you don't say anything, Aquitane laughs. A full, deep belly laugh. The kind you envision paired with old men, or bitter housewives. "You know, I went for that once, too. In middle school. A real low period. And let me tell

---

4 At least that's what they say.

you, there's all kinds of guys who just wanna come up and *eat* you. They'll say anything to make you fall for them."

"But…it always sounds so…*nice*," you say.

"That's when you know it's bullshit!" Aquitane says, her voice loud and accusing. "Those men, they don't exist. They're just made-up personas. That's all they are, Elizabeth. Got it?"

> Nod to be nice.

You nod, even though you want to believe they're real, somewhere.

"It's like their full-time job, to scam college girls." She shakes her head. "But listen. If you want to meet someone right for you, I'll bring you out on Friday. We'll find you someone real."

> Try to not laugh at the irony.

> I feel safer with online men, I think.

> Mention Jeremy.

Your body folds in on itself, your hands plucking at your skin defensively. Aquitane takes the hint. "We can start you off slow. Maybe we can do a rave this weekend. Just meet some people, dance, no promises. Then you can go from there. Who knows—you might find someone you like."

You tell her you'll think about it.

You are back in your room with a box of leftover dinner. You really should be doing some art homework, but instead, you check if there's any update from your dating site. In your inbox, there's one new message from TheDisasterRoom. It says:

HIYA BUFFY, HOW ARE YOU? I WAS WONDERING IF MAYBE YOU'D LIKE TO MEET UP, YOU KNOW—IRL. I LIVE RIGHT OUTSIDE BALTIMORE, BUT I'M WILLING TO DRIVE. ☺

Exits are: close laptop lid.

> Contemplate this option way longer than appropriate.

You stare at the computer screen for a while, realizing you actually live somewhat near Baltimore, and that this is a viable option. Now that Merrill's out of your love life, you feel a need to celebrate, to splurge. Even if splurging means going out with a complete stranger.

> Ask—

Are you sure?

> What now? What'm I doing wrong now?

Don't jump into something so fast, Buffy. Maybe get to know some people on campus, see who you might meet...

> That takes time.

Quality takes time.

Despite your better judgment, you ask him when and where, adding a suggestive smiley face at the end. Then you slam down the laptop lid and take a shower.

And as much as you try to stop, you keep scratching at this one part of your chin for the whole night. In the morning, it's red and oily.

THEDISASTERROOM PROMISED HE'D WEAR A fedora and a brightly colored bowtie to your "date."

The very thought of the word "date" makes you flustered.

You're in the garage of Towson Town Center, looking for fedoras. A boy walks by who looks familiar. He's from your art class, but you don't know his name. He waves at you. You wave back, and he keeps walking. You wonder for a moment if you should've said something.

Above you, there is a Rainforest Café and a video game store. On the sidewalk, there is a McDonald's bag filled with trash, and some scattered change. Exits are: parking lot, inside, up escalator.

> Examine parking lot.

You look over the cars, and from the distance you see a fedora. At first, you think to yourself, he doesn't look half bad. He notices you staring and waves back. Then you notice the dog collar around his neck. And a feeling of foreboding washes over you.

The boy stops about three feet from you, then gets on the ground and starts rolling between empty handicapped spaces.

> Um, excuse me?

You just stare at him, regretting this whole internet dating decision.

He gets up off the gravel, onto his knees, and you notice some people stopping outside their cars, staring. You look at the trashcan, afraid to be associated with all this.

> This is why I don't have nice things!

I'm sorry. I don't understand "this is why I don't have nice things!"

On his knees, he reaches for the dog tag around his neck and looks up at you with big eyes. "See?" he says. "I'm a ferret. It's right here." He points to the line on the tag that says *STRIPES,* along with an address you can't read. You wonder if you can throw him in a mailbox somewhere, and the postal service will return him to that address for you. It'd certainly make things much easier.

You open your mouth to say something, but what do you say to that? Seriously, what can be said?

He examines you, a look of disappointment dripping over his features. "Wait…" he says. "Didn't you say…you were a fish or something?"

"I'm *sorry*?"

"The name just escaped me…" He scratches his head. In the dim garage light, you can see the slight, but disturbing, resemblance to a ferret. "It wasn't a whale, but something like that…"

"A narwhal?"

"Yeah! You said that on your profile."

You don't want to correct him and explain that you wanted to *date* a narwhal, because that could only make things more complicated.

"It was a metaphor," you resolve with.

His eyes open wide, as if this idea never occurred to him.

You both stand in the garage in silence. You are in a garage. Exits are: mall, car.

He looks down at the ground. "I thought you'd—that it was understood— look, maybe this just isn't gonna work out."

Before you can thoroughly agree with him, he gets up to his feet and shuffles away, his head hung, eyes on the gravel. People are still standing beside their cars, parents afraid to open the doors to let their children out.

And as happy as you are that that fiasco's over with, you can't help but feel at a loss, being dumped two minutes into a date. Because in the end, you weren't the one who dumped him.

You're driving home when you realize you haven't eaten in eight, nine hours. You thought you were going to eat with TheDisasterRoom, but well, you didn't really feel like eating after that fiasco. Your head starts to spin, and you feel like vomiting.

One moment of not looking at the road, you swerve into the car in front of you and get sandwiched between two SUVs. It doesn't take long for you to die.

But thanks for playing POST–HIGH SCHOOL REALITY QUEST! Would you like to load a saved game?

Because you forgot to save. Again. And let me tell you, that was your worst mistake.

Post—High School Reality Quest

Merrill says this'll be funny a few years from now, but you still have your doubts.

You are in your bed. Next to you, your phone goes off.

It's a text from Merrill, inviting you over to his place today, before you go back to school.

> Still can't say no.

You resisted once in your memory. It wasn't very easy, and the idea of having to do it again, only to go on a not-so-pleasant date with TheDisasterRoom is less than appealing.

And unfortunately, that file was never saved. It was only a dream, you could say.

You're unsure of whether it's fear of internet men, or guilt for denying Merrill before, or your suddenly developed lust for attention, but you call Merrill and ask if he'd like to go to a movie with you this afternoon.

He doesn't say anything for awhile, then manages, "This was Chase's idea, wasn't it?"

You shake your head and then remember he can't see that. "I'm sorry about that time—"

"It's no big deal. Really."

"But I didn't act right. It just startled me was all. There was a lot on my mind."

"Look, Buffy… I'm not sure what you're getting at, but—"

"I might like you," you say quickly, before you can retract it.

A pause.

You open your mouth to say things you don't really mean. But you really shouldn't do that, you know. You can't take back those kinds of things.

> But Merrill is sad :(

He'll be a lot more sad if—

> Make Merrill feel better.

Your heart beats faster. "You're kinda cute," you say. "And I don't know. It might be fun. If we go out, we won't have Tristan and Sephora getting in the way." Even as the words escape you, your mouth gets bitter and heavy.

Merrill laughs. "Okay, Buffy. How about at six? And if this is some prank by Chase, I'm gonna kick his ass."

The word discomforts you, but you laugh because it's your obligation. This is what girls going on dates with boys do.

AND HUN, LET ME JUST say—if disaster falls on you, don't say I didn't warn you. This is your own side quest, after all.

YOU'RE TOO EAGER TO HELP people. That's your problem.

At least that's what you tell yourself as you try to not throw up on your dashboard, turning your car off in the parking lot.

You are parked outside the movie theater. There is a ticket booth. Next to the ticket booth, there is a bulletin board. Merrill is standing in front of it, playing with his phone.

Exits are: inside car, ahead, back.

> Do I have to go in?

Too late to go back now.

> Ahead.

You walk toward Merrill. He's reading the movie listings like they're cheat codes he has to memorize on the spot.

At the sound of your coming, Merrill turns around. He looks you over. "You look nice," he says. You notice his clean polo, ironed khaki pants, and not-tennis shoes. No pizza stains or bacon odor. You blush at his attention to detail.

Merrill says he already has tickets. You pull out cash and try to pay him back but he refuses.

WITH EVERY STEP, YOUR GUILT level rises.

When you two sit down, Merrill picks the seats toward the back. You know what the back of the theater means.

You feel like you might bite your own heart as it jumps up your throat.

Merrill pulls out a box of Mike and Ikes. Your favorite.

He asks if you want any, and you can't pretend that you don't. He pours so many into your hands that they overflow. You thank him, but it doesn't feel adequate. If you were dating, this is the part where you'd kiss him.

> Save before anything crazy happens.

You save over slot one in Bed Bath and Beyond, and brace yourself for the movie.

As the movie starts, you become aware of Merrill's presence. His breathing is rhythmic above your ear, steady like an air conditioning unit. You almost feel drawn to his shoulder for reasons you can't explain.

He adjusts himself closer to you. You know what's coming but have no contingency plan.

During a fight scene he whispers in your ear, "Buffy, would you believe me if I said I've had a thing for you for a while now?"

You turn around to look at him but know he's not making it up.

No one's ever said anything like that to you before. You don't know how to respond, how to explain how that idea amazes you: of someone being drawn to you before you were drawn toward them. You consider telling him about the dating service online, how men spam you with emoticons but it's like junk food. You don't really even know what you want or love anymore.

Instead, you bury your face in his arm and hug it close to your chest, afraid of thinking about letting go.

You accept Merrill's kisses because even in the dark of a theater, you can't find yourself able to push him away, or deny him. Not only that, but the feeling of kissing is nice. And being kissed. How Merrill leans in to find you. How when he looks for you, there's a moment of vulnerability. How when he finds your lips, he leans in eager, like you're a new, unlocked bonus level in his favorite game. Like you're the prerelease demo that he's been waiting months, maybe even years for.

And best of all, how you're not rejected when you kiss him back, even when you miss.

```
> No, actually—the best part is that you can't
stop me.
```

I'm sorry. I don't understand "you can't stop me—"

```
> That's right. You can't understand losing your
own game.
```

Buffy. You do realize how this game works, right?

```
> I understand that I'm winning, because you aren't
making me do anything. I'm making my own decisions.
Like an adult. I'm making my own game, dang it. And
you can't stop me, or ruin this, or anything.
```

...Buffy. You really don't understand how this game works.

It's only once the credits start rolling that you notice Tristan's head just a few rows ahead, and Sephora's hair draped over his shoulders.

Sephora's the first to notice you two. She turns around and lets out a whistle. "Lookin' smoking, guys!"

Merrill fixes the collar of his polo, and you redo your ponytail, but it doesn't do much good.

"Wow—so it's getting serious between you two!" You wonder what will ever shut her up. "We should totally go on a double date sometime!"

You feel Tristan look over you, like this is the first time he's realized you're a girl. "Yeah," he says. "That'd be cool."

Merrill shrugs and puts his arm around your waist, like you're something that has to be held onto in fear of it running off.

You are something possessed, and you know it.

As long as you've known Sephora, she's given you things. She says it's her love language. The first week of sophomore English class, she brought you one of those old *Pokémon* Burger King toys. It had scruff marks on the back and the eyes were faded. "I found it while cleaning up this week," she said. "It made me think of you."

The real reason she does this, you predict, is to make people feel indebted to her. Because that's exactly what it does. It makes you feel like you have to give something back. And you hate that feeling.

After the movie when you get online, Sephora messages you and says, *I have something for you.*

You don't believe her, but you thank her for her kindness.

It's so cute, you and Merrill.

You've said that…

And I mean it. Merrill needs a woman in his life. And deep down, he's pretty sweet.

You rest your fingers on the keys.

Let me tell you a secret…

You can't help but want her secrets.

Merrill's had a thing for you for forever. Since he first met you. He told me that, years ago. Like freshman year.

When you don't reply, she continues, *And he'd do anything for you. He just doesn't know how. I was hoping you'd catch on, but…*

Why are you telling me this?

Because…I know you're into Tristan and all, but it just won't work. You guys aren't really, well, compatible. But you and Merrill have a chance.

You wonder who Sephora is to tell you who you do and don't have a chance with. You think about your time at high school, and try to imagine the possibility that Merrill has, in fact, liked you this whole time. And you think about how, since that first day in freshman keyboarding, he's driven you insane. How he always corrected the teacher and called himself the computer god. Really, it's impressive you two ever became friends.

> We're just so different...but they do say opposites attract, right?

What're you asking me for? This is *your* side quest, remember?

> Side quest? What's that even supposed to mean?

You type, *But you and Tristan? You think you two are compatible?*

Sephora's status shows as idle for the next couple minutes.

Let me tell you another secret, she says.

What?

I always hated you for it.

> Ask for clarification.

?

That he wanted you like that. Everyone wants someone to care for them like that, you know? Sorry, it's stupid for me to say that. But I guess what I mean is, don't screw this up. You could really fix him up, and be just what he needs. I don't know. You two might actually be happy or something.

Your status becomes inactive.

Campus:
October 5, 2009

YOU SWEAR TO YOURSELF THAT no one will ever find out about your dating site.

It's Monday, and you're in a lecture hall. The lecture is very boring. Exits are: out, internet.

> Pull up dating site.

You pull up your dating site and check for any new messages. None.

In front of you, a boy pulls up an internet browser full of porn. He must feel very confident about himself, you imagine. Or else just be really stupid.

On Facebook, you notice Merrill's sent a request to update your relationship status. But you don't answer. You don't know how to answer.

> Break up with Merrill. Send him a message. Anything. Please.

Sometimes, Buffy, we say one thing and do another.

> I mean it this time. I like the whole feeling of being with him but...

And you think that'll make everything okay, just like that? Don't think this game is *that* easy.

The lecture is still going. It takes a long time. On your shoulders, you feel this constant heaviness, like someone's standing behind you. But every time you turn around, you can see that no one's there.

All the same, you can't help but feel like Merrill's following you.

On your instant messenger, you notice that Sephora just logged in.

> Message Sephora for help.

Hey, Sephora... you begin.

Buffy? What's up? OMG Congrats on Merrill! You two official?!?!?

Well, not in so many words. But what else can you be? Clearly, Merrill's in favor of something more official.

I...don't know what we are, you write. *And I don't really want it to be anything. Merrill does, though, and I don't know what to do.*

The weird thing about all of this is that Sephora's the one you're going to for help.

Hm... Sephora types, erases, and retypes. While you wait, you try to listen to some of the lecture. And by try to listen, I mean, you try to *look* like you were listening.

Merrill's really sensitive, she says at last. *You have to be easy on him. Better to say it in person. Or, you can tell him there's someone else. That it's not going to work out. It's not his fault, you've just figured out what you need. That when he totally snuffed you out, it made you want him all the more—well, okay maybe not that part lol.*

You roll your eyes, wishing Sephora could not talk about Chase and/or her own relationship problems for at least two seconds of her life.

But the thing is, with Merrill, he can't just discover it. You have to tell him. You got that? I'm dead serious.

You want to ask Sephora how she knows Merrill so well, and why, but in the end, you know she's right. You tell her you have to go, then log off your IM and start shopping online. Because you always have to do something with your hands.

"HOW HAVE YOU BEEN, BUFFY?" Jake stands at the front of the ESOL classroom, wearing a kilt.

> Holy crap—people actually wear those in public?

Jake must notice you staring at his kilt, because he laughs and says, "Got this at the local Renaissance festival, but it's so comfortable, I don't know why we all wear pants."

It's a reasonable question. "I guess I feel safe in pants." You look down at your jeans. "Is that weird to say?"

"Well, we're not in a therapy session, so maybe?" Jake laughs. "But I can respect that. Did you remember to bring the bag of clothes?"

You stare at him blankly.

"You know, for the *clothes* unit? We talked about bringing in props to go over vocabulary." He looks down at his kilt. "Or maybe you just *said* that so you could make me look like a freak in a kilt."

"No! No, I didn't mean to—I just forgot." You let out a sigh. "I'm sorry, there's been a lot on my mind."

"It's fine." He laughs. "I guess we'll just get to talk about jeans and T-shirts. It's a shame though—you said you had some cool costumes to show them."

"'Cool' isn't exactly the word I'd use to describe them."

"Hey, I'm a nerd, too! It's not like I'd judge you or anything."

When you don't say anything, he continues. "Let me guess. You're a closet furry? An otherkin? A weeaboo schoolgirl cosplayer?"

You break out laughing. "Uh—not quite. Unless you were about to say 'gothic Lolita' somewhere in that list."

"That stuff looks pretty cool—why would you be all weird about that?"

You shrug. "I'm weird about lots of things."

He nods. "Hey listen—you know, after we're done and everything, I was gonna grab food. You can join me, you know—if you want."

You are in a classroom. No one's ever asked you out before, unless you count Merrill—

"I'm good," you say. "My boyfriend's gonna want to hang out."

"Oh, that's cool," Jake says, turning to the board to write the day's agenda. "I feel ya—"

> Why did I just say that?

You start rubbing your sleeve. "Thanks, though—"

"No sweat. Hey, are you cold?"

You look down at your arms. "No, I'm fine." On your shoulders, you feel something heavy, as if someone's standing behind you.

Turning from the board, Jake says, "You said you do art, right? You think you could draw a person on the board for me? With all sorts of different clothing articles on?"

You chuckle. "Clothing articles."

"Pieces of clothing? Outerwear? I don't know. Why's it so awkward to talk about clothes?"

"Probably because people have to be so weird about it." You go up to the board and grab one of the markers. What do you draw? You draw every day for class, yet as you stand there, you feel your hand go numb.

Jake smiles, then turns away. Why did you mention a boyfriend? He didn't have to know. It might be easier that way, to leave Merrill that is—if there's someone else instead.

As you draw, your hand shakes. You erase the head you started with your fist, leaving a purple dust on your hand. Several times, you try to draw the same head but it doesn't work. It's like you're self-conscious or something. Like someone's watching you. But beside you, Jake's sitting down, looking over today's lesson.

> Why does it feel like Merrill's watching me, everywhere I go?

ONLINE, YOU TELL MERRILL: *THERE was this guy in class today who tried to get me to go get dinner with him.*

Merrill starts typing something, then stops, then is silent.

And I was like, my boyfriend—

☺

> Wait a minute.

Your face becomes warm. *I—well—d'uhhh.*

So it's official then ;), Merrill says. *:kiss:*

You reply with the obligatory *:kiss:*

There it is. Anything you do now will break something that officially exists.

Your head spins, and you open a new tab on your computer, checking your dating site frantically, like you might never get to see it again.

A s soon as you get home on Friday, you see Merrill in your driveway, hands in his pockets, looking up at the trees. A numbing sensation shoots up your throat, and you feel like you might vomit, or pass out.

> I'm seeing a theme of me vomiting a lot…

> Also, Merrill's everywhere! Are you sure there's not like, a glitch in this—

There are no such things as glitches, Buffy.

"Oh, look," your mom says, pulling in. "There's your boyfriend!" How your mom knows this when you yourself are unsure of this status, you don't want to know.

She turns away from the wheel and smiles at you. You wonder if she means it just as harshly as it sounds, or if she's truly naively happy for you.

Your mom stops the van midway up the driveway, rolls down the window, and waves at Merrill. "The princess has arrived!" she shouts, and the two of them laugh. Your mom really doesn't understand you at all.

Your mom puts the car in park and as you open the door, Merrill catches up to the side of the car. He opens his arms for you, and his empty embrace is so pitiful that it's endearing. How can you leave him standing there like that?

> Hug.

You hug Merrill, your arms light and tentative.

The hug doesn't end.

Merrill holds onto you tighter, like he's afraid to let go of you.

> This is really weird.

You giggle and he steps back, looking you in the eye. Taking your face in his hands, he kisses you. And once he does, you grip his hair between your fingers, like you're about to juice an orange.

> Please tell me this is some, like, alternate universe dream state—

"I missed you," he says, his voice mumbling.

> This isn't how it's supposed to—

I'm sorry, I don't understand "this isn't how it's supposed to—" This is what happened. This is what you chose, Buffy.

You are in your room. Even through the walls, you can hear Merrill and your mom, chatting away. She says he's charming. Since when were they so compatible? And why can't you two be compatible, too?

This is when you're supposed to be with them, socializing. He's your "boyfriend," after all—

> We've never made that official.

> Besides, I'm not up for that right now.

You hope that maybe, if you stay in your room long enough, no one will bother you. Maybe Merrill will get the hint and go away on his own.

"She's putting away her things. She always has so much *stuff* she brings from campus to home and back..." your mom complains.

It's been six hours since you last checked your dating site. This guy BBQ_ Muffin's been sending you messages, and as much as you tell yourself to wait and check it out later, you feel an almost-biological compulsion to check immediately.

> Open internet browser.

You pull up your horrible addiction site.

> You shouldn't use such emotionally loaded/biased language.

You pull up your horrible addiction site. No new messages.

> Pull up followers page.

You look at the profile pictures of the men following you. None of them look terribly attractive, but then again, you're optimistic that the pixels aren't doing them justice.

> I have no good options.

You bury your face on your desk and want to cry. Maybe if you cry enough, an attractive, all-around good guy would drop from the sky.

"Buffy?" your mom calls through the wall. "You ready?"

> Ready for what?

You've been found out. Time to socialize and whatnot. You leave your laptop open on your desk and go to the other room, where Merrill and your mom are standing there like best friends.

Before you or Merrill can say anything, your mom says, "I'll leave you two *alone*. I'm going out to get groceries—you all want anything?"

If only you had one of those overprotective moms who refuse to let their daughters be alone with any male.

Once she closes the door, Merrill sits on the couch, his legs wide and full like a chair. He motions to you, for you to sit on his lap.

> What is he, Santa Claus?

You are in the living room, alone with Merrill. Exits are: hallway, outside, mind.

> Sit.

You bend over slowly, settling on his kneecaps, and slowly drawing yourself closer to his body. His warmth is incredible—you feel your body tingle with a dopamine rush. From behind, you feel Merrill's arms shake as he holds you close to himself. This is the kind of intimacy you used to spend all of Algebra dreaming about, but right now, all you can think about is how badly you need to pee.

"How was your week, Buffy?" he asks, his voice humming in your hair.

> What even happened this week?

"It was okay," you manage. "Classes. Lots of homework. I sometimes help out with an ESOL club after class."

He nods, and you feel your hair bob to the rhythm of his movement.

You squirm on his lap, but he holds you closer. Eventually you say, "I have to go to the bathroom—I'll be right back."

He lets go, and you're free! Running down the hall, you get into the bathroom and close the door. It is very dark in here.

> At least it's away from Merrill for a little bit. Maybe I can pretend to poop and take a long time in here…

You sit down, heart racing. If there's any time to tell Merrill, it's today.

> But how exactly do you launch into that sort of conversation? "Hi, Merrill, so I just don't like you enough to date you"?

As you think about what to say, you hear Merrill walk down the hall, toward your bedroom.

"Merrill?" you call, but know your voice is soft.

> What's he doing?

You are on a toilet. Your pants are pooled at your ankles.

> Flush toilet.

You get up and pull your pants on, forgetting to wash your hands.

But by the time you get to your room, it's too late. Merrill's bent over your laptop, silent and still.

> Distract him.

You come behind him and throw your arms around his neck. He doesn't move.

"Merrill?" you say. "What're you doing, messing with my laptop?" You try to laugh. "Creepin' on my stuff?"

He moves his shoulders to shake you off. You let go, your smile disappearing.

He lets out a chuckle. "I was just gonna change your relationship status." He turns red. "You know, with what you said earlier..."

Neither of you say anything for a while.

"Seriously, what the fuck, Buffy? One minute you call me your boyfriend, all the while having this?" He points to your dating site profile, with your description about narwhals.

"It's a *joke*, Merrill. You know that, right?"

"But it's not, Buffy." He doesn't look away from you. "If you were joking, you'd say some shit about wanting a big black dick—"

"You know I don't talk like that—"

"You still can't get over him, can you?"

Some valve breaks inside your chest. "What? What's that even supposed to mean?"

He turns around, looking at your bed. Then he shakes his head. "It's okay. I mean, I don't know what you see in the guy, but I get it. Just admit it, instead of trying to convince me that you don't."

Merrill gets up and walks out of your room.

> Follow him.

"Merrill?" You call after him, slipping on your bedroom slippers, carrying your laptop with you.

Merrill goes downstairs, out the kitchen door.

"Merrill, can we at least talk, like civilized people—"

"It's okay, Buffy. Not even a big deal or anything, gosh." Merrill chuckles under his breath but it sounds more like a sob. "You've got your obsession. I get it."

It's dark and cold outside, and you want nothing more than to just curl up under a bush and never wake up.

"I—" You begin, reaching your arms out.

The idea of being single—even after one week of a relationship—sounds exhausting.

But instead of comforting Merrill, all you manage to do is drop your laptop on the pavement. It makes a noise that is far from reassuring. The hinge squeaks like an injured animal.

Apparently, it's not that simple.

> Freak out.

You hit a melting point you didn't know existed.

"What the heck, Merrill! You guys probably look at porn every night, and we can't hate you for that because 'that's what guys do'—but I joke around with strangers on the internet for the lolz and suddenly that makes me *undateable*? How'd you feel if I opened up all your computers and creeped on your browsing history and found pictures of naked women! You think that'd be okay? Would you like it if I left you because of that? It's not fair!"

Merrill looks down at the pavement. After some thought, he says, "Buffy. You know that's not the reason this isn't going to work out."

If only he wasn't in some way bizarrely right.

LATER THAT NIGHT, YOU SEND Merrill a link to the profile page from your desktop computer. "You can look at it if you want. There's nothing I have to hide." You think that's a reasonable thing to say, even though you know the damage is done.

In the end, you know you don't—and never can—love Merrill. So why do you keep trying? Maybe, just like Merrill hopes, you hope you can learn to love him in time. He's better than nothing, right?

Because that totally doesn't sound like Sephora or anything.

> I don't need commentary on my choices, especially not from you.

The next morning, Merrill sends you a text that says maybe you guys shouldn't be trying so hard. Maybe you both should forget this ever happened.

You cry. You cry as if a fetus just died inside you. Like you felt you had something with the potential for life, then felt it heavy and dead in the pit of your body. And no matter what you do, it won't come out of you.

You wake up in your room at home. On your desk is a condolences card from your mom. Like the kind you buy when somebody dies. It's got these lilacs and some ghastly font like Monotype Corsiva on the front[5]. Mom said it was the closest thing she could find to a "I'm sorry you broke up with your first boyfriend but there are many other fish in the sea" card.

> Examine laptop.

You open your laptop. It cries when you do that. The screen pops a little and it feels like the end of the world.

Well, you needed a new one anyway.

Dad offers to buy you a new one this afternoon. You're grateful for his offer, but after all of Sephora's gifts, you're afraid of having love bought for you. And worse, having to find a way to pay it back. You tell him you'll pay.

In the meantime, you have nothing to do. There's an unfinished painting that's due tomorrow, but all you can do is think of Merrill.

> Run after Merrill.

Seriously? It's forty degrees outside.

> I really think I should see Merrill.

It's forty degrees outside, but you run outside in your Xbox boxers[6] and jog to Merrill's house. *It's not that far,* you tell yourself.

> Save over slot three.

You run and save over the party.

You are in front of Merrill's house. It looks more nonexistent than usual. It's daylight so you only now notice the peeling paint on his mailbox and siding. Dead branches collect on the roof, threatening to fall and impale someone.

> What time is it?

---

5 Personally, I'm more of a Miriam Fixed type of person. Not that you care, or anything.

6 From the men's section in Kmart. No one ever seems to notice that they're underwear, though. Guys keep coming up to you saying, "Nice Xbox skirt!"

You check your watch. It's seven thirty-five in the morning on a Saturday. Merrill's not going to be awake, let alone interested in seeing you.

But you don't let that stop you.

> Go to the back door and try to sneak in.

You don't want to wake anyone up. Therefore, you decide to sneak in. It makes sense in your head.

The back door is locked like you expected, but then you think about the window you climbed through before. The window is left unlocked like a doggie door, as if Merrill expects someone to come in and out whenever they need to.

> Climb into window.

The metal's cold under your hands, but you climb. And you fall. But not the way you want to.

You crash and crack your head open. There's blood on Merrill's couch. How sad.

Thank you for playing POST–HIGH SCHOOL REALITY QUEST! Would you like to load a saved game?

YOU ARE IN FRONT OF Merrill's house. There is a front door. That's what normal people use when they want to approach someone. Exits are: in, down street.

> Knock on front door.

You knock because there's no doorbell. You've never come to the front door before. Merrill totally won't see it coming.

No one answers.

> Knock again, dang it.

You knock again. This time you hear someone moving inside. Something jumps in your chest. Maybe you just expected no one to answer you.

Behind you, someone pulls into the driveway, which throws you off guard even more.

The car stops and someone gets out. You realize it's Merrill's mom, even though you've only seen her once before. When you last saw her, she was going to work. It was nine at night. Merrill's mom is known for her late-night shifts at the hospital and her daytime naps. Hence why Merrill invites everyone over so late.

> Defend yourself.

"I'm so sorry—I know it's early—"

"Elizabeth? Is that you?" Merrill's mom smiles at you despite the bags under her eyes. You're impressed that she remembers your name in the first place.

"Merrill's mad at me, I think," you say. "It's not my fault, though. He seems to think I'm doing things I'm not." Your face must be getting red, because Merrill's mom smiles. Like you two are just so cute, and she can't wait to take you in as a daughter-in-law. Gah.

"Oh, sweetie." Merrill's mom wraps her arms around you in an embrace. Your body stiffens. "Don't worry about him. Merrill overreacts sometimes. Just be persistent—he'll get it at some point."

"Thanks," you say, trying on a smile.

"Would you like to come inside? Merrill should be waking up soon anyway—he sleeps in too late on weekends."

As Merrill's mom walks you to the door, you notice her hands. How red and ripped her fingers are. You don't ask where the wounds came from.

"Would you like anything? Did you have breakfast?" she asks.

You shake your head, and realize just how awkward of a time this is to arrive. "I'm fine. I'm sorry for coming—"

"Don't be—I just wish I had more…"

You wait for the end of her phrase but it hangs there. She walks into another room as if she's a desktop computer, being rebooted after freezing mid-task.

Above your head, you hear steps. Merrill's steps, heavy and confident.

Merrill comes down the stairs in his boxers and a T-shirt. Your face gets warm. Merrill stops mid-motion and looks at you like you're a wild animal. His usual calm is disrupted.

"Buffy—what are you…?"

You know this is your moment to explain things. That if your life was a movie, this would be the scene with the dramatic violin music and everything would be okay from now on.

But everything's not gonna be okay, and you can tell from the way Merrill's looking at you.

> Attempt to confess your love to him, just like the movies.

"I—I—"

I can't figure out what to do with you, is what you want to say.

Merrill rolls his eyes and goes down the stairs past you. "You have no balls, Buffy. I don't know what you expect."

"I—I don't want you angry at me, Merrill. Especially when I don't even know—"

"You do know, Buffy. You do." He walks in the kitchen and grabs a mug from the cabinet. "Look, let's just forget this happened. I don't care enough to try differently—let's just go back to normal. We'll tell everyone it just didn't work out."

You want to start crying but can't muster the tears.

But maybe you don't have to. He looks up to your eye and, for a second, and matches your feelings.

> Be a scumbag.

Without another thought, you force yourself forward and kiss him long and hard. He drops the mug he was holding and starts kissing you back. It breaks but you both don't stop. He holds your lower back and you can feel his excitement. His longing.

You want to tell him Tristan doesn't haunt you. That this could be enough for you. That if you try hard enough, you can replace Tristan's light, thin features with Merrill's dark, robust—

But somewhere in the middle, Merrill stops and pulls away.

"I'm not Tristan," he says suddenly.

And it's like he broke through every holy barrier you set up. Like he really does know you.

Which, oddly enough, makes you want him more.

He shakes his head and goes back upstairs without the shattered mug.

Your life is not one of those happy movies.

You ARE ONCE AGAIN IN front of Merrill's house. But don't worry; you didn't die this time. You might as well have, though. Your chest is heavy. It is very early in the morning. You don't know what you want anymore.

> Seek closure.

You don't knock on the door. You don't climb through the window. Instead, you walk to the back door and pull out the empty character sheet from your inventory. Where it says NAME, you write, Despite what you think, I do actually care about you. Just maybe I don't love you yet. It's the boldest and longest thing you've ever written on a character name slot.

You fold it up, write MERRILL on the front, and slip it under the doorway. Then you walk away.

You ARE ON THE ROAD. It is very long and winding. Exits are: north, south.

> Go toward home.

You start heading north. You know it's the responsible thing to do. Your parents will wonder where you are soon. And even now, you're not sure how to explain your departure. You'll say you just needed a walk. Yes. You needed some fresh air.

You think about Merrill's words: *I'm not Tristan.*

True. Merrill ≠ Tristan.

And you never thought you'd like Merrill.

Can you like everyone and no one simultaneously?

> Do somethin' crazy.

You turn around and go on a manic sprint south. You run past Merrill's house, past the closet taxidermist's house, past the woman who sunbathes topless in her front yard. You run past everything recklessly toward Tristan's house.

> Save over slot three.

You save over Merrill when you get to Tristan's house.

YOU ARE IN FRONT OF Tristan's house. Your parents are going to wonder where you are. There is a tacky birdbath in the front yard.

> Examine birdbath.

You've only been to Tristan's a couple of times, and you've never been farther than his yard. Even though he lives close, he always said you all should go to Merrill's instead. You always wondered why, but never had the courage to ask.

The birdbath still worked the first time you came here, but sometime during junior year, it broke. The birds still came to it though. And sometimes, you guys threw stuff in it when you were bored and had nowhere better to dispose of your horrible English Lit textbooks. Even now, there's the edge of Richard Rodriguez's *Hunger of Memories* you had to read freshman year. Before throwing it in the bath, you all took a page and ate it. Like some cultish twist of Communion.

> Take the book.

Despite your better judgment and phobia of getting bird flu, you take what's left of the Richard Rodriguez book and put it in your inventory. It's so water damaged that the only word you can make out from it is *HUNGER*.

> Walk up to the house.

You walk up to Tristan's house. None of the lights are on. It's eight-thirty now, late enough that Tristan is probably up. He works on the weekends, after all.

> Knock on the door.

You knock on the door. No one answers.

> Examine door.

It is a door.

Your hand stumbles over the doorknob, and you realize it's unlocked.

Forgetting all kind of propriety, you step in.

YOU ARE IN TRISTAN'S FOYER. It's very different than you imagined it to be; you've had dreams about it before. In your dreams, it has bright red shag carpet, like your old house when you were little. Instead, everything is ivory and celadon. Distant and elegant, but cluttered.

The hallway is full of boxes of half-opened boxes of china plates and brand-new electronics. The walls are crowded with mounted animal heads and framed pictures of Tristan as a little kid, alongside various academic awards he's won over the years. You blush at the invasion, and realize that Tristan's smile hasn't changed since he was five. It makes him all the more endearing.

"Hello?"

Your body freezes at the voice. You hope it's Tristan but realize the voice is much older and louder. It's Tristan's dad.

"Do you just walk into houses for fun? There's a door for a reason you know." As he comes down the stairs, you notice how different he is from how you remember him.

You said I could visit anytime, you almost say, thinking of the last time you saw him—how long ago was that? Your hands begin to shake. "The door was unlocked," you say. "I was looking for Tristan."

"He's left for work. Shouldn't you be somewhere?"

"It's Saturday." Your voice is fading. "When will Tristan be back?"

"Not for a while I suppose. You're one of his friends, aren't you?"

Slowly, you nod. "I'm sorry. I don't know why I'm here. I just hoped seeing Tristan—"

A small smile comes over his lips. "You startled me is all. It's a bit early for me to expect people, but I guess robbers come at any time of day they please."

You don't want to think of yourself as a robber, but maybe you are. Are you?

"Do you want some coffee or something? I'll have to head out soon, but if you like, you can leave a note for Tristan."

"I'm not sure what I'd write," you say, fumbling with your inventory straps.

Tristan's dad shrugs and starts the coffeemaker.

He motions to the kitchen counter. "There's some paper and pens in there, if you wanna write something."

You nod and walk over to the counter.

> Write a note.

Pulling out the paper and pen, you begin to write:

Dear Tristan—Merrill hates me, and it's all because I still have a crush on you. I thought I was getting over it, but it's like Merrill won't let me get over it. Whatever. I don't really know what to do with myself right now. I'm probably creeping the heck out of your dad right

You stop writing. This is way too honest. You might as well add:

My period just started yesterday, and I didn't change my pad before coming here. It's probably all brown and gross and stinky. I'm glad you don't have to smell it right now. Because it smells very, very bad.

But it doesn't matter anymore. You crumple the paper up and stick it in your inventory to hide the evidence.

"Have writer's block?" Tristan's dad asks, looking over.

You nod, covering the paper with your hand. "Some things just don't come out right, no matter how hard you try."

He laughs and takes a swig of coffee. "Unfortunately, that doesn't change when you get older. I have to get going, so if you want to leave anything for him, you should do it now."

He's probably making a mental note to make sure all his doors are locked at all times.

When you get to the stairs, he points at which door is Tristan's. You go up, your legs shaking.

You ARE IN FRONT OF Tristan's bedroom door. It has a sticky note with a heart on the front. You recognize Sephora's handwriting.

> Make an ambiguous, yet dramatic, statement.

You pull out the class photo of Tristan from your inventory. The corners are bent and it's kind of embarrassing, thinking about how much you've held onto this. But you take it and slip it under his door. You don't need it anymore. At least, you hope you don't need it anymore.

"Buffy. Buffy?"

The doctor's hand is warm on my back.

"Do you want to come back to your chair?" he says, bending over me. I must look like a kid, squatting on the floor with my head in my hands. A mediocre and brief relationship like mine shouldn't be traumatic, yet...

"Take a deep breath, Buffy. Deep, slow breaths."

I breathe.

"Thank you, Buffy. Now listen—I understand you've been going through a lot of stress. This stage of life is probably one of the most stressful periods that a person goes through. But I'd like to better understand this relationship you went through. What is it that upsets you so much? Everyone goes through breakups. Heck, most everyone's been on at least one or two obligatory dates." He laughs.

But he doesn't get it—how can he? I broke Merrill. I broke him, and it's something I can never be forgiven for, no matter how much I wish I could be.

Outside Your Dorm Window: October 11, 2009

I T'S TWO IN THE AFTERNOON. You are back at college. It's a relief, in some sort of weird way.

You realize now that you can't say you've never dated. Is that a good thing? Or a bad thing?

You were in a relationship for a whole week and a half. But even Alice and Aquitane never knew. You'd rather keep it that way.

> Get ready for class.

Class is in an hour, but before you go you set up your new laptop and try to transfer over as many old files as possible.

Alice and Aquitane aren't back. You wonder if they're still at a party from the night before. Or maybe they were kidnapped. Maybe they're dead. Who knows.

You hear a tapping at the window.

> Hide under blanket.

The side text reads: *Post-High-School Reality Quest*

You get on your bed and hide under your blanket. If kidnappers got your roommates, it's entirely conceivable that they'd come to get you, too.

The tapping continues. "Buffy?" You hear muffled from the other side, somewhere down below in the courtyard.

> Be adventurous.

You peek out from underneath your blanket and lean toward the window. You're on the second floor, you remember, so it's not like someone can just jump in.

Looking down, you see someone throwing rocks at the glass. It's someone you hoped you'd never have to see again for the rest of your life.

It's Jeremy.

WHEN YOU GOT ONLINE THIS afternoon, Sephora gave you unsolicited love advice. She said, *I'm sorry things aren't working out with you and Merrill. It's a shame, but at least there's other fish in the sea!*

You hate that phrase. Men ≠ fish.

But as you think about it, you let yourself have some hope in that phrase. Other fish in the sea. It's what lonely people tell themselves to feel better.

The first place you went to go fishing was with your dad, in some Virginian lake. The water was scummy and you wondered if anything alive could be found in there. Kind of like your first attempt at finding men, in the lake of online dating.

You don't feel like you can seriously use that site anymore, but whenever you see dating ads on the sidebars of your web browsing, you can't help but imagine Merrill. And you really wanna kiss someone again.

YOU ARE LOOKING OUT THE window. There is Jeremy standing there, throwing rocks at your window. Exits are: door, window.

> Hide under blanket again.

Not sure what to make of his presence, you hide again. Maybe he'll go away on his own. Or maybe you'll wake up from this nightmare.

You hear another rock. The glass scratches, and you imagine it cracking.

Not so much.

> Escape.

You run out of the room for the stairs but then realize he'll just be there, waiting. That there's nowhere to run.

> Go to the bathroom.

You walk into the communal bathroom. There are three stalls and three sinks. Exits are: stall, out, window.

> Escape via window.

You're becoming experienced in climbing out windows, but unfortunately for you, this one is screened in and locked. That, and you remember you're on the second story. That, and you can still see Jeremy from here. He's wearing a nice clean shirt and a bowtie. You're not sure whether to be impressed or creeped out.

> Go back to your room and re-evaluate your life choices.

You leave the bathroom and return to your dorm room. Aquitane is there, her hair cut up short and shaved on the sides, but all the more blue. She opens the window and leans out with half her body exposed to the cold.

"Yo! I don't know what you're doing here, you little shit, but you should go away."

"I'm here to see Buffy."

> Why can't someone who's actually dateable chase after me?

Aquitane pulls herself out of the window and straightens what's left of her hair. Looking at you with the disgust reserved for expired fridge food, she says, "You? And Jeremy? Seriously, you out of your mind?"

Your feelings on Jeremy are complicated. You feel a blush run up your cheeks. Though you know there's absolutely nothing of substance in him, and that he's clearly emotionally unstable, you can't help but feel a little flattered by the fact he came here to pursue you, or that you're not the only one who can't get over someone you love.

> Play it cool.

"At the party last month—" you say, taking a deep breath. "He kept following me around. Remember? How I wanted to leave?"

Aquitane stares at you for a minute, her lips forming into an O. "The little dickwad," she says.

> Talk before thinking.

"I can take care of it," you say. "I don't want you all mixed up in drama."

"You sure?" Aquitane squints her eyes at you, and you notice just how thin her eyebrows are, like she's plucked them herself, one hair at a time.

Are you sure?

You nod slowly and she turns to her desk. "Have fun then. Just know you can always call for backup, okay?"

You run down the stairs before you can stop yourself.

And as you run, you nearly trip and fall flat on your nose and break it. Nice.

When you open the door and walk into the courtyard, Jeremy looks at you shyly like he's filled with guilt. He says, "You didn't have to come down."

"My roommate was up there."

"You mean Alice's friend? I don't get why they hate me. If anyone should be hating, it should be me."

You don't know enough to make a fair judgment. "So, what's up?" That's your nice way of saying *what're you doing throwing rocks at my window? If you're gonna say something, just say it, dang it.*

He stares at you blankly. "'What's up?' I don't know. I just wanted an excuse to talk to you. I talked around and learned you were Alice's roommate. Go figure."

Contemplating the drunken circulation of information makes you feel suddenly naked.

"I...need to go to class soon."

"Oh. I see."

"But—maybe we could hang out another time?"

He smiles. "Yeah. Sure. I just—" He looks at the ground. You wonder why he couldn't just text you if this is all he was going to say, why rocks had to somehow get involved. "I just wanted to thank you, Buffy. You being there that other night that really helped me through a hard time. I know we haven't known each other long, but you're pretty amazing. Just saying. And, well, I'd like to get to know you better."

Your heart starts freaking out in your chest. This is like all those movies. And as much as you know that the movies don't always work out perfectly, you've always wanted your life to resemble a movie.

> Be nice, but not too nice.

"Thanks. That means a lot." You smile and turn back to the door.

"And Buffy?" He says, standing straight and still. "Sorry, one other thing. Do you know when Alice might be around? There's something I need to get to her. If not, I could maybe give it to you to get to her."

What are you, the new mail woman?

You shrug. "I never know where Alice is, honestly."

"Okay. I hear you." He turns to go. "Thanks, Buffy. And I want you to know, you're different than Alice. I mean that as a good thing. Don't change, okay?"

As you wave goodbye, you laugh: as if it's possible for someone to *not* change.

AFTER CLASS, YOU GET ONLINE in your dorm. No more online dating. What are you supposed to do with your time now?

> Haha. Very funny.

A message from Tristan appears. *Buffy?*

The thing that regulates your heart stops working, the way it does whenever you see a super cheap auction listed for the collector stuffed animal you've always wanted. Like your head is about to float somewhere high above you. But you're head's still there. Your fingers shake as you type.

Yeah?

I got home last night, and Dad said you were here. That you were looking for me.

Oh…

Is that true?

Maybe it's the ambiguity of chat-speak getting to you, but it almost sounds like he wants it to be true.

Yeah, you write. *I'm sorry. I was feeling kinda weird.*

Sorry I wasn't there. What's going on? You doing okay?

The idea of Tristan caring and worrying over you makes you want to giggle excessively. *I'm fine, I guess. Just went to talk to Merrill. He doesn't wanna talk to me. Like I broke his trust or something.*

Weird. Was it still about that internet dating site?

Yeah. You wonder how he knows about that. *I feel bad about it now—it was just something silly…I don't know.*

You can't say that it was a joke because it wasn't.

But you're so reliable. Some stupid joke with a site shouldn't affect that.

You blush. *Thanks* ☺

No problem. I don't get Merrill, but if you wanna talk, I get home at four most days.

Your mind starts going all kinds of places, and it causes this warming sensation in your toes.

Tristan has one more question. *Oh—I got back and there was a picture in my room. Did you leave that there?*

Your status says that you're offline.

TRISTAN TELLS CHASE THAT SEPHORA'S been calling in the middle of the night, asking for him to come over. And as much as Tristan would like to have Sephora in his bed in the middle of the night, the logical and moral confounds...confound him. You aren't supposed to overhear this, but Tristan says he doesn't get Sephora. She'll call like that, but then won't speak to him during the day. He finds it weird, and very counterintuitive.

"Do grudges hold over to the next day?" he asks, the sound of faucet water overpowering him.

Chase coughs. "How should I know? Women are weird, and Sephora's weirder than most."

You aren't supposed to overhear this because you're not supposed to be in the men's bathroom.

Sometimes, you do this when you're not thinking straight. Bathrooms look too similar if you ignore the signs above the door. And what's more is you're at an anime convention, so it's not like anyone pays much mind to someone in a black lace dress going into a men's stall.

Tristan laughs, but it sounds more like a recording.

Maybe it isn't your place to know these things, but you wish it would be. That maybe it would become your place, soon. Especially if this whole SephoraxTristan thing doesn't pan out.

> Blend into environment.

You flush the toilet.

YOU'VE BEEN WAITING ALL MONTH for this convention. You reason it might be a time to meet new men (or even friends) and get over the past few weeks of your disastrous life.

Because gaming cons are totally an abundant spring of emotionally stable bachelors and girls who can keep your secrets.

FOR THE ENTIRE DAY, MERRILL'S been starting all his stories out with "when Buffy and I were dating..."

It impresses you how many dating stories he can make when you two were dating for only a week. That and, perhaps more troubling, the fact that he's telling unsolicited dating stories to all your friends.

This convention is the first time you've all been together since the breakup. People don't ask questions. They don't have to. You reason that Merrill tells these stories to make it sound like he's re-acclimated to the single life. But it comes across as just the opposite. No one bothers to tell him this, though.

Merrill is wearing a dark cape and camo cat ears. They really don't go together at all except that they're both geek ware, but no one cares to tell him that cat boys don't typically also have dark mage powers. But nobody likes correcting Merrill anyway.

Tristan compliments your signature Lolita lace dress. You blush and thank him. Sephora eyes you two carefully, her hands on her disturbingly bare hips[7].

"I have your gift for you!" She says, pulling out a wrapped box. You open it and inside there's a chainmail necklace. You've never been into chainmail and it doesn't match your dress, but you can still admire its handicraft and Sephora's supposed thoughtfulness. Underneath the necklace, there is a folded letter.

> Question whether Sephora has ulterior motives.

Sephora smiles like you are the sunshine in her life. You know better than to believe that.

> Thank her and put the necklace in inventory.

"I found it in my jewelry box. I don't really do chainmail anymore, but I thought you'd like it." She winks and you realize she's leaning toward your ear.

"Wait to read the letter when you get home, okay?" she says.

You muster a nod.

YOU ARE IN A HOTEL lobby. Around you, there is an anime convention going on. Next to the elevator, there is a boy dressed as Link from *The Legend of Zelda*, playing a french horn.

Suddenly Merrill stops walking and makes an audible groan. Only when Tristan calls out, "Hey, Lawrence!" do you understand why. You all didn't exactly leave high school with warm feelings for Lawrence the hacker, who repeatedly squeezed your butt during Intro to JAVA, then swore it couldn't have been him because he's gay and doesn't like girls' butts. On Wednesdays, his excuse was that he mistook your butt for the guy next to you.

> No joke.

---

7 When Sephora told you she was dressing up as Slave Leia, you thought, *How appropriately whorish.* But you typed, *That sounds nice. Make sure to bring a T-shirt, just in case.* Sephora signed off then.

Merrill looks like he wants to side-tackle, Tristan but you know it's too late. Lawrence has spotted you and is coming over. His gamer belly is rounder than you remember, his bright red beard full and thick like a man's. He looks like he's twenty-seven, not nineteen.

"Well, time to make our escape," Merrill says, his voice surprisingly close behind you. You turn around and his head is just above your ear. Just as quickly, he disappears into the crowd of nerds and is gone.

"Hey guys, long time no see." Lawrence smiles and you try to muster a smile back. "Where's Merrill?"

"Oh, you know," you say. "He's got a lot going on."

> See? I can lie sometimes.

"How've you been, Lawrence?" Tristan grins, as if Lawrence is the kind of person who can be a good, long-time friend. "Still doing Yu-Gi-Oh?"

"Yeah, I guess you could say that. Have been playing in the tournaments here, but have been getting my ass handed to me on a silver platter." Shaking his fist, he says, "Tabletop club! May you be anathema!"

Well, *that's* a two-dollar word you haven't heard since theology class. Even so, the idea of damnation makes you shiver. How much do you have to hate someone to hope they'd go to such a horrible place?

Tristan laughs. "Yeah, there were totally some characters there. Do you remember Adrian—"

And the two start yakking like schoolgirls. Merrill's still nowhere to be seen.

Chase coughs, nudging you. What's he expect you to do?

"It's great seeing you, Lawrence. We should catch up sometime," Tristan says.

"You know, I'm heading over to the artist alley, if you wanna join me."

"Actually," Chase says, "we were heading to a panel."

"That's fine." Tristan pulls on his backpack straps. "I'll catch up with you guys later."

"You don't mean—" Sephora's shoulders drop. She looks so small that even her tiny costume engulfs her.

"I'll text you, and we'll meet up tonight, okay? Have fun!" Tristan and Lawrence go off in the crowd, chatting about something from high school.

Sephora watches them go. "Really?" she says, crossing her arms over her bare stomach. As if she might actually miss Tristan.

You think about following after him for a minute. If he sees something good in Lawrence, maybe you can, too?

THE CONVENTION HOSTS A DANCE party in one of the hotel ballrooms, and Sephora makes it the goal of the day to convince you all to go.

When you all walk up to the room for the dance party, a man says that you can't bring bags in there. You look down at your inventory and start to get all shaky, like you do when your blood sugar gets really low. Sephora just throws her purse in a corner of the hallway. The man says she can't do that. She asks why not, and he says there might be a bomb in it.

Chase laughs, but the guy isn't joking. He asks Chase to empty his pockets. Chase gets quiet then, and pulls his pockets inside out, making a 10-sided dice fall onto the floor, along with a crumpled piece of paper and a green penny. The man waves him through, and he walks into the dance party, just like that.

You are all in front of the door for the ballroom. There is a man with a beard and a yellow security smock. Exits are: elevator.

Merrill pulls out his cell phone and calls Tristan. "We need you up here," he says.

"Why?" You can hear Tristan's voice, distorted but defiant.

"Because." Merrill grips the phone until his knuckles turn white. "We need you to hold our stuff. They won't let us into the party with bags."

Tristan laughs, "Whoa. That's your problem, man. Explain to me why would I would hold onto your shit?"

Then he hangs up. Just like that.

Merrill stares at the phone in his hand in disbelief, like it's broken or something.

"It's no big deal," Chase says. "We can just drop them off in our room and come back."

But it is a big deal. You all know that, but nobody wants to say it. Merrill's lost his lackey—and if that isn't enough, he's lost you too, in the same week.

For the rest of the night, everyone is careful when they talk to Merrill. Even people like Sephora, who never seem to be careful with much of anything.

YOU ARE IN THE DANCE hall (a.k.a. a badly executed rave). There are lots of lights and a smell that you determine to be pot. So much for the "no bag" policy.

From out of her skimpy costume, Sephora reveals a pack of glow-sticks. You wonder how she could hide much of anything in her lack of clothing. She hands you a green glow stick. Breaking hers, she starts jumping up and down and screaming.

Exits are: out, stage.

> Climb on the stage.

You think about climbing on the stage, but you're smarter than that. Haven't you gotten the whole climbing on stage thing out of your system yet?

> Attempt to dance.

You dance in place and Sephora joins you, throwing in unsolicited pelvic thrusts. It makes you very uncomfortable. She laughs at your discomfort and continues violating your private space.

> Protect yourself from Sephora.

You dance away from Sephora and attempt to keep the façade of having a good time. Unfortunately, you aren't looking where you're going and run into Merrill, who's just standing there, not dancing.

He stiffens at your touch. You look up and apologize, but he shrugs like he doesn't mind. But he totally minds, and you know it.

"Where's Tristan, anyway? He's been gone for a few hours now." Sephora's thrusts get more intense. "Don't know what he thinks better about Lawrence than us."

Merrill shrugs. "This isn't daycare. If he wants to go off and make bad decisions, that's his own business."

No one else says anything about it. It makes you wonder: If you walked off too, would anyone care? Would anyone fight to get you back?

You look down at Sephora's ankles, which even in the dark you can see are red and swollen. "It's the straps," she says, as if reading your thoughts. "From the sandals. Not the most comfortable costume, but hey—beauty isn't painless."

You nod.

> What do I know about beauty?

You are in a dance hall. The music is very loud. If this day was up to you, you'd be anywhere else: probably a quiet panel discussing the top most underappreciated games in video game history.

"Hey, guys, how's it going?" You turn around and see Tristan.

"So you survived," Merrill's voice drops. If you didn't know better, you might think you heard a tone of disappointment.

"I know Lawrence was a jerk in high school, but he's not really that bad of a guy. And it was nice catching up, remembering some of the funny stuff that happened. Good times."

Merrill snickers, and the music gets louder, drowning out any attempts at real conversation.

"You've been gone so long!" Sephora whines, reaching her hands out. "Dance with me."

Tristan looks at her like she's asked him to eat a puppy. You're pretty sure Tristan doesn't have a coordinated bone in his body. Yet Sephora grabs Tristan's hand and tries to get him to move. At first he rolls his eyes at her, but then she smiles at him, and he follows her obediently. Once she gets him close enough, she gets her other hand on his shoulder and tries to lead him in basic dance steps. As you already know, Tristan's uncoordinated and he falters, but the two start laughing and trying to make something out of their poor dance moves. It's adorable, really.

You despise it.

Chase pulls out a camera from his pocket and tries to snap a picture of them, but you walk in front of it and cut off half the shot. Totally not intentional or anything.

They keep dancing. You wonder for a moment if there is in fact something, deep down, that's compatible about their relationship.

You tap your foot in solitude.

Sephora shouts over to you that you should dance with Merrill. Merrill frowns. Tristan and Chase look at her with sharp alert glances, like they're afraid a war's about to break out.

> Make the moment light despite your loneliness.

You walk up to Merrill and start doing the only dances you know: the ones from the internet.

Everyone laughs, even Merrill.

Crisis averted.

Despite it, Merrill doesn't say anything to you for the rest of the night.

JUST AS YOU ALL ARE getting bored of the dance hall and want to leave, the room fills with a pungent sulfur smell. You've smelled it once before: that time some kid decided it'd be funny to bring a stink bomb to school. Everyone stops dancing and puts their hands to their noses. A worker motions for everyone to evacuate the room. Once in the hallway, nobody moves. They all just stand there, complaining, frozen in place. Nobody goes to other panels, or returns to their room. You're all victims of the same experience; what could be done after that?

Shortly after, you see security escort someone out of the dance hall. In his dark cape, you're pretty sure it's Lawrence.

"What a surprise," Merrill snickers. "Funny how some people never change."

He looks at you when he says this, and for the rest of the day you try to figure out what exactly he meant.

You get home late that night. You're grateful to be in your own home, not your dorm, considering Aquitane and Alice are hosting a party in your cramped dorm room. You almost wanted to be there just to see how that would be physically possible, but you decided to just trust the careless Facebook pictures that would inevitably show up, and save yourself.

It's one in the morning and you want to go to bed, but your body's been up long enough that it doesn't know what to do with itself. Every few minutes, your legs twitch and you bite your pillow. You keep thinking about Tristan and how happy he looked with Sephora and how you blocked their picture. You wonder if you're the evil villain in this story.

> Remember to open Sephora's gift.

You dig in your inventory and find the box for the necklace. You have to dig under the packaging, but there's Sephora's promised letter. It says:

HELP ME. Get online as soon as you can.

> Those who fall behind get left behind. Right?

You consider throwing it away and never thinking about it again. Heck, what would Sephora ever need help with?

> Return SOS note to inventory.

You put your letter back in inventory and try to think about something else.

An hour has passed. You've been laying in bed in your underwear and knee-high socks. No matter how many pillows you add or subtract from the bed, you can't fall asleep.

> Distract yourself with silly pictures.

You get online and look for silly pictures of cats. You hate cats, but it still makes you feel better somehow. When you get tired of cats, you look up memes and can't help but see yourself as Hipster Ariel, who looks kinda like this:

And you can't help but imagine Sephora as Annoying Facebook Girl, who looks kinda like this:

That is, assuming your life could be broken into JPEGs.

But you get distracted from distractions when you see Sephora pop up online. You can't help it. It makes you get all self-conscious and even more anxious.

> Solicit the inevitable conversation.

Hey, Sephora—your note... you type.

Buffy! Hey listen, give me a sec.

You have nothing better to do so you just sit there and think about your life choices.

Sephora comes back online and says, *Sorry. Tristan was here.*

At two in the morning?

Yeah. We were fighting about earlier. He said he's sorry but I'm still ticked.

About what?

How he totally ditched me the whole day, hanging out with that asshole Lawrence. :sigh: We ditched that dude ages ago, for good reasons. And seriously— wtf was up with that stink bomb?

Yeah, that was weird—but Tristan wasn't involved in that, I'm sure.

Dunno. You can imagine Sephora shrugging her I-don't-care-about-other-people shrug. *What pissed me off was that he left. That's the thing I liked about Tristan—he never left. Now, I don't know. What if he does it again? I think I need to break up with him.*

You can't say you didn't totally see this coming. You begin typing *bitch,* then erase that for *slut,* then erase that. The cursor blinks.

It's not just about that. You remember the other day we were all at Merrill's and Merrill kicked us out and Tristan started bitching about it? You probably already knew this, but we all planned to do that to give you and Merrill alone time—you know, to see if anything would happen. I guess Tristan changed his mind about wanting Merrill to possibly get something that he wanted—and I don't know, it was just weird. Not to mention embarrassing. What's he, a kid? Sometimes I feel like I have to be his mom or something, and I don't like it. In fact, I don't know if I like him enough for that to be worth it. And I hate that I don't love him. But I need help.

THERE IS NO "MY FACE When" for this moment. The closest you could get is a cross between Overly Accusatory Donald Sutherland:

…Dubious Mila Kunis…

…You Don't Say Nicholas Cage…

…with a little I Know That Feel, Bro…

...and maybe even some Success Kid:

I know you're probably totally judging me right now, but hear me out...

Scrolling through your message history, you conclude that in the past three to five months, Sephora has had crushes on at least fifteen different boys, most of them people you've never actually met before. That must be some sort of record, you imagine.

When you don't say anything, she continues, *It's a lot of things, I guess. But I can't stop thinking about this: So the other day, we were in his bedroom, making out—wait, not like doing it, you know—just kissing and making out. We had all our clothes on, I promise—*

You're not sure what to say to that.

So anyways, I was on his bed, and we were laying on our sides, and I was on the edge of the bed when I saw something peeking out from underneath it. At first, I was like, I must be seeing it wrong. But when I looked again, it was still there. Tristan said he was going to the bathroom, and stepped out. So, when he was gone, I got up and looked under the bed and I was right—it was a gun.

You suppress the urge to laugh. For as long as you've known Tristan and Merrill, they've had all sorts of guns: the NES Super Scope, water guns, firework pistols, BB guns from when they were kids, paintball guns...

And I don't mean like a play gun, Buffy. I mean this thing was real.

Doesn't his dad do some hunting sometimes? you ask. *And I know Merrill's started going to the shooting range. So that doesn't seem—*

But this isn't Merrill, this is Tristan, Buffy. Tristan isn't someone who would go hunting. He always hates when Merrill does his fireworks and does all that loud stuff—I can't see him going shooting for fun. But whatever. It's weird, and I don't like it.

Your whole body is shaking. *You don't know jack shit about Tristan!* you send before you can stop yourself.

Silence.

There's no turning back now. *Look, Sephora—just because you make out with him all the time doesn't mean you know Tristan. He's a good guy, yes—but he does do lots of the same stuff Merrill does. Just because he has a gun doesn't mean—*

Oh, and you think you know him?

You stop and stare at the screen. The cursor blinks.

Sephora continues, *Just because you've been crushing on Tristan since forever doesn't mean you know him. But that's just it, Buffy—you're right about one thing. I don't know who Tristan is anymore. And that's the problem with us being a thing. Like, I'm scared to ask him about the gun. I told him I needed to go. I didn't want to be in that room anymore. Maybe it's just that we're out of high school or something but he seems different.*

We all change, you say. *That's natural.*

I guess... You see that she's typing, then stops.

The screen stays like that for a while.

You're tired. It's two in the morning. Exits are: sleep.

But Tristan's a good guy, you say. *You're tired. You're probably misinterpreting things.*

Tristan's the best guy I've been with. It's not like he's done anything wrong, and I like him for that.

You like that he'll come talk to you at 2 a.m.

Sometimes I need someone to remind me that I'm not going to wake up as the last person on earth.

> What can someone even say to that?

On your desk, your Pikachu alarm clock ticks too loudly, and you throw it across the room. The batteries pop out and Pikachu's tail breaks off. But at least it's quiet now.

You don't hear anything from her for several minutes. A world record. Maybe she's dead. Maybe you're the last person on earth.

Despite how many daydreams you have about this scenario, you don't actually want her to be dead.

After a few minutes, she says: *Buffy—have you ever worried that you'll never find someone to be serious with? That you'll get old but no one will ever stick with you, and so you never get married or have kids or anything?*

You try to remember the last time you had this serious of girl talk with Sephora. You type, *All the time. Don't we all?*

☺ *Okay. I guess that makes me feel better. Well...Imma go to bed.* Sephora pauses for a minute, typing then erasing then typing. *Buffy, you're a really good friend.*

You almost say, *you too,* but you know that'd be too much of a stretch.

Before you log off, you check your home profile. On your feed, you see the much anticipated party pictures. There's a boy posing on your bed, a red cup in hand.

It's Jeremy.

Treatment III:
June 21, 2010

WEEK TWO ON HALOPERIDOL. I'M supposed to journal what I'm feeling, but I haven't done it yet, so here it goes.

Sometimes I have this incredible silence in my head. It's absolutely terrifying. I should be happy—maybe this is working after all. But I hate the silence. It's like someone's carved me out of my own body and all I'm left with is an abandoned building.

I've been having trouble going to sleep—something I never had until starting college. Sometimes I just lay there for hours, my heart beating frantically, like I'm waiting for something to come and eat me. But when I do sleep, I have the trippiest dreams. I could write one down here, but they're kind of embarrassing. And they're so real—I feel everything as if it's actually happening. Plus, all the senses are heightened; everything smells stronger, the colors are all brighter. Is this what it's like to take drugs?

In all my dreams, there are pieces of flashbacks. When I'm awake, I feel like I'm trying to relive memories. I can't help but wonder what would've happened if I had said something else, if I had made different decisions, would I be here right now? I don't go to sessions with Dr. Moritz right now, but the sessions are continually happening in my head. Sometimes I just start shaking or pulling at my hair because there are some things you can never undo, and that kind of guilt makes me want to break my body in half as penance.

I looked at the side effects on the pill box. A lot of this is normal. I told the doctor, and he said to give it some more time before making any judgment calls. But right now, as I'm writing, I know something's wrong. Something that they don't warn you about on the box labels. I can't explain what it is, or why I know something's going to happen, just that I keep looking out the window, waiting for the world to end.

Y**OU ARE IN** T**RISTAN'S BEDROOM**. You've never been inside Tristan's house but it smells like him. There is a dog. You know its name is Skip-a-dee-doo-dah because you've read one-too-many Facebook posts.

Exits are: ?

> What's that supposed to mean?

You try to move but your legs are heavy.

Tristan's dad comes in the doorway behind you and asks, "You're Tristan's friend, right?"

> Check inventory!

You nod and try to check your inventory, but it's not available at this time.

> ...Pick up magazine off the floor.

You bend to the floor and pick up an old *Nintendo Power* issue from 1998. The floor is covered in them. It's like your childhood, in the form of a makeshift carpet.

"Tristan loves those things. I try to tell him to throw them out, that if they're ten-plus years old, they're probably worthless."

"He could probably sell them online," you say. Internally, you think it's cute that he saves them. "Is there anything else he likes?"

"Sorry?"

You remember why you don't always say just what you're thinking.

Exits are: forward, backward.

> Walk backward, like a boss.

You start walking backward, imagining what he'll tell Tristan after this: *Don't talk to that girl in the weird, lacy clothing. She doesn't seem to be all there in the head, if you know what I mean.*

"No, I'm sorry—" Tristan's dad says. "I didn't hear."

"Is there—anything else Tristan likes? Anyone else, I guess I mean."

"Oh. Well, I try to not interfere with his—"

"I should probably go," you say.

"No, stay!" Tristan's dad motions to a chair. Exits are: chair.

> Chair.

You sit on a chair and remember that Tristan's dad grew up in Australia. He tells you there's no income tax (a statement that you question), and that unlike the Chesapeake Bay, the water's very nice.

"I want to go there one day," you say. And by "one day," you mean now. It's one month before you move onto campus, but it feels like the world's about to end.

"Oh! I'll take you and Tristan there one day."

"Me—and Tristan?"

"Of course! He needs to get some fresh air. You know, my son can sometimes be a little odd… Doesn't get out of his room much. But he's still a boy, I suppose. If he says anything that bothers you, don't take it too seriously. He'll learn in time."

He hands you a whistle. It looks like a unicorn horn.

"You seem like a good girl, though. Good for him. If you ever need help, just call with this. Help will come. Help always comes."

> Blow the whistle.

You blow the whistle, but it makes no sound. You put the whistle in inventory and say, "I really should get going. Even if I don't want to."

Tristan's dad nods. "I understand. Feel free to visit any time, especially for Tristan. I'm sure he'd be glad to see you."

> Walk forward.

You get up and walk forward, only to wake up.

You check your inventory. There is no whistle.

You forgot to save again, didn't you?

Your Roommate's Closet: November 2, 2009

FIRST THING ON YOUR MIND when you get back to your dorm room is the bed. When you see Aquitane at her desk, opening and closing textbooks, you ask her what Jeremy was doing in the room, not to mention on your bed.

"Jeremy?" she says, looking at you like you were the one wasted on Saturday.

"Jeremy," you repeat. "On Facebook, there's a picture of him here. At the party the other night."

"Really?" She scratches her now-blue scalp. "I don't remember seeing him there."

> Bury her in the couch.

You don't want to be a suspect for the murder of your roommate. You hold your hands inside your pockets.

> Show her the picture.

You pull up the picture online while Aquitane complains about the lack of vodka in this room. You remind her that Alice refills her stash behind the cleaning supplies in the closet when it runs low. Because that's where you would totally put a stash of vodka, if you were an underage drinker.

You realize that, in her own way, Alice is looking out for her roommate.

Aquitane goes looking for vodka right when you pull up the picture. "See?" you call. "Here he is. On my bed. I thought you guys hated him or something, but…"

Aquitane can't see because her butt's up in the air, her head searching through bottles of chemical and alcoholic substances.

"I don't see any vodka," she says, her voice rough.

"Then talk to Alice later. But look."

She gets up and looks at your screen. "Holy shit, it's him."

> Be a detective.

You nod and look up at her. "Alice's story's more complicated, isn't it? With Jeremy, I mean?"

Aquitane shakes her head. You wonder if the high concentrate of blue from her head will splatter across the room. "If you mean that Jeremy's still obsessed with Alice, then yeah. When she didn't want to be as serious, I guess he didn't know how to take it. It's freaking her out. He doesn't know how to deal with 'no.' You know one time, he had this giant bouquet of flowers delivered to Alice's door. And let me clarify: This wasn't to her dorm, it was to her house. Like, her *parents'* house. How he got her address, I don't even want to know."

"Okay, so he's weird—I get that. But I mean on Alice's end."

Your roommate frowns. "What are you getting at?"

"I just mean—it seems weird that he can get this much info out of Alice and all. He found me, he found our room, he found a way *into* our room—is it possible that Alice is letting him get away with it?" A revelation hits you. "That maybe she still likes him a little? And she can't completely turn him down?"

"He's a *creep*, Buffy. It's what he does. He doesn't have a life, Alice *is* his life—"

"But like, if Alice is so creeped out by him, then why are they still Facebook friends?"

"Alice doesn't like dickwads like him!" Aquitane says, her voice getting loud. "She doesn't *do* relationships. Got it?"

"I'm just trying to help," you say. "Maybe we could get him to go away—"

"It's no use." Aquitane huffs and says, "Better to just ignore him. But whatever, I'm going to class. Try to get your nose out of trouble, Elizabeth."

Great. It's only been a few weeks of school and your roommate already has shouted at you.

> Also, made false accusations about needing to get
my "nose out of trouble." My nose is *not* sniffing up
trouble. I just don't understand how I'm supposed to
feel about Alice and Jeremy. And shouldn't I wonder?

THERE'S **ESOL** CLUB TODAY, BUT you know it's going to be a low turnout. They're all studying, or at least that's what the emails say. You're tempted to skip—it's not like your presence would be missed, after all. But you don't have any homework, or anything to do, and you feel the need to talk to someone, even if they don't speak your language very fluently. Maybe, in a way, that would be an asset.

When it's time for the club to start, no one has shown up. There's just Jake, sitting in his usual spot, looking over notes.

"Do you know if anyone's coming?" you ask, questioning the goodness of your heart that convinced you to come today.

Jake shrugs. "I was just gonna wait it out for a while, see if anyone shows up late."

"Don't you have other things you have to do?"

"Yeah, but these students are more important."

You smile. "You're a guy. Maybe I can ask you about something."

"Why, yes, I am." He laughs. "Give me a shot."

"So if you found out your girlfriend was using an internet dating site while you two were dating, what would you do?"

He raises his eyebrows. "What would I do? Well, first I guess it depends on what kind of site we're talking about—is this glorified porn like Chat Roulette—"

"Oh gosh, no!"

"Or something really serious like Christian Mingle or eHarmony.com—"

"I think you're using the term 'serious' a bit loosely..."

He laughs.

"No, it's like one of those silly ones where you just make a page and describe yourself and people message you if interested. It's not serious questions like "do you wanna get married" and "how many kids you want." It's just meant for fun."

"Well…I guess I'd be wondering why my girlfriend was doing that. Seems…questionable."

You bite your lip. "But what if it was just a joke, just something for fun? How could you know the difference?"

"Maybe if you're single, it's funny to get a site, but if you're dating someone already, where's the joke?" He taps his fingers against the desk. "Are you going to actually tell me what happened, or keep talking in hypothetical stories that are totally not hypothetical at all?"

You turn red, looking at the wall. "Well—it's just…"

He watches, waiting.

You let out a sigh. "I started this internet dating site—I didn't mean it to be serious, it just seemed like a fun thing to do. You know, people message you, and the attention's nice. But then I started dating this guy—this guy I went to high school with and, well, it wasn't going to work out anyway, but then he found the site and dumped me."

Dumped. You envision a dump truck with you in the back, lowering your body into a landfill, Merrill at the wheel.

Jake nods. "High school romances don't really seem to work well anyway."

"We weren't—"

He laughs. "It sounds like it's probably for the best anyway. But let that be a lesson to you: Internet dating is no joke. There's some weird stuff that goes on there."

You roll your eyes. "It's not like I'm giving strangers my social security number or anything."

"Well, in the end, it's your choice. But if you wanted advice from a guy, there it is." He shoots you this smile that appeals to you, despite the fact there's nothing about Jake that you find particularly physically attractive.

Looking at the clock, Jake stands up. "It looks like no one's coming today then. It happens this time of year, with all the project deadlines and exams coming up."

"Yeah…"

He turns off the light, but you stay at the front of the room. "You coming?"

> Right. Reality.

You nod and follow him out.

As he locks the door he says, "Thanks for coming; sorry to make you come all the way out here just for no one to come."

"It's okay. Thanks for listening to me—sorry to be all weird like that."

"Weird like what? It's fine; I enjoyed talking." He smiles. "See you around, Buffy."

See you around, you think but forget to verbalize.

See how easy that was?

> How easy what was?

Talking to someone else about your life? Making new friends?

> If you mean talking to Jake, then yeah...it was easy talking to him, I guess. Maybe I should talk to him more often about stuff.

Maybe you should.

A Place with Evidence of Decay: November 4, 2009

YOU HAVE A DREAM WHERE you win an all-expenses-paid trip to Romania. It's good enough for you; you're just waiting to get out of this place, anyway. The sponsors tell you that you can invite five friends to come with you. To go to Romania with you. In November.

You think about who you'd want to invite.

You think about it really hard.

Way harder than you should have to.

You should really have more friends than this.

You settle with bringing Alice, Aquitane, Sephora, Chase, and Tristan. You know Merrill won't go with you after all this.

When you guys actually get to Romania, there are a bunch of old ladies in hot springs outside the airport. You suspect that they're gypsies. Aquitane jumps right in, clothes and all, which is when you realize all the old ladies are naked, which makes you very uncomfortable. Then Alice starts trying to strip in front of Chase, who pulls out a Barrett M98 from his backpack and threatens to blow her brain out. And the only question that bothers you is: how did he get that through airline security?

As you're watching them, you think about Jake from ESOL. Maybe you shouldn't have brought anyone else: just Jake. Your body throbs with regret, and without saying anything you get back on the airplane and return home.

From the airport you walk to Jake's house (wherever that is) and make out with him in the front yard, which oddly reminds you of Tristan's house, with the defunct birdbath and the way the trees are laid out. When you wake up, there's a pool of drool on your pillow.

The idea of Jake makes you confused to say the least. Usually when you have dreams of making out with guys you hardly know, you wake up grossed out and confused. You don't quite feel that way right now though.

> Would I take Jake with me to Romania?

> Who else would I bring?

You think about it for a while, but still don't come up with any real answers.

IN YOUR BED, YOU THINK about going to ESOL today. Remember? That class you allegedly teach?

You've already had excuses of being sick, having too much homework to do, and not sleeping well. The director of the program should be asking why she's giving you service credit for this, assuming she's actually paying attention to what the students in her program do.

But every time you think about going in, you feel like you want to vomit. And every time you actually get the guts to go up there in front of all those students, you can hardly get yourself to speak, as if English isn't your first language either.

> I don't know why, it's just something that happens... I'm busy, you know? Maybe I'm just not good at that. Lesson learned.

What's so bad about Jake? Okay, he's a little quirky.

But so are you.

> I'm not sure what that has to do with anything—

Are you really going to stop going because of him?

> I've had enough dating advice from you. I'll tell him I'm sick...or something.

One time at ESOL, a couple students complained about feeling like they're completely segregated from the rest of the school. "We never meet Americans," they said. "It's like most people try to avoid us."

You relate to that feeling all too well.

TODAY IS YOUR BIRTHDAY. Y**OU** should really be more excited than this.

Mom left you a gift on the counter, like this is Christmas and she's an impersonator for Santa. There's an envelope with *BETH* on the front.

Dang it, Santa doesn't even know your name. You're known by so many names at this point that you feel a little bit like Sephora.

> Open.

You open the envelope. Inside there's a card. Inside the card is a gift card to a local supermarket. The card reads: *Sorry I'm out today, but there's a meeting I couldn't reschedule. Hope you understand. Get something delicious and have a very special day! Love, Mom*

Translation: Mom's too lazy to figure out what counts as vegan anymore.

Today is your birthday but you have no idea what to do to celebrate. Last night, Merrill sent you a text to invite you to his place for a day of video games and November fireworks. You say you're busy, but busy with what?

It's the first time you've turned down Merrill, probably in forever. Which is really weird when you think about it.

> Do whatever it is that you do for fun.

Since no one's home, you go into the rec room and unfold your easel from the closet. You set an empty canvas on top. There's an art project due next week, so you might as well get a head start. Because that's fun. And birthday-ish.

The project is to paint an animal. You look out the window and catch a squirrel in your periphery.

> Paint the squirrel.

You get some brown paint and start shaping the basic body of the squirrel. Your model starts scaling the house and attempts to jump off the roof.

A squirrel was a bad decision.

> Paint from memory.

You try to remember what a squirrel looks like for painting, but you forget some of the crucial parts. You begin to question if squirrels have whiskers or not, and what their toes look like.

The light brown starts making you think of Tristan's hair.

Dang it, does *everything* have to be about Tristan?

Seriously? He's not even that incredible of a guy.

> Ignore inappropriate commentary.

> Try a different technique.

You start throwing paint. If you had to nail down what exactly caused this frustration, you'd blame:

- Your period (though that was a week or two ago, so that can't really be starting up again now)
- Your sucky birthday
- Tristan
- and possibly Sephora, too.

Your phone goes off. It's a text from Tristan. It says, *Facebook says it's your birthday, so happy birthday!*

You're glad Tristan trusts such a reliable source for his information.

Another text comes. He continues, "Also, you coming to Merrill's tonight? I think his mom made a cake for you or something."

You love Merrill's mom, even if you've only met her a couple times.

> Reply.

You say, "Thanks! And I don't know. Not sure I feel up to it."

What does that even mean? It's not like you're sick or anything.

Paint's gotten on the floor, somehow. You tell yourself it's not your fault, that if Mom asks, you'll say it was the pet you've never owned. And when she asks why you didn't just put newspaper down, you'll have to think of a better explanation.

Because apparently, your excuses suck today.

IT'S 8:39 P.M. AND YOU lay on your bed, wanting to fall asleep. Somewhere outside your window, Chase is lighting fireworks in the cold dark. Even from here, you hear a soft popping noise above you.

YOU GET A CALL FROM Chase. It's ten o'clock at night. "Buffy, my car just flipped over into a ditch," he says.

You start hyperventilating like you were the one whose car just flipped over.

"I'm *fine*," he qualifies for your sake. "Merrill's bringing me to the hospital. But I need someone to come and help with the car."

> Prepare for an overnight hospital trip.

"Do you need food? Drinks? An oxygen mask?" You start going across your dresser, sweeping everything into a bag.

"You don't have to worry about *anything*. But if you could show up, that'd be amazing. I'm on the street right outside Merrill's house. Oh look, someone's getting the gurney now."

"They're putting you on a *gurney*?"

"We're not sure what's up with my leg. It's kinda just not doing anything."

"Oh gosh, Chase!"

"I've done worse—merk!"

The phone line disconnects. You hurry and call Merrill.

"Huh?"

"Merrill—is Chase okay?"

"Chase? He's right h—I mean, yeah. They're taking good care of him. Don't worry."

"I'm on my way," you say, and instead of walking over, you get in the car and drive the couple of blocks.

You are outside Merrill's house. There are no cars in ditches. In fact, there are no ditches. There are no emergency vehicles. It is late, and your brain reasons, *Man, we sure have efficient emergency care around here.*

You knock on Merrill's front door. There isn't enough time for the back. You're in your unflattering aqua sweatpants, but you can't be worried by things like that right now.

Merrill opens the door.

"Merrill—is Chase—"

Behind you, you see Chase standing there—no casts, no gurneys, no sign of bodily harm.

> Embrace Chase.

Without thinking, you run past Merrill and hug Chase, without considering that there could be hidden injuries. He hugs back.

"Chase! I was so—"

Sephora looks at you with jealousy. You let go of Chase but hold onto his arms, more for the sake of making Sephora angry than anything else.

You look around the room. "Wait…you…"

Tristan motions to the cake on a table. It looks store-bought, but someone took the time to write *Happy Birthday, Buffy!* Except in binary.[8]

Sephora says, "Surprise!"

"We knew you'd come if we…you know," Merrill says, his eyes on the floor.

This is the part where everyone is supposed to start laughing and celebrating, but no one laughs. No one teases you for being a concerned human being. They all just look at you with these semi-sad eyes, as if realizing that no one's cared about them that much before to be so worried.

> Cry.

You want to start crying—whether it's from birthday loneliness, or fear of Chase in a ditch, or late-night confusion, but maybe you're just too overwhelmed and dumb-struck for crying. So you just stare.

Tristan walks over and hugs you. "So… Happy birthday and Chase-not-being-in-a-ditch!"

There are a few laughs.

> Save over Jolt soda encounter.

You save. Man, that was a while ago. You still had that there?

Tristan is still hugging you. His body is warm and firm. You wish you could just crawl into his chest and fall asleep between his lungs.

> Hold on for as long as you can.

You hug Tristan tight and squeeze the back of his shirt. He must feel it because you hear a soft, but present, gasp. "You doing okay?" he asks, his smile disappearing. "Did the Chase thing really freak you out?"

> Remember yourself.

You let go and nod. Sephora walks behind Tristan and begins nibbling on his ear, looking at you with spite the whole time. For a girl who isn't even in love, she sure is possessive of her property.

Merrill cuts you a slice of cake and hands it to you on a napkin. He tries to not look at you when he hands it, but your eyes meet for a second and he smiles, looking away.

> Put aside vegan values.

The cake is stale and sugary, mainly due to all the binary icing. You eat until you feel sick because Sephora insists she's not hungry and you hate the idea of

---

8 01001000 01100001 01110000 01110000 01111001 0100000 01000010 01101001
01110010 01110100 01101000 01100100 01100001 01111001 0100000 01000010
01110101 01100110 01100110 01111001 0100001

having to throw away any of it. You don't feel you can leave any earlier. They're trying to love you in the way they know how. That much you can tell, and it's sweet. But you sit on the couch and chew and think about the new life you want to start: the life where you're not naïve, and you aren't coerced to go to someone's house when you don't want to.

In your dream world, you carry shotguns in your purse, and everyone buys your paintings because they just love you so darn much in your adorable lace dresses. And Tristan takes the hint that you love him, and asks you out for dinner. And you laugh out loud to everyone's jokes and put your feet up on the coffee table, because you aren't afraid of things.

> So what do I have to do?

Sorry?

> What do I have to do, to change my character? Do I need to earn up some kind of currency? Buy mods or something? Whatever it is, just tell me.

I'm sorry, it's not that—

> I don't care. I'm going nowhere in this. In fact, it feels like things are getting slowly worse, like I'm sliding off the edge of a table. That's not how games are supposed to work. There's supposed to be action, adventure, romance, easter eggs—

Around you, the room's fallen into conversation about video games you've never played. The air smells sweet and thick with icing. You can't help but feel cheated.

> Start a new game.

Treatment IV:
July 3, 2010

I SAW A FACE IN THE window last night. I've never had visual hallucinations, and I know that's what my doctor would call this, but the face was so real—it glowed like it was made out of gold leafing illuminated by one of those day lamp bulbs. All I could think about are those pictures of angels from the storybook Bible my parents got me when I was little. What I mean is—I'm not saying I saw an angel or anything—but if I didn't know better, I'd say that's exactly what an angel looks like.

"You *saw* something, you say?"

I nod. I don't tell him what I saw. "I've never seen anything before. It's always hearing. Nothing I see changes." I pull out the pill bottle and slide it across the table. "This thing's doing something janky to me. I can feel it in my body. I need to get off of it."

He examines the pill bottle. "There are still quite a few pills left in here, even though your prescription should just be running out right about now. Did you take a pill three times a day, like it said on the instructions?"

I scratch the dead skin behind my ear. A glorious snow shower of dandruff rains down on my shoulder. A bad habit that started about a week ago.

He leans over the table. "Buffy. I know that this is a very strange place to be. Sometimes, it doesn't feel like anything's wrong, or that you can handle all this on your own. But the medicine is here to help you. And if you only take the medications on and off, it won't help you—it'll just bring you back to square one. And we've been at this for almost two months already—do you really want to go back to square one?"

Maybe if I don't say anything I can disappear into the floor.

He taps his fingers on the desk, looking at me without blinking, as if that'll break me into saying I'm sorry or something. When that doesn't work, he lets out a sigh. "I can't do anything until it's clear this one isn't working. Finish up the rest of the pills, and if it's still not working, we'll switch you to another one."

A package on my desk. It's the new prescription, a second chance at killing the thing inside me. Why does taking these pills make me feel like I'm performing my own abortion?

They aren't supposed to have a taste, but they taste bitter and powdery, like old people's breath. Sometimes I wonder if I actually want to end this game or not. It's been going on for so long now that I almost don't know what I'd do with myself, not playing it.

I swallow. Maybe it's all in my head, but already I feel it change me. I feel like I'm back two years in the past, and it's the end of the world—my hands start shaking, and my breathing gets fast. Why? What am I afraid of?

Just as suddenly, I feel a weight on my shoulder, warm like a hand. I turn around but there's nothing there. The weight lifts, replacing the warmth with an empty chill. Yes, it's official. I've gone off the crazy deep end.

WELCOME TO **POST-HIGH SCHOOL REALITY** QUEST! Would you like to load a saved game?

> No. I'd like to start a new game.

I'm sorry, I don't understand—

> I want to start a new game. Forget the save slots. Forget everything. Forget Buffy—

Whoa. I don't think you know what you're saying.

> Yes. Yes I do. I'm sick of this crap, and I want a redo. What do I have to do, blow on the cartridge and plug it back in?

Don't be silly. We're way beyond that point. What I mean is—it's impossible to completely erase saved data. In unfortunate circumstances, some data might be corrupted—

> And what corrupts it? Sand storms? Exposure to moisture?

You're missing the point. Buffy, there are two ways to play this game: You can follow the hints I give, or you can continue to crash. I can't make you do either.

> And you can't just start everything over and fix it all.

No, Buffy. You have to choose that.

THERE WAS A FIGHT. YOU can gather that much.

It's 2:00 p.m., and you're Skyping with Tristan when his phone starts ringing. He rolls his eyes and lets out a dramatic sigh.

"What?"

"It's Sephora."

You frown despite feeling incredibly excited. "She's your *girlfriend*, Tristan. Shouldn't you be happy to hear from her?"

"Yeah. If Sephora was ever the bearer of good news."

You open your mouth to ask why he's dating a girl he can hardly stand to talk to, but he's already stood up from the computer and answered the phone.

"Hello?" he says. "Hey, Sephora—what's...you *what*...hold on a sec." He covers the mouthpiece of the phone with his hand and says, "Sorry, I'll be right back."

He closes the call from his end and all you have is an empty chat feed to stare at.

It's Tuesday, and class was cancelled due to November snow. Seriously—this state can hardly seem to handle snow when it comes in the normal months. When it snows in *November,* everyone freaks out like it's the apocalypse.

Unfortunately for you, you're stranded on campus because no one could pick you up with the short notice. You've resorted to emulator games on your laptop and talking to Tristan. Which really, when you think about it, isn't a half bad way to spend your day.

LAST NIGHT, ALICE WENT ON a midnight 7-Eleven run and got five Coke slurpees, two hot dogs, and a giant bag of chips. She said she was stocking up for the storm.

But before it even got to snowing, she'd eaten half the bag of chips and chugged four slurpees. At 3:00 a.m., she vomited it all up on the carpet, moaning, "I just can't believe...there wasn't room for it all." She left the fifth slurpee sitting on her desk, where it's completely melted now. Your room smells sticky with Coke.

Outside, the ground is covered in snow. Some kids have made a snowman that is at least one story high. You look out your window again and he's gone. Not melted. Just plain gone.

A message from Tristan pops up: *Gah.*

?

Sephora wants me to drive up to see her.

Doesn't she go to school like an hour away? And didn't it just snow? Like, a lot?

She says she's lonely. I've tried telling her that that's not realistic and then she freaks out and calls me a horrible person. And now she won't shut up.

> Say something mean.

Tell her to get over herself.

Haha. Maybe at some point.

> Say something more helpful.

Tell her you have to go. That you have more important things to do, too.

She'll get even more mad.

Tristan?

Yeah?

Do you love Sephora?

No typing icon shows up. Five minutes later, his name shows up as idle.

On Black Friday, Tristan has news for you all.

Thanksgiving night, Sephora was found at two in the morning outside Chase's house. Chase refused to answer the door. And when she started stripping outside his window, he called the police. They took her to the police station because they didn't know what to do with her.

This morning, Tristan said they might just be better as friends.

When Tristan tells this story in person, Merrill laughs and says, "Man, you got off easy."

You laugh in your hand, but it's actually to try to stop yourself from vomiting with nervousness. You are on Merrill's couch. It's just you, Merrill, and Tristan in the basement. Everyone else is out for obvious reasons. This is an annual tradition: to barricade away from the crazy shoppers and watch movies. Only none of you are watching movies right now; there doesn't seem much of a point with only three people.

"Yeah." Tristan scratches the back of his head. "I'm blocking her number from my phone and everything. I never want to hear her voice again. So I guess that's what I'm thankful for today."

> This is what starting over feels like.

You become fascinated with the couch fabric, the way the pattern weaves in and out, and in and out...

"And now there's no more reasons to invite Sephora over. Finally," Merrill says, leaning back until the couch creaks. "You should find someone with good taste, Tristan. Go out with someone like Buffy or something."

> What!

Your eyes open wide and wanting, your chest throbbing until it feels like your whole body might suddenly burst, if held too tightly. You bite your lip, all to stop yourself from screaming, *Yes! Yes!*

You look up at Merrill, trying to read him and understand why he's helping you. He doesn't look at you, but instead at the dead TV in the corner, and the musty VHS tape pile beside it. And that's when you realize, without a doubt, that Merrill really does, intentionally, love you.

After break, Tristan asks online if you want to go out. *Not like it's a big deal or anything,* he says. *We can hang out, just casual. What I mean is—we don't have to do anything official, if you don't want to... Gosh, why's this stuff always so complicated? I feel like I have to make, like, ten disclaimers with just proposing the idea.*

You're okay with complicated, as long as the complicated is with Tristan. Preferably, that complication wouldn't be happening so close to finals, but hey—you can't get everything.

You find it cute that he can handle the complexity of theoretical math equations, but not females or emotions. You want to tell him how much you love him, how you've loved him for a while now, and how you'd love nothing better than to bear his children. How if anyone had asked you what you were thankful for this Thanksgiving, he would've been the answer.

You have to type and retype *Okay* three times before your shaking hands get it right.

As you hit enter, Alice walks in the door and throws her bag on her bed.

Alice isn't exactly the person you want to go to for love advice, but you can't help but squeak, "Tristan just asked me out!"

She turns to you, her eyebrow peaked. "Tristan?"

And then you vomit out the whole story.

She makes a face like she just chugged a glass of vodka. "Whoa—talk about being the rebound!"

"Rebound?"

"Buffy. Get out while you can. Rebounds are *shit*. You don't want to be some old whore's replacement. Guys can't handle being single for five seconds. You're only there to make him feel less lonely."

You think about Alice's exploits and wonder if she's someone to speak on loneliness.

> Defend yourself.

"I know Tristan," you say. "I went to high school with him. Plus, he probably doesn't even know what a rebound is. He couldn't hit a squirrel with his car, even if he tried."

Alice keeps her hands folded, fingers tapping. "All I'm saying is—a guy doesn't ask a girl out right after breaking up, and want more than some nice comfort food, if you know what I mean."

"I'm not looking for anything serious," you say. "I just want some fun."

But you know it's a lie as soon as it comes out of your mouth.

Aᴏᴜɪᴛᴀɴᴇ ᴛʜɪɴᴋs ɪᴛ' s ᴀᴅᴏʀᴀʙʟᴇ ᴛʜᴀᴛ you're finally going out. She demands to help figure out your first-date outfit. Afraid of arriving to Tristan's with bright magenta hair, you say you'll be fine on your own.

"I mean it though. Think of it as me buying your dinner."

It's Friday and you feel like you might vomit from excitement. You finished your last exam at noon, so you have nothing to work on, nothing to study for. Nothing to do but wait.

Exits are: out, window.

> Window.

You walk toward the window but Aquitane gets the hint. "Come on, hun," she says. "At least see what I come up with. You might even like it."

Aquitane walks over to her dresser and pulls out a giant fold-out box of make-up that makes you think of your paintset back home, containing pretty much every conceivable color. Aquitane has colors you didn't think were used in make up like gold, green, orange, white, but apparently that just shows how naïve you are.

It's only when Aquitane colors your lips a dark purple that you realize just how light your lips naturally are, how light all of you is. She asks what color of eye shadow you'd like and you pick the most absurd one you can find. You feel like a kid in a beauty salon, or a candy shop: someone's actually asking for what *you* want. Needless to say, that doesn't happen very often.

"So how'd you meet him?" Aquitane asks, brushing on some eye shadow.

> Trust your roommate with your story.

"We went to high school together," you say and blush. "I've kinda always had a thing for him…"

"Aw—that's so cute."

You wonder if that's all your life is: cute.

"Do I look okay?" you ask suddenly, examining your pasty skin and flat hair. You haven't given these things much thought before. "Do you think he'll—"

"It'll be *great.*" Aquitane smiles a way you've never seen her smile before. Almost motherly, really.

She reaches over and outlines your eyelashes in mascara. "Just have a good time for me, okay?"

You wonder what she means at first—wondering if there's something that you possess that Aquitane doesn't.

She steps back, examining your face, and smiles. Before you can fully examine her, she turns to the wall and rubs her eyes. "You're all good," she says, and leaves you alone in your room.

In the Rain:
December 4, 2009

YOU ARE EVERYTHING YOU EVER wanted to be. Plastered in Aquitane's battle armor, you feel like you could punch Sephora in the face right now.

The bottle of raspberry rum Aquitane gave you is also helping. You feel like you could conquer the world. And vomit. You didn't want to be one of those drinkers, but you reasoned, this one time…

> She said it helps with nerves.

Inside your chest, your body moves in sequence, thinking about how monumental of a turn this is in your story.

> This has to be the last level, right? I'm almost done. I'm gonna win.

I'm sorry. I don't understand "last level." What is that?

YOU ARE IN YOUR KITCHEN at home. Your dad just brought you back from campus. When he picked you up, he said, "What's with that make-up? Don't tell me you're going through that goth phase again."

You said something like, "I thought I'd give it a shot today—the make-up I mean, not the goth thing."

For the rest of the ride back, your dad didn't say anything. Now, you feel a nausea that even medicine won't get rid of.

You think about Sephora and wonder if you can't compare to her whorish magic. If Tristan will regret this as soon as it starts, or if Sephora will come bursting through the window—right when you two are about to kiss and everything—and throw pies in your faces. You wouldn't put it past her, really.

Dad's already started dinner. Cilantro and chicken, from what you can smell. *What will it take for someone in this house to remember that I'm vegan?* "I have plans for tonight," you say.

He turns from the stove and looks at you. "Another Friday party? In that?"

You look down at Aquitane's outfit and wonder if he has a point. The skinny black jeans with chains and the sequinned top look a bit too mainstream for you. But it's the thought that counts. "It's only down the street," you say, like that makes it any better.

"I thought you were just hanging out with a buncha kids and playing video games."

"I am," you say, because it's true.

"Then what're you all dressed for?"

You are in the kitchen. The stairwell's just a few steps away. If you run fast enough you can get upstairs before having to give an answer.

> Stay.

You don't answer him but instead just stand there, your body rigid. You want food, you realize.

"Your mom should be home soon," he says, turning back to the chicken. "She might be able to give you better advice."

Advice about what, you wonder?

> Go upstairs.

You go upstairs to your room. Outside, the sky looks clear. There is an umbrella by your door.

Your room is covered with lots of things you don't need. Only now do you walk in and really realize that. You're not sure what you're supposed to bring to an unofficial first date but you grab your purse and throw in duct tape (always handy) and breath mints (because they're always in the commercials).

At the bottom of your purse, you find Sephora's necklace and her SOS note. For a moment you toy with the idea of wearing it. But instead you toss it on the floor and head for the door.

Downstairs, you hear the front door open and Dad say something. You imagine your parents embracing and blush when you wonder if you and Tristan will be in a similar arrangement one day.

Your mom's heels click up the stairs. She walks past your bedroom but then does a double take when she sees you. "Beth?" she says, looking over you. "You look *great!*"

Exits are: under your bed.

"You going somewhere tonight?" she asks.

> Tell her without really telling.

"I can neither confirm nor deny my plans for the evening."

Your mom smiles and walks into your room. You aren't known for taking advice from your mom. She once tried to buy you a Gucci purse for your birthday. "It's good quality," she said. It was supposed to be her way of telling you that she loves you. And you tried to act thankful, but it still sits in your closet somewhere, unused. It's been her life goal to relate to you, and as much as both of you try, you are not the daughter printed out of a Forever 21 catalogue.

She examines your outfit and says, "You missed a button." Bending over you, she unbuttons part of your shirt and re-buttons it correctly. "Seeing a boy tonight?" she asks.

You're not sure how to answer that question.

She laughs. "I was eighteen once, too. Let me just give you one piece of advice." Then, in a way only your mother could get away with, she takes your breasts and fluffs them to try to make them look larger. But you know it's a hopeless case.

"It's not like I'm big myself. But you've gotta use what you've got, right?"

You nod because it seems right. You'd rather not talk about breasts with your mom.

"You want a ride over?" she asks.

"I'll just walk."

"You sure? I'm heading back out anyway. You'll get there faster then. Plus, I hear the weather's gonna take a turn tonight."

The idea of riding in a car with your mother sounds far from appealing. "I want the fresh air," you say.

She nods and, for once in your life, you feel like she understands you. "You'll have a great night, I know it." She pulls a stray hair off your pants. "You're growing up, you know."

You know.

She steps out, pulling the door with her. "If you ever want to talk about boys—"

"I know," you say. You try to imagine how you'd explain your feelings about Tristan to anyone, let alone your mom.

The door closes. You're alone in the dark. Exits are: out.

It's 6:45 p.m. You're supposed to meet Tristan in fifteen minutes.

> Brace yourself.

Aquitane let you borrow these incredibly spiked high heels, which now seem rather impractical. You kick them off and put on your tennis shoes. You can feel your feet again. You put the shoes in your inventory though, just in case.

> Go outside.

You leave the house without having any of Dad's dinner.

You walk to Tristan's house and begin thinking about all the possibilities, your face warm and tingling.

Above you, the sky is dark and restless. You feel something drop on your forehead but try to tell yourself it's just imagined.

A few minutes into your walk, and you can't deny it anymore: the sky is crying. Full-blown menopausal crying. Your scalp feels wet—only slightly—but you still have another block to go.

> Pull out umbrella.

There is no umbrella. You make a note to put that in your inventory next time instead of a pair of useless but pretty shoes.

> Cover self with old dating flyer.

You still have that in your inventory. Man, you're weird.

It's small and doesn't cover much, but you carry it over your head until it gets too heavy and full. Then it breaks, soaking you in all that compiled water. So much for that idea.

> Crumple up useless flyer and throw it on the ground.

That's littering, you horrible person.

> Ignore good conscience and throw it anyway.

You horrible person.

You break into a sprint, and your tennis shoes start to get muddy. All of this is making you very sad, and with you already being nervous—in combination with the rum—you're getting dizzy and delirious with feelings you can't begin to understand. Your arms begin to shake, but that might be the pneumonia kicking in. Mom always said you could get pneumonia if you didn't dress properly for the rain.

You make the turn to face Tristan's house. The decrepit birdbath is overflowing with rainwater, like some deranged tropical waterfall. You walk up and knock on the door.

When no one answers, you knock again and fumble for your cell phone. Your fingers are wet and you hit the wrong keys. What would totally top this off is if you realized this was all a joke on Tristan's end. That there was no date. That you really *were* just the rebound girl.

> Lose control of yourself.

Your period must be about to start because you start coughing up little sobs, right there, on the door step.

The door opens and it's Tristan in his favorite XKCD T-shirt, looking at you with these big, horrified eyes, probably because he's never seen a girl cry before.

"Oh my gosh—Buffy are you okay?"

You try to wipe away your face and say you're fine, just wet, but it's too late for that.

"Why are you so wet? Why don't you have an umbrella? Did your car break down or fall in a ditch? Why are you wearing make-up?"

It's the last one that catches you. "My make-up?"

"I've never seen you wear make-up before." His face turns red. "It's weird—I mean, since I'm not used to you wearing it and all. Didn't recognize you at first."

> Kick him in the balls.

You don't kick him in the balls. If you did, that would definitely qualify as *worst almost-date ever.*

> Cry again.

You almost start crying again, but then Tristan catches himself. "I didn't mean it like—look, let's get you inside. You must be freezing!"

You nod and step into the house. That's when you feel the squish in your shoes and look over Aquitane's wet top and jeans. It's only water, you tell yourself, but the damage looks so permanent.

You both stand in Tristan's hallway. You have a momentary nostalgia trip looking up the stairs and fill with longing for Tristan's room.

> Go into Tristan's room.

No. You are not going into Tristan's room. That'd be weird.

Neither of you say anything for a moment, and the only sound is the sound of you dripping. Tristan looks at the pool of water and gets back into focus. "Right—we should get you dry." He steps onto the stairs, but when you don't follow, he turns around and says, "You coming?"

> Follow.

You follow him upstairs and your heart returns to its thudding dance party.

Tristan doesn't bring you to his room, though. He brings you to the master bathroom just a few doors down. Its age is evident, but to you that gives it charm: the grime between the off-white tiles, the crusty toothbrush above the toilet, the towels on the floor. Unlike the hallway, which has a sort of grandness to it, this is normal, relatable, down-to-earth. If you could, you'd camp out in the bathroom forever.

Exits are: bathtub.

> Climb. Into. Bathtub.

Um, seriously—are you *trying* to ruin your own first date?

Tristan walks over to the hair dryer mounted on the wall and turns it on. He blushes. "Mom uses the hair dryer to dry stuff off quickly."

Your face flushes.

He motions you over, kind of like how airport security wand people over with a metal detector. Except this is gentle and well-meaning. You hesitantly step toward him as he starts blowing the hair dryer over your wet hair, smeared-mascara face, and ears. You start laughing and he grabs you from behind, holding your body close and blowing your hair back with the hot air.

His face is so reachable.

You realize his arms are much more effective in warming you than the small hair dryer.

Small puddles pool on the tile. Tristan looks just as surprised as you, but he doesn't pull away. Neither of you pull away, you just look at each other, like you're realizing for the first time what it means to encounter someone of the opposite sex.

"Oh—sorry," he says, but doesn't break eye contact. You smile.

"You're still wet," he says and lets go, circling your body with the hairdryer. You throw your arms out and take it all in.

He starts with your head and gradually goes lower. With your arms out, he dries your sleeves, torso, and goes down your jeans to your ankles. He bends to the ground and tries to dry the ends of your jeans and your socks.

"You don't have to—" you begin.

"It's okay," he says, and bends over with focus, like your dampness is an equation for him to solve. The way he hovers over your feet, you can't help but think of the story of Jesus washing his follower's feet at Passover. The implication of love makes you blush.

"Are you feeling any better?" he asks. There are wet stains on the front of his shirt from embracing you.

> Be chaste.

You nod. "Much better. Thank you so much—"

"I'd give you clothes to change out of, but that seems a bit fast for a first—"

He stops and shakes his head. The warm air rides up your leg.

"Look, I'm sorry, Buffy. This must be really weird. You can always tell me to shut—"

"No," you say. A blush rides over your nose. "So it *is* a date?"

"It doesn't have to be anything you don't want it to be—"

"But I want it to be." You close your eyes. "I kinda hoped it was, but I didn't wanna make anything out of—"

Tristan stands up, the hair dryer still on in his hands. He steps close to you, and you're afraid you might fall on the tile and crack your skull open. Because that happens in all the love movies: people get so dizzy in love that they fall over and crack their skulls open.

You seriously need to watch more romance movies.

"Is it okay if I kiss you?" he asks, his eyes on your lips.

You think of how Merrill leaned in before you could stop him. Tristan doesn't move. He watches, waits, hopes. You're amazed Sephora didn't ruin this about him.

You nod, stepping toward him. You brush his nose with your own and you kiss.

And it's way better than when Merrill kissed you. It's like the movies. Maybe you should thank Sephora for giving him some practice.

> Go all out.

Any inhibition you had is gone. You lean onto Tristan, run your fingers through his hair, and press his face to yours. Every dream you've ever had about Tristan collides all at once. And it feels. So. Good.

> Remember this moment forever.

Don't worry—you'll remember. Trust me.

WHEN YOU PULL AWAY FROM each other, you both just start laughing. You tell yourself: life is perfect, the game is completed, and it can all end now.

Unfortunately for you, there's another third or so of this game left, so clearly, it's not the end yet. Good luck with maintaining your happiness, though.

Treatment V: August 1, 2010

"THIS IS KIND OF WEIRD to share."

"It's okay, Buffy. This is a safe space. Right, everyone?"

A bunch of people smiling. On the edge of the circle, one girl breaks out into spontaneous crying. How did I get here?

"I didn't used to see things. I just heard this voice, this game telling me what to do. You know, like a text adventure game, except this text adventure game is my life, and the game is really sassy." A boy laughs. "So anyway, I used to only hear it, but recently I've seen something. It's so weird to talk about, but it's this angel-like figure. I see him sitting outside my bedroom window sometimes. And the other day, I was taking a walk with my mom, and we were crossing the street when this car came speeding out of nowhere, and then I saw this light—it was shaped almost like a body—that went in front of the car, and it stopped. My mom and I, we were staring at the car there, in the middle of the street, and the guy driving just sat there, staring at the wheel in disbelief, and my mom said, 'Wow, our guardian angel must really be on overtime!' And I thought about asking her if she saw that light there too, but I didn't. I haven't told anyone, except for you guys right now."

There's a moment of silence. Great. I've managed to even weird out the weird kids.

"Wow," a heavy-set girl says at last. "That sounds so…spiritual."

"I guess you could say that," I say. Spiritual experience is the last thing that came to mind. The last thing I want is to sound even crazier than I am already. "But I'm not sure if I believe in spiritual experiences."

"Neither did I," a boy with braces says. "But then, when I was feeling really low, and was thinking about killing myself, I went into the kitchen and got this knife, and I tried to dig it into my wrist, but it was like there was something there. I tried pressing harder, but it wouldn't touch my skin. I tried that a few times, standing there—I even tried a few more knives—but nothing worked. I decided in the end that there was something out there that didn't want me to die, and that I was supposed to keep living."

The instructor and a few other students clap.

"Thank you for sharing that, Brandon," the instructor says. "Sometimes we all need the reminder that someone's watching us, and that there's a meaning to this whole existence."

"But what *is* that meaning?" My voice gets loud. "If we're all just some cosmic dust, then where's the meaning *come* from? I mean, *fuck*, who cares if one cosmic accident disappears, because another one will just come to replace it without anyone remembering who I am!"

Everyone looks at me with an uncertain distance, and the girl who cries spontaneously begins to cry again. I look down and realize that in my weird, little speech, I've stood up without realizing it, my fingers balled up into small fists.

I can't believe I just said the word "fuck." Have I ever said that before?

"Sorry," I say, sitting back down.

The instructor nods. "I appreciate your honesty, Buffy. Does anyone have a response to that?"

This is a non-religious setting. How can anyone respond to that? The room is silent.

Then suddenly, the crying girl lifts her head and wipes her eyes. "I guess that's assuming we're all cosmic dust. What if we're something different?"

I think about Tristan and cup my face in my hands and start crying.

A Date:
December 21, 2009

Y OU ARRIVE AT TRISTAN'S HOUSE for your date. But when the door opens, it's not Tristan. It's his mom.

"Oh, hi, Buffy! I'm sorry, but you just missed Tristan."

You frown. "What do you mean? We had a date planned."

She smiles in what you think is meant to be sympathy. "I'm so sorry—you probably know, he can sometimes be a bit absentminded."

"Do you know where I can find him?"

"He said he was going by the high school. Talking to an old teacher or something like that."

> Go find Tristan.

You thank her, and drive to your old high school.

As YOU PULL IN, YOU see Tristan's car: an inherited station wagon, complete with fake wood siding. It's old enough that Tristan has it registered as a historic vehicle. It's a miracle it still runs.

You find Tristan outside your old high school. From your car, you watch him for a minute: walking around the perimeter of the old brick façade. You remember being forced to come here for school. Seriously, why would anyone voluntarily come here?

You get out of your car, parked in a bus lane. As you head over to the school, Tristan looks up at you and smiles, waving you over.

> Follow.

You approach him, passing empty park benches and a pretty pathetic-looking tree. It's a Saturday and everything looks dead.

"Funny, how it's been six, seven months already." Tristan admires a rather unimpressive brick wall.

> How do I even respond to that?

"Tristan," you begin, "I was worried about you—"

He turns to you, confused.

"Remember? Today we had a date set up."

"A date? Oh—gosh, I'm sorry, Buffy." He turns back to the wall. "I got distracted, I guess."

You want to tell him that's no excuse. "Why are you here? Isn't someone gonna tell you you're trespassing?"

He smiles. "I come here sometimes to think. Like, when I'm stressed, I like to remember what high school was like."

"Yeah—so you can remember how good you have it now?"

He looks at you as if you just spoke to him in Klingon.

"Tristan, you were totally bullied for being a dork. We all were. Everyone thought we were complete weirdos. Remember? That's why we became friends in the first place, why we stuck together until now." The "until now" in your mouth feels bitter and heavy, like a hunk of raw ginger.

Tristan shrugs. "I hung out with Lawrence the other day."

"Really?"

"Yeah, ran into him at Best Buy. It was good talking with him. We talked about high school, about Mathletes—and it was fun. I forgot how funny he is."

All you remember of Lawrence is how at Sephora's pool party one year he kept brushing up against your butt, and how he kept insisting it was an accident and that he was gay so why would he want some lady parts and no matter how many times he apologized you knew he was totally doing it on purpose.

Tristan says, "Sometimes, don't you wish we were back in high school?"

> LOL

You start laughing when Tristan puts his hand on your arm. His fingers feel cold against your skin. "I mean it, though—in high school, we didn't have to worry about what we'd do with the rest of our lives. We were great at everything. Our parents took care of us. All teachers did was tell us how special we were."

"Tristan, they told *you* how special *you* were. They threw marker caps at the rest of us for not being able to decline basic Latin nouns."

He smiles. "But you must miss *something* about high school. You had more time for your drawings, right? And we all got to hang out all the time. It was so much easier to see everyone then."

"Honestly, I'm glad to be out of high school," you say. "All I remember from high school was being depressed and crushing on you."

You both chuckle.

"And in high school, we were told who to be. Now—I'm figuring out who I am. And I like that."

Do you, though?

"It wasn't perfect, I guess." He kicks at a fallen gumball on the sidewalk. "But this semester was hard—and school's never really been hard for me. I still feel exhausted from it. I'm not sure I'm ready to go back."

"The first semester's always hard—it takes adjusting," you say, as if you know anything about what's normal. "I'm sure you'll do better next semester."

"Maybe." He doesn't smile.

You are outside of your old high school. You reach your hand out toward Tristan, but it hangs there bare for a minute. You nudge him with your elbow, and he looks down at your hand, smiling, and taking it in his.

Tristan's Bedroom: December 27, 2009

Your body becomes unfamiliar to you. You find yourself urged by strange sensations, none of which you want to go into further detail about.

The last time you were with Tristan, the two of you were in his car, in the parking lot, and he pulled you onto his lap. Even though "nothing happened," it totally did. In your head, at least.

And at that sensation of warmth underneath you, you felt something awake inside you: the kind of thing that can't be revoked, or forgotten.

You find yourself running in the dark, which is rarely a good idea. If Mom knew, she'd tell you all those stories about girls that get beat up and raped on their own street, because of being in the dark and alone. She thinks it'd help, but right now you're not thinking. And as you know, advice does little good when you aren't able to think.

You arrive at Tristan's house and open the door like it's your own home, and that you totally have the right to just walk inside whenever you feel like it. It's even unlocked for you, like Tristan said it would be.

Tristan asked if you'd like to come over to see a new game he just got. But both of you know you're not there to see the game. That you'll probably never get to the game. If you can resist the urge to kiss immediately and actually have any kind of conversation, you'll be impressed.

A feeling of guilt and excitement overwhelms you. You don't know which feeling is stronger.

YOU ARE IN TRISTAN'S HOUSE. The hall is unlit. Exits are: up, kitchen.

> Take off sneakers.

First things first.

> Up.

You step on the stairs, and hear movement above you. A light turns on, and Tristan comes down. His shirt hangs loosely on him, like his body is just a hanger in some forgotten closet. Only then do you realize just how empty the house is.

"Where're your parents?" you ask.

"Dad's at work still. Said he's gonna be home late tonight. Mom's out for a conference." He gives you a smile, like the kind men give on TV when they're about to lure a woman into a dark alley. As weird as it is, you find that both sexy and discomforting.

He steps down one stair at a time and puts his hands around your waist. You've habituated to this routine. First, he lowers his chin onto the top of your head and buries his nose in your hair. Then you sigh. Then he squeezes you close to him and grips the back of your shirt. You lean in and rub circles over his back. He bends down and kisses the edge of your chin, by your ear, then goes down your neck and hits the edge of your collar. The routine is comforting in its predictability.

But today, he doesn't stop at your collar. You're wearing a button-down top, a detail you gave little thought to, except a silent hope that it might lead to something more. He unbuttons the first button and kisses your collarbone. Then you realize you didn't actually prepare for that to happen.

You jump back at the new feeling and he laughs. "Problem?"

Internally, you wish you could devour him similarly.

He steps back from your opened shirt and takes your hand. He leads you upstairs, and you obey.

> Is this okay? Can I have him?

> Hello?

> ...You still there?

You choose your exit, Buffy. I'm only here to facilitate.

YOU KNOW THE IMPLICATIONS OF bedrooms. They unsettle you. You always judged girls who'd go up there with guys they hardly knew. Said they shouldn't be surprised when they get into compromising situations. And by compromising situations, you mean pregnant.

You told yourself that when you'd start dating, you'd never go into bedrooms with a boy. You also said you'd never call each other horribly affectionate nicknames, but clearly you didn't stay true to that promise either[9]. You want to tell yourself that it's religious guilt, after the hoards of commandments your mother integrated with her delivery of the puberty talk in sixth grade. Not that you blame her, but as you follow Tristan up the stairs, you begin to wonder: if he put his hands on your ankles and slowly reached up, how far would you let him go until you told him to stop?

And afterwards, would the guilt be unnecessary, or entirely justified?

TRISTAN OPENS THE DOOR TO his room. You open your mouth to say something.

> He doesn't want to have sex, does he?

Exits are: downstairs.

> I mean—of course that'd be nice, but—

There is a bathroom next door.

> Conflicted morals.

You stand at the threshold. Tristan stops, turns around, and sees you in place. "You okay, Buffy?"

He blushes, and you notice just how thin and amazing his fingers are.

> Nothing will go wrong. We won't do anything, really. I promise—

Teenagers are known for dramatic ranges of passion. It comes and goes pretty quickly. There's so much to regret—

> We're not like that.

---

9 > I think you're making horribly unsupported claims.

So far, I've heard: "dearest," "darling," "my love," "sweetest," just to name a few.

> ...

> Go in.

You step inside Tristan's room, realizing it looks eerily similar to your dream. When you walk in, you wonder if you've suddenly been transported into an old video game store from the nineties. The room's dimly lit, and the walls are covered in bookshelves of old games, all categorized and alphabetized. Above his bed, a neon *NINTENDO* light. Even the carpet, a dark maroon, makes you feel like you're travelling back in time. A TV hangs on the wall, and the floor is covered in old issues of *Nintendo Power*. There is a bed. The sheets are pulled tight and flat, in what looks like an attempt to impress. You blush at the implications.

> Tell him about your dream.

"You know," you say, the words coming out hard and rapid. "I had a dream about you. And your house."

"Oh?" He sits down on his bed and smiles. "Is it everything you hoped it'd be?"

"I hung out with your dad."

"My dad? That's weird."

"Yeah. I'm sure Freud would have a blast psychoanalyzing me—"

Tristan leans back on his arms. "No, not just that. It's just that my dad doesn't talk very much. Especially to people he doesn't have to."

"Really?" You sit down, thinking of how much dream-Tristan's dad talked.

"He must like you a lot," Tristan says.

"It *was* just a dream."

"Yeah. But still. He talked to you when you came over, didn't he?"

Only now do you notice that the picture you slipped under the door is on his nightstand. He walks over to it and picks it up. "You left this here, before we were dating and all—didn't you?"

You nod, feeling a heavy, stone-like sensation in your throat.

"Why? You were trying to say something, but I don't get it. I look at it before sleeping some nights, trying to figure out what this means. But I've got nothing. Is this some girl thing that I just don't get?" He laughs.

What were you trying to say? You think about it, how you carried that picture in your wallet for months, like Tristan was some saint you prayed to for good luck on math tests.

"I don't need a picture anymore," you say. "I used to, when I could only... like you from a distance."

He looks at you with awe, then back at the picture. "Is that why it's creased? You carried it around?"

For a minute, you wonder if it's that you no longer needed the picture, or that you no longer had interest in it. That you could cope with the idea of living without him. The latter makes you shake your head in denial.

"It's kinda embarrassing when you put it like that…"

"No—I didn't mean it like that!" He reaches over and hugs you. At his warmth, you relax. "I'm just, I don't know—flattered—you've really felt that way, Buffy?"

You nod. "Since sophomore year."

He leans over, holds your chin in his hand, and kisses you.

"I thought we could watch some TV. Sound good?"

You nod. He turns on the TV and leans back on the bed. You watch him as he lies back, situating his head on the pillows. When you don't move, he opens his arms expectantly.

> Move toward him.

> Wait—

> Save over slot 1.

You look over at the picture on the nightstand, then back at Tristan. It's strange how different they look in just a short amount of time.

> Did you save?

|----$@V!NG----|

Your file is saved.

> Join him.

> …

> Hello?

> I lean beside him. His arms wrap around me and he brushes his nose against my forehead. He lowers his chin, down my neck then stops. Turning away from me, his face turns red.

> I watch him. He becomes small and childlike. He pauses near my chest, and I know that somewhere within me an old law is being overwritten.

> What about what Sephora saw—should I look under his bed?

> Pull him in.

> I take his head in my hands and pull it to my breast. He lets out a quick, barely audible gasp, but sinks into me. Warmth.

> He tells me he doesn't deserve me. That I'm so good and kind. Am I, though?

> Slowly, I feel him grip my wrists and move from my side. Looking up, I watch as he climbs over me, like I'm a bridge, and he kisses my collarbone and between my breasts.

> He examines me, his eyes wide with awe, like I'm the first woman he's ever looked at up close. "Buffy…I—"

> This is what I've been dreaming of. How long's it been?

> This is what you wanted, right?

> Tristan says: "I lo—"

> Wait.

> I put my finger to his lips, and smile.

WHEN YOU GET HOME, ALL you can think about is Tristan finishing that phrase, and what would've happened, if you'd let him continue.

> I don't get it. It should be over. Right?

I'm sorry, I don't understand—

> This whole game. This whole nightmare. It should be done. I got what I wanted. It's done.

But did you, Buffy? And besides, is that really what games are about: getting what you want?

Treatment VI:
August 10, 2010

I T'S COMING CLOSER. AT NIGHT I feel this weight—like someone's thrown a blanket over me—and it's like I'm being watched. It's not something I can explain, but it's gotten to the point I have to close all my window blinds each night. I think about that face in the window—was someone actually watching me? What, then? My mom said that one time: a guardian angel. Is that what this is, a guardian angel? Is there even such a thing?

Outside the door, two doctors are talking. It's been twenty minutes of sitting on this patient bench. Why is this so complicated, to get my mind back?

The door opens, and one of the doctors steps in. "Buffy," he says, "we're trying to figure out what exactly your next step should be. We have to admit that your case isn't exactly typical. Usually, if patients are consistently taking the medications, they should see the symptoms alleviated pretty soon after. Before we continue, we really need you to be honest—have you been taking your medicine regularly?"

I nod. "I've taken all of them. It only gets worse."

The doctor nods, jotting something down on an iPad. Is he actually taking notes or just playing with an app?

"If that's the case," he says at last. "We need to re-evaluate your diagnosis. It's possible that this isn't in fact schizophrenia..."

Haha! Knew it!

"But it's going to be tricky. Your symptoms pretty clearly line up with schizophrenia, so figuring out what's really going on isn't going to be easy. It's going to take effort—on both ends."

"Right."

"Buffy." He leans back, eyeing me. "Could you tell me why you stopped going to your therapy sessions?"

"Sorry?"

"You stopped coming—it's as simple as that. But why, I'm not sure. Your mother's said you've not been feeling well..."

"Yeah, I've had something. Maybe a flare-up of mono. I'm gonna come back once I—"

"But that's just it, Buffy. I feel like you don't want to come back. That you're delaying coming back because there's something you don't want to talk about. And I wish you understood—I'm not making you talk to make you feel embarrassed, or to learn all your secrets. I want you to talk so it can help *you* overcome whatever it is that's holding you back right now."

Should I tell him? About the thing that keeps coming closer to me? I don't know how to feel about it, though. Whatever it is, as it comes closer, it's like it wants to kill off a piece of me—or maybe, all of me?

Post-High School Reality Quest

IT'S WINTER BREAK, AND EVERYONE'S in Merrill's basement for the traditional New Year's gaming night. To celebrate, everyone is wearing dollar store party hats, and they all look appropriately silly. There are also some of Merrill's mom's famous cookie sandwiches.

Tristan gets up when he sees you and approaches, his arms open. You feel like the friggin' queen of England. When he reaches you, he pulls you in and kisses you. It sure is nice to be loved. Merrill and Chase pretend to be watching TV.

Tristan puts his arm around your shoulder and announces to the room, "So in case you didn't know, Buffy and I are official now."

"Haha." Chase changes the channel. "That totally wasn't fast at all."

"What?" Tristan frowns.

You say, "It is what it is."

Chase looks you in the eye, like he wants to really understand what you're thinking, but can't figure it out. He shrugs and returns to watching TV.

Merrill doesn't say anything, either. Tristan rubs your back but you step away from his hand. You almost feel ashamed, being so happy.

A few minutes later, the doorbell upstairs rings. Which is weird, since only new people use the doorbell. Merrill goes upstairs while everyone else watches the stairwell.

"Who's that?" Tristan asks.

"You'll see in a second, dumbass." You watch Merrill go up the stairs and notice just how light his feet appear.

Merrill returns down the stairs with a hooker on his arm.

Really, you're pretty sure she's hired. Real girls don't have breasts that buoyant and full. She looks like she's only a year or two older than you, but her habits of bright lipstick and overdone eye shadow are too hard to hide. Her tank top seems out of place for the season, and the straps keep falling over her shoulders. Whenever she adjusts them, she giggles.

"Everyone, this is Alice—she's in my Javascript class."

While you're skeptical about her being in a Javascript class, let alone Merrill's, the biggest load of bullcrap you find in that statement is that her name is Alice. Her name is *totally* not Alice. It's probably Jasmine or Stacie or Crystella. You can tell because you've never met a hooker named Alice before—

Wait a minute.

Unlike your Alice, the hooker has bright California-blonde hair. She looks like she's supposed to be in a *Playboy* magazine, not Merrill's moldy basement. She looks just as confused as you are, like Merrill told her she was getting paid to dance naked out of a cake, not pretend to be a nerd for a night.

She looks around to us then remembers her place. "Hi, guys," she says. "I brought some CDs."

Out from her purse she pulls out dance remixes of Lady Gaga. Tristan looks at them with suspicion of a foreign object entering his skin.

The doorbell rings again. "What is this, Merrill—a fuckin' party?" Tristan says in a very loud, deliberate voice.

You frown at him.

Merrill says, "I didn't invite anyone else."

The doorbell rings again.

"I'll get it," Tristan says. But when he opens the door, you hear a familiar nasally greeting. Something inside you involuntarily reels.

When Sephora walks down the stairs, you wonder if she's the real hooker Merrill hired: she comes down each step with intentional hip sways, her stomach so flat you can see the indent of her hip bone. You touch your stomach, imagining it flatter. Also, her breasts look much larger than you last remember.

> It's probably pillows. Or implants.

For a minute, you feel a need to fluff your own breasts.

She stops at the base of the stairs and claps her hands together. "Hey, everyone—long time, no see!"

The hooker pretends that she recognizes Sephora and waves. Like that's part of what she's paid to do. Sephora waves back and smiles like she's the long-lost *actual* queen of England. Tristan follows her, his face pale.

"Why are you here?" he asks.

"I missed you guys! Plus, I ended up having some time over break. I saw the invite on Buffy's page." She eyes you like a piece of meat. "You're all such good friends," she says. "Especially Chase, he's always been so good to me."

"No, I haven't." Chase has loaded up the Xbox and gotten on *Halo Live*. For all you can tell, he's left this world.

The hooker isn't sure what to do with herself. She looks at the chairs, and you pat the empty seat next to you, like the nice person you are.

Tristan returns and sits on your other side, rubbing your lower back. You look at the hooker Alice, un-embraced, and feel guilty.

> Try to make the hooker Alice feel better.

"So how did you meet Merrill?" you ask. Tristan puts his head on your shoulder to look over at her.

"I forgot to do my code one day, so I asked Merrill if I could look at his."

You totally feel like this is a backstory Merrill paid her to say, so you ask, "What're you guys doing in the class?"

"We're learning how to create arrays." The hooker pulls back her blonde hair and sighs. "Gag me with a spoon. What're we, middle schoolers? But this class is a prerequisite, so they make you take it, if you wanna do anything fun."

"*Oh.* What is it that you want to do?"

"Theoretical mathematics."

> Vomit your thoughts.

"So, you're *real*—I mean."

Alice laughs. Her breasts jiggle. You really hate her. "I'm only at community college to get general credits. I'm hoping to transfer to State next year and study Comp Sci. Or math. I'm not sure yet—maybe I'll do a double major."

Sephora takes an unsolicited seat on the floor next to Chase. Her skirt rides up so it's barely covering anything of redeemable value.

Alice whispers in your ear, "Man, what a *slut*."

> Cover mouth to prevent laughing too noticeably.

Chase mutters under his breath, "I thought you were still under custody at the police station."

Sephora lets out a loud cough-laugh. It sounds like a goat, or a wild animal dying. Tristan watches her with these big horrific eyes, like he can't wake up from a nightmare. He squeezes your hand, and you squeeze it back.

Merrill looks at everyone with a death sentence.

Already, you see tonight's going to be a long night.

> Make things better.

You get off the couch and put on your perkiest smile. "Hey, everyone—we should have a dance party! Alice, you got those CDs?"

Sephora gets up and shakes her hips. "Aww, yeah!" Maybe this wasn't the best idea.

Alice puts her Lady Gaga CDs in Merrill's desktop computer in the corner of the room. As she bends over, you catch Merrill watching her shorts pull down her butt just slightly, showing a crack of skin. Part of you wishes you could throw a blanket over her.

The speakers were selected for gaming—for hearing gunshots and an enemy's footsteps—not techno bass. But you all make do and turn the volume as loud as it'll go.

This Alice, like your roommate, has an intuitive sixth sense for partying. Her dancing looks as natural as walking. While you shuffle your hips awkwardly and blockish from side to side, Alice whips her California-blonde hair and lifts her arms to show clean, spotless armpits. You're afraid of lifting your own arms to show a very different picture.

Tristan gets up and dances over to you, only he's a worse dancer than you.

> Make fun of your new boyfriend.

You laugh at his attempts, but he just runs up and throws his arms around you, swinging you around. It's like that thing you always see all those annoying teens in the mall do, how when you were single, you despised them for it.

> Forget yourself.

You giggle at his touch and he buries his nose in your hair. You feel his breath in and over you. You let yourself forget there are other people around.

When he lets go, you start dancing the way you dance in your dorm room alone, with your iPod ear bud in one ear, the way you dance when you're tired and happy and lonely. You dance until you open your eyes and catch Merrill looking at you. It's only for a moment, but it's enough to remind you that he will always want you.

Your dancing slows down.

Tristan catches the change in your eyes. "You okay?" he asks.

You nod.

He smiles and leans close to your face. "You'll have to teach me how to dance—you're really good!"

> Remember yourself.

You laugh and wish you could bury your face in his chest and find a hiding place there. But when he touches you again, you draw back. You whisper, "When we're alone."

The implication makes him beam.

Merrill walks up to Alice and starts dancing next to her. She laughs and dances closer to him, her hips moving with skill like a belly dancer. You look over to Sephora, who looks like she despises everyone in the room. She throws her hips with vengeance, like keys sloshing on a key ring. But nobody looks.

You want to ask Alice about her non-computer class side, but as if reading your mind, she turns to you and says, "I have a weekend job as a pole dancer downtown."

Which would explain lots of things.

> Ask her what her stage name is.

Merrill smiles at her and she smiles back, but you can tell it's the customer smile. You're not sure Merrill can tell that, though.

What Alice tells you later is that her pole dancing is less for the sexual image and more for physical fitness. "It's becoming a sport now, you know—outside of strip clubs and all. It's what Chinese acrobats do." She adds, "The sex part sells, though."

And in the corner—Sephora keeps dancing, even when Chase refuses to join her and Tristan refuses to look at her. It's her best drug. Sometimes you notice her catching glimpses of herself in the reflection on Merrill's computer monitor. She dances even when Merrill asks Alice to demonstrate her pole dancing on the basement's awkwardly centered pole. Even when Alice refuses and everything gets so uncomfortable that you suggest turning off the music and watching the New Year's TV special. And through the whole thing, Sephora keeps dancing like she's happy in her loneliness, but no one falls for it. No one gives a crap about Sephora's happiness, or lack thereof.

But as you dig into your inventory, you find her old *HELP* note and feel a sliver of pity.

DURING THE SPECIAL, MERRILL GOES upstairs to get some snacks. Tristan motions for you to follow him into the office.

You're not sure that's such a good idea. "We're at a *party*, Tristan. That means we *stay* with the group."

He frowns, like he doesn't understand the word "group." "I need to talk to you," he says, looking serious.

> Follow him.

That totally worked on you. You follow him into the office, like you're still in school and scared of getting in trouble.

He closes the door.

"What's wrong?" you say.

"What's wrong with you?" he replies back. "Is there something about me that makes you...uncomfortable? I don't get it."

Your body feels weak and confused. "What's that mean?"

"It means every time I try to be close to you, you keep stepping away. What's up with that?"

```
> We've been dating like a whole week, Tristan.
Calm your pants.
```

"First off, I love being close to you." Your face flushes. It's true—even if it has only been a week or so, you can't believe you somehow functioned without Tristan's warmth: his hand squeezing yours, his smile, how he holds you when he hugs you. His affection is like your fuel.

You continue. "But I—"

```
> How do you explain how you're trying to protect
the people you didn't even think you cared much about?
```

"Do you remember what it was like to be single?"

Even though he's been single most of his life, he looks at you blankly.

"Well, I remember," you say. "And it really sucked when I saw couples being all affectionate around me. It was like they were laughing in my face."

"Maybe that's exactly what I want."

"*What*?"

He sighs, and sits on the office chair. He puts his head in his hand, and you notice just how tangled his hair is. You want to fix it for him.

```
> Fix his hair.
```

You reach down and try to touch him, but he turns your hand away. The rejection feels hot on your fingertips.

"You know how annoying it is to have Merrill make fun of you all the time? Or what it was like dating Sephora? How it's like they do everything to spite me?"

You want to point out that he chose to date Sephora, but realize this might not be the best time to do so.

"They deserve it, okay? If they want to tell me how I'll never—" He sighs again. "You know what I've always wanted?"

"What?"

"To love someone so much that I could fall asleep right next to them and wake up the next morning with them beside me."

You smile.

"And you know what? Merrill and Sephora are never going to get that. They're too selfish for anyone to love them like that."[10]

You watch him sitting there. The light casts shadows on his cheeks in a way that suddenly makes him look older, more knowledgeable than you've ever given him credit for. Full of more anger than you could imagine him filled with. It doesn't scare you—it only comes as surprising—but you wonder if you should be afraid.

"I want them to see what it's like, to actually be—" Tristan says, leaning forward. He cuts himself off and kisses you slowly.

You take his face in your hands and bend down to his seat. He puts his hands on your waist, as if trying to steady you, or plant you into the carpet.

When he pulls away, he says, "You're too good of a person, Buffy. You're too wonderful, and I'm sorry it took me so long to realize that."

"You're wonderful, too," you say. "That's nice for you to say about me. I don't know if I'm good."

"I don't deserve you," he says, looking up at you. "I'm horrible—I really am."

"Why would you say that?"

> Attempt to fix his hair again.

You reach down and touch his hair, and this time he lets you. You brush his bangs away from his forehead and he looks at you like you're an angel, or some other unfathomable being. It's flattering. The feeling hits your stomach.

And he pulls you onto his lap.

When Chase gets up to go to the bathroom, he sees the office door cracked and finds you on Tristan's lap, your faces pressed together like fruits being juiced. He doesn't say anything but goes upstairs.

You didn't even notice, really.

FROM THE STAIRWELL, YOU HEAR Merrill call, "Buffy, you should press charges on sexual harassment. You can do that as a woman. Maybe you can even get some of Tristan's money!"

You don't know how to tell him that it's all right, so you tell Tristan you both should leave the office and keep it together just for the night. Tristan says, "Didn't you hear what I just said?"

And you say, "Didn't you hear what he just said?"

---

10 For a moment, you wonder what'd happen if Merrill and Sephora hooked up. Man, what a disastrous fanfiction that'd make.

Tristan sighs and says something like, "For now, fine. But you're too good to Merrill. He doesn't deserve it."

"I know," you say. "But...he does, too."

Tristan shakes his head. "I'm only putting up with this because I like you, Buffy. I really do."

A feeling of power surges through you. This must be what Sephora desires, you realize. And suddenly, you feel very hungry.

SEPHORA AND THE OTHER ALICE[11] are the only ones watching the special when you return to the living room. The plate with cookie sandwiches is empty. Under her breath, you hear Sephora complain about eating too many cookies. The ball is dropping and people in Times Square are counting down the end of the year. The Other Alice isn't paying attention to anything, but flipping through formulas on her phone. "I'm studying for Monday's test," she explains. On the back of her phone, there's a decal for the *Playboy* bunny.

YOU ARE ON THE LIVING room floor. Tristan sits close to you, but doesn't put his arm around you. What you wouldn't give to be alone with him right now, and have his arm around you. Man, this is harder than you thought it'd be.

The ball drops, and Tristan kisses you. You think about 2010 and imagine it'll be the best year yet if Tristan's in it.

Upstairs, you hear Chase shout an expletive. He does that sometimes, but now, you realize, it's not for the laughs.

> Figure out what's going on.

Shouting up the stairs, you ask, "Is everything okay?"

When no answer comes, you run upstairs. Tristan follows after you. Everyone else returns to watching the movie, assured that you'll handle the situation.

"Merrill?" you ask, peering around the corner of the stairwell.

You are in the kitchen. Merrill's standing there over the kitchen counter and a bag of cheetos. Chase has a bloody nose, and some red stains on the front of his shirt.

On impulse you scream.

If you hadn't screamed, maybe things would've worked out all right. Maybe the drama would be mendable. But once you scream, the Other Alice and Sephora come up.

---

11 This is what you call her, to avoid confusing Merrill's computer-programming hooker with your roommate.

> Sephora's probably just coming up for the action.
Let's be real.

But when Sephora sees Chase's bloody nose, she freaks out. She runs over and pulls the end of her shirt up to wipe away the blood. Her stomach shows but no one's noticing. Not even Sephora. You wonder if she'd rip her shirt in half to save Chase.

The Other Alice freaks out on Merrill. "Did you *punch* him?" she shouts.

"He was taunting me," Merrill says, looking at the floor.

"You're really good at first impressions, Merrill. Asking for a striptease, punching your friend out, disappearing for no reason—"

"It was a joke—" Merrill says, his voice dropping. Everyone gets quiet, like they know they're intruding.

The Other Alice rolls her eyes and pulls her tank top strap up her shoulder. Like that does much good. "I'm just saying. You've really got a lot to learn, don't you. You nerds—you don't think of anyone except yourselves, do you?"

"I'm behind you with that one, sister!" Sephora raises her hand for a high five, but the Other Alice doesn't take it.

Chase and Merrill exchange a look. With his bloody hand, he pats Merrill on the shoulder, looking down at the floor. "I should get going," he says. Sephora walks Chase to the door, her hands steadying his arm, like he's old or fragile. He doesn't shake her off.

The Other Alice grabs her bag and says, "I'll see you in class."

"Do you need a ride?" Tristan asks.

"It's okay—I can take the bus."

Something feels heavy in your throat.

"Happy New Year, Merrill. It was cool times," Tristan says.

"Cool times," Merrill echoes as the door closes.

You walk with Tristan to his car, secretly hoping for a "bad girl" experience. Like the things girls sing about in techno dance songs. Something involving the terms "dirty," "get it on the floor," "baby, shake it," etc. You never elaborate mentally on what exactly those terms mean. You're too ashamed to.

But with how physical Tristan's been, your body can't help but be excited, anticipating something it knows nothing about.

Tristan offers to drive you back to your place, which you find funny since you're all within walking distance, but you say yes and get in the car. It's dark and he doesn't start the car right away.

Leaning over the armrest, he kisses you lightly on the lips.

It's quiet in the dark, and you look over to Merrill's window. The light's still on in the kitchen. For a moment, you wonder if he's watching.

Tristan speaks in a low voice, like he's afraid of someone overhearing. He says, "Buffy, promise that whatever happens, we'll always stay in touch. No matter what."

And he kisses you again.

You wonder what "whatever happens" means.

AFTER TRISTAN DROPS YOU OFF, you get changed into your PJs and get online. That's where you seem to live these days: on the internet.

> I know, I know. Our whole generation is "corrupted" with technology.

> It's funny, because I definitely agree that *your* technology is corrupting me.

I guess it all depends on perspective.

You log into your Steam account. Maybe a good calming first-person shooter will help you fall asleep.

As you log in, you notice that Merrill's online. Not a shocker, really, considering he breathes games. Maybe with the whole fiasco tonight, you thought he might not be online.

> Say something comforting.

You open a chat window with Merrill. *Hey,* you type. How do you exactly comfort someone who invited a hooker over and punched his friend in the face? *Gee, I'm sorry you make bad decisions, but you're still my friend anyway?*

No response. Odd. Well, not really odd. It's not like you and Merrill have really done a lot of messaging online. Particularly recently, your conversations have all been strictly business. Maybe you hoped he would answer, though, that there would be a moment like your brief time dating where you see another side of Merrill that you didn't know existed.

All of a sudden, you start seeing Merrill everywhere. He logs into Facebook, Twitter (ugh, you actually *use* Twitter?), Steam, YouTube, everything. And it all happens in sync, as if the great power button of all of Merrill's accounts was just pressed at once. Heck, you forgot Merrill even *had* some of these accounts. For all you know, he might even be back on that horrible anime-themed forum game you all were into freshman year.

> Just for kicks...

You log onto that unmentionable forum site. It's impressive you still remember the username and password for that.

And sure enough, you see Merrill logged in. You also have to re-encounter your old avatar, with her bright purple hair and dramatic fairy wings. Some things are better left abandoned.

> Chat with Merrill.

You attempt to bring Merrill into a conversation for the second time. *What are the odds we'd both be on this site again at the same time lol.*

> Retry.

You erase that. Try to not sound too weird.

Don't tell me you're trying to relive your past lol.

> Probably still sounds weird but whatever.

> Send.

You wait for a response. Nothing.

> Okay, so maybe Merrill's ignoring me. Whatever. That's cool.

You flip back to Facebook. On your home feed, you notice Merrill's status has been updated. It says: *YOU JUST GOT HACKED YOU IDIOTTTTT.*

A few people you don't know have liked it.

You freak out for a moment.

> Wait…this is a joke, right?

It's getting late, and you're in your room while Merrill is (presumably) in his. It seems like a weird thing to say, but at the same time Merrill is known for saying lots of weird things.

BEFORE YOU GO TO BED, you see a new status update from Merrill. It says:

Did you know? Merrill totally steals everyone's shit and keeps it locked in his bedroom closet. Why? Because his goal in life is to be the biggest dickwad possible! In fact, he don't just fucking hate everyone else but himself, too, because his New Year's resolution is to continue being more and more of a dick until he watches the news and sees one of his friends has gone out and shot everyone's brains out. And you know why, Merrill? You know why I'm gonna do it? Because you made me. You made me fuckin' crazy. That's what they'll say in textbooks— they'll say that you made me like this. That you killed all those people. You've fucked up my life, Merrill, and now I'm going to fuck yours over and haunt you like a ghost. Just you wait.

Comments include:

- *...da fuck?*
- *since when did you talk to yourself in the third person lol*
- *Do you believe in ghosts? There's significant evidence that they do in fact appear in abandoned places (link to: <www.myfriendstotallylegitghosthuntingblog.blogspot.com>*

You get the idea.

Does this disturb you? Yes, it tottally does. But it's late at night and you tell yourself that there's nothing you can do to fix this, not now at least, so you turn off your lights and try to go to sleep.

But you can't sleep. You know something's wrong, and no matter how many cups of chamomile you drink, you keep thinking about Merrill.

> Call Merrill.

In the dark, you can't find your phone. Weird.

Closing your eyes, you say a prayer for Merrill (and yourself), but your mind refuses to stop.

> So what happened, exactly?

What do you mean?

> I mean between Chase and Merrill tonight. Upstairs. I guess I could ask Chase, but...

But what?

> I don't think he'd tell me truthfully. I don't know why, but I have a hunch it has to do with me and Tristan.

Would you like to see?

> Yes.

Close your eyes.

So it happened like this:

When Chase got upstairs, Merrill was pouring the same cheese curls into a bowl and then back into the bag.

"You were totally right," Chase said. "I just saw them downstairs. Kissing and shit. I don't think I'll be able to sleep tonight."

Merrill rolled his eyes.

"I mean it! It's sick. Just thinking about biting that black lipstick—"

"Seriously, Chase. Fuck off."

"It's just not my thing, that's all. I just can't sit well on that." Chase put his hands on his stomach, like he might vomit right there.

Merrill continued working the cheese curls, and even though he was holding the bag and the bowl, neon orange cheese flakes still got on his fingers. "I just wish Tristan wouldn't be such a dick about it."

"What'd you mean?"

"As soon as they became a 'thing,' he messaged me online and was like going on about dating someone he was friends with and how Buffy's 'so different' than Sephora. He was like, 'It's weird making out with someone that you've beat up in *Halo Live*, you know what I'm saying?' I mean, I can't tell if he really is that stupid, to not get it, or if he's *trying* to be a dick."

"Tristan isn't exactly known for his social-cue reading…"

"And then he was like, 'Do you have advice?' And I was like, what the fuck's that supposed to mean? He even had the balls to say, 'Got any insider tips?'"

Chase shook his head. "Again, we're talking about *Tristan* here."

"But that's just it—maybe he's playing the stupid card to fuck with me. Maybe he's actually like one of those insider terrorists, and he's doing all this Buffy stuff to get me pissed off, but let's be clear on this: it's not going to get to me."

Chase nodded, sucking air in between his teeth. "You know, Merrill… there's a *lot* more fish in the sea."

And that's when Merrill punched Chase in the face.

> Oh. okay. Wow, I don't know what to think of that…

> Or really, that whole experience just now.

> I thought you were just going to tell me, but then you *showed* me.

> Like my life is an episode of some weird sitcom.

> …Wait. Is this *real*? Did we just time travel?

> Maybe I'm just really tired, and I've forgotten how to distinguish between dreams and memories. Or maybe I'm just going crazy.

> …

> I guess you're not going to answer me, are you?

A magician never gives away his tricks. But I want to show you something else.

> I'm sorry?

It won't take long, and it's not like you're getting any sleep as it is. Besides, this is important. Just think of all this as one giant "cut scene."

> What's that even supposed to—

It'll be important later. Trust me.

YOU OPEN YOUR EYES. YOU are in Merrill's basement. It's dark, then suddenly a light turns on.

> So how am I going to explain this one to Merrill? Sorry, but I'm clearly going crazy, because somehow my mind teleported me into—

> Wait. Why am I even trying to justify this? This is obviously a dream. That's right, a dream.

You don't wake up.

Merrill emerges from the stairs. The room's still dim.

"If anyone's there, you'd better tell me now before I shoot your fuckin' brains out," he says.

You freeze. You are in the middle of the room, and there's nowhere to hide. You open your mouth to tell him, but no sound comes out.

> That's right. You can't talk in dreams.

Merrill looks right at you, and maybe it's the dim light but he doesn't acknowledge you. It's like he's seeing right through your forehead.

He lets out a sigh. "I'm just going crazy I guess."

Just as he's about to go back upstairs, he looks over by the television. You see it, too—it's too dark on the shelf. Something's missing. And then he turns, as if he heard a sound.

You heard it, too—a rustling sound.

Merrill walks over toward the couch and turns on his cell phone's flashlight. You hear a grunt of surprise.

"Tristan, what the fuck are you doing here? I thought you went home with Buffy." Merrill tries to snicker, though you catch the edge in his voice. "Look, I know you have a crush on me, Tristan, but for serious—I'm not that into you."

From your angle, you can't see Tristan's face, but you imagine he's not smiling. "Lawrence told me the real reason you've kept me around," he says.

Merrill stiffens. "Lawrence? You still hang out with that asshole?"

"Just because someone doesn't bow down to you, you call them an asshole."

"What's with this new attitude, Watson?" Merrill leans against the couch. "That Lawrence kid is a no-good dickwad—you know that. Don't you remember when he—"

"You've known about my condition all along, haven't you?"

Merrill is still. In the dark, the silence feels like duct tape over your face.

"It's fine," Tristan says. "I don't expect you to say anything."

"Whatever Lawrence told you, it's bullshit and you know it."

"You can't talk to me like that anymore! okay? I'm doing better than you. I'm in a *real* college. I have a girlfriend. I have real *friends*. I don't need you to tell me what to do anymore. Got it?"

Merrill snickers. "If you don't need me anymore, then why are you here? Why'd you even come at all?"

"People don't come over here because they like you. You know that, right? You're not the only one stuck with friends you don't want. But at some point, you're gonna realize what all your screwing around has really done. It might seem funny to you now, but it won't be when you have no one left in your life, and all you have to keep you company is all the shit you've stolen from me over the years."

"Get out of my house, Watson."

Tristan gets up, and for a moment you see his body—his legs, two shadows stretching across the room.

Merrill puts his head in his hands and lets out a deep breath. In the dark, you see the silver curve of his back bent forward. You reach your hand out toward him, but as soon as your hand is about to touch him, you're suddenly back in your bed, staring at the night-blue ceiling fan quietly turning.

Home II:
January 2, 2010

YOU WAKE UP IN YOUR own bed, in your own house, panting.

> That...wasn't a dream.

Whether it was a dream or not doesn't matter. Don't forget what you saw—it might help make sense of things later on.

> You mean you know what's—you have some explaining to do.

You are in your room, and there is a phone vibrating on your desk.

> Don't think you can distract me that—

There is a phone, still vibrating on your desk.

> Get up and examine phone.

You get out of bed, only to realize it's not your phone. It looks way too nice to be your phone. It actually has a screen with color and a keyboard. It folds. A new text comes in.

> Read text.

You tell yourself that reading it might help figure out whose phone it is.

The text is from Merrill. It reads:

Some dumbass from high school thought it'd be funny to screw over my computer. Looks like he hacked it and streamed it online. I need you to come over and help me out.

You frown, wondering if this is your phone after all, and if the magic Phone Fairy just replaced your five-year-old piece of crap with this overnight.

> Examine the text again.

It is very long, coming from Merrill. It makes you think of the time Merrill was totally into you and would say things without really saying anything, the way girls do, like the time he sent a text that read, *I wonder if it's raining outside…*

And you totally mentally replied, *You should look out the window and check.*

But you didn't reply. You didn't know what he wanted. You never know what he wants. And you don't reply now.

> Do some exploring.

You feel like a horrible person, but you wonder if you look at some more texts, if it'll clear who this is. These are the texts that you find:

- From "Jimmy-jang:" *What'd you mean, you won't do the late shift? That's what's on the schedule, that's what you'll do.*
- From Merrill: *Want to come to my place Saturday for video games and lolz? You can meet some of the people I've been talking about.*
- From Merrill: *Thanks for the "homework" advice—that helped a lot. ;)*
- From Mom: *Please come home for break. We miss you!*
- From Sears: *Thank you for your application. Unfortunately, we currently have no openings available to offer. We'll keep your application on file for the next six months should anything come up.*

- From "Jimmy-jang:" *Where are you? People are coming in already, and they want you here. You can't just leave whenever you feel like it.*

YOU DON'T KNOW ANYTHING ABOUT the Other Alice, but you know this is hers. The phone feels hot and heavy in your hands. You feel an urge to throw it out the window.

> Ask for help.

You can't call Merrill. And as much as you want to talk to Tristan, there's a moment of reluctance when you think about what you saw last night.

> Was that even real?

> How do I know?

> It's not like I can trust you, anyway.

I'm sorry, I don't understand "it's not like I can trust you." If you don't trust the person who brings you back to life every play-through, who can you trust?

You call Tristan, on your house phone that is. It's been a while since you've used one of these. When you plug in Tristan's number, you feel proud of yourself for remembering it.

> Hey!

He picks up almost immediately.

"Tristan—I need your advice."

"Oh? It must be serious."

"You see—I somehow have Alice's phone."

"Who?"

"That girl from last night. You know, the one Merrill invited."

"Oh right. That was kinda awkward."

"You think?" You try to laugh, then remember what you saw last night and fall quiet. "But anyway—I have her phone and I don't know anything about her."

"You have to ask Merrill about that."

"But if he knows I had it…"

"What?"

"You know—he might get the wrong idea."

There's silence. You realize you're thinking like a girl and he doesn't get it.

"Maybe I'll just drop it off at Merrill's. Leave it in the mailbox or something."

"That sounds like a good idea."

Talking things out makes everything feel better than it actually is. You should really get back into the habit of talking out loud to yourself when trying to figure out what to do in ambiguous situations.

You think about asking him about last night but stop yourself. You don't even know if that's real or not—remember?

You're about to hang up when Tristan says, "Buffy?"

"Yeah?"

"You got time this week for some hanging out?"

You're still totally not used to this dating thing, especially because nothing's been made official—at least, in the terms you consider "official." That is to say, he's never called you his girlfriend. There is no status update of "in a relationship." You wonder if that's the kind of thing a girl's supposed to ask about or wait for, and if love ever comes in whole increments.

You blush, but he can't see that. "I should have time."

"Great! I've got this movie I think you'll really like."

"Awesome." Your head becomes full and dizzy with thoughts of Tristan kissing you. "Well, I have to go. I should drop this off to Merrill."

"Okay. I'll be online if you wanna talk."

"Great. Thanks, Tristan." You hang up.

> Brace yourself.

Putting on your snow boots and a torn-up hoodie, you head over to Merrill's.

YOU ARE ON THE STREET, facing south toward Merrill's house. It is very cold outside. Much colder than you expected.

> Build a bonfire.

You are in the suburbs, Buffy.

> But there are twigs and stuff…

I don't understand "but there are twigs and stuff…"

> Walk faster.

You walk faster. You are still cold.

> Stop thinking about the cold.

Cold. Cold. Cold. Cold.

> Run away from life.

You try to run away from life, but it always catches you.

YOU ARE IN FRONT OF Merrill's house. It took a long time. But you're here.

There is a mailbox. It looks like it's in need of a new paint job. Exits are: north, inside.

> Examine mailbox.

It is a mailbox. It holds mail and other things, like a nest of baby birds. Isn't that cute?

> Put The Other Alice's cell phone inside.

Just as you're about to put the cell phone inside, the door opens and Merrill's standing on the front porch in his boxers. They have a Halo Spartan centered on his crotch. It makes you uncomfortable, so you look away.

"Buffy!" he shouts but doesn't move.

You don't know what to say to that.

"Buffy—I need your help for a sec. Can you come in?"

You look at the ground. It looks cold.

Finally, you mutter, "You're not dressed."

He sighs and rolls his eyes. "There's no time for that! I'm not gonna rape you, Buffy. I promise."

You totally think that's what a rapist would say.

> Go in and get warm.

You go inside anyway.

MERRILL SHOWS YOU THE CRIME scene, which you realize you've already seen. The empty spot on the shelf—you can see it clearly now—was where Merrill's prized cartridge of *Pokémon Stadium* once sat. In the corner by the fireplace, you see his computer blue screening.

"You probably saw it earlier, but all my accounts were hacked too."

He holds up a PlayStation memory card. Sticking it into the PlayStation, you see the screen reveal its save files. Tristan and Merrill have shown you this before: bragging about the scores in *Tony Hawk Pro Skater 2* and *Crash Bandicoot* they achieved in middle school. But now, you see that those files are gone, only to be replaced with file after file of *Bubsy 3-D*.

"*Bubsy*..." Merrill murmurs under his breath. "You know, it'd be kind of a funny prank if it wasn't Tristan who did it. Tristan doesn't know how to do funny."

You look up at him. You were there—you know he's right. Yet at the same time, you can't believe it. "Tristan? Why would he—"

"That's a good question, Buffy." He leans toward you—but not in any sensuous sort of way. "Do you have any insights?"

> ???

"What? What would *I* know?"

Merrill studies you. You're such a bad liar. "Maybe you don't know anything. Or maybe you don't realize that you know something."

"I'm not going to be interrogated, Merrill."

"That's cool, that's cool—but I have to ask one thing."

"What is it?"

"Tristan said something about Lawrence. That he still hangs out with him or something. Do you know anything about that?"

"Well, I know he's hanging out with Lawrence again for some reason. Said something about missing high school, about wanting a nostalgia trip or something. But that's all I know."

"That kid's a dickwad, and he's ruining Tristan. Not that Tristan is really that hard to mess around with."

"Don't say that."

He glares at you, then remembers he's in his boxers. He walks over to his bedroom and puts on a robe. You feel better, but still don't know how to help him.

Nobody says anything. Seems like a good time to save, if you ask me.

> I didn't ask you.

> Save over running to Tristan's house.

You have saved.

THERE'S SOMETHING THAT STILL BOTHERS you, though—something that you've been thinking about all night, preventing you from falling asleep. Before you can stop yourself, you ask, "What did he mean—his condition?"

Merrilll looks at you like a deer that just realized it's not alone on a road. "Condition? I didn't say anything about a condition."

> Undo this whole thing.

I'm sorry—I don't understand "undo." What do you think I am, a time wizard?

> Kind of, yeah.

"I know, but—" How can you explain this? You let out a sigh. "I overheard you and Tristan last night."

Merrill's eyes get big, his face reddening until he looks like a cartoon. "You—he brought *you* into this?"

"What? No! I—I forgot my phone last night." You reach to pull out Alice's cell phone, but you remember that you put it into the mailbox. It must be cold and lonely in there.

"I accidently grabbed the wrong phone, and—and I came back to grab mine. Instead I found you two."

He studies you like he doesn't fully believe you. Heck—you don't even believe yourself. "Whatever. If you two are dating, and Tristan hasn't even told you about that, maybe that says something about him. Or maybe how compatible you two are."

"Is it serious?"

"If you want to know about it, you go ask him yourself." He looks back at the shelf, where the empty spot is blaringly obvious now, and you wonder if anything else could ever be placed there to make it feel full again. "It's not a big deal. Just some stupid save files and an old game cartridge. Not like I was ever going to do anything with that old stuff again, anyway."

"Tristan doesn't steal. Are you sure it's him?"

"I'm not worried about the blue screen." He laughs, but you don't believe it. "Tristan thinks he's so smart, but he was never that good at hacking. I think I'll be okay."

He takes the memory card out of the PlayStation and throws it in the trash.

"I'm so sorry, Merrill," you say. "I'm sure he didn't really mean it. Was probably just ticked about something stupid, and will call you apologizing—"

He eyes you strangely, like he doesn't know what to make of apologies or sympathy. "You really do see the best in people, Buffy."

You're not sure what that means, so you smile. For a moment, you wish you could hold him and reassure him that everything will be fine.

> Reach out to touch him.

You realize you no longer have the authority to do that. You pull your hand back. It burns with a sensation almost like regret.

YOU ARE IN TRISTAN'S HOUSE. Before you can say anything, Tristan insists on showing you something upstairs. "You have to swear to not tell anyone," he says, pulling you by the hand up to his room. You try to remember the last time you saw him so excited over something.

As he opens the door, you see it right away: the *Pokémon Stadium* game, front and center on his games shelf. He's shown you his shelf before; looking at it is like walking into an old used games shop. Heck, one of his bragging rights is that this shelf came from an old shop. It has the original Nintendo logo on the top and everything. He has games from every classic system you remember playing: Sega Genesis, Dreamcast, PlayStation, SNES, and of course Nintendo 64. You're used to them being neatly organized alphabetically, only the spine of the case showing. But the Pokémon Stadium game is covering all those labels now, perched so the fading sticker label of Charizard and Blastoise is showing.

He gestures to the cartridge. "Guess where I got it?" He's biting his lip as if that'll hold in his smile.

> He's so cute when he's excited like this.

"GameStop?" you say, even though you know.

He shakes his head. "It's Merrill's. I *stole* it. Can you believe it? I know, I know—that's not really my thing: to steal. But it's all in good humor. You know." His smile drops. "It's not like he really cares about it anymore or anything."

Letting go of your hands, he walks across the room and picks up the cartridge. Facing the shelf, he says, "You know, I still haven't decided what to do with it yet. Should I destroy it? Or hold onto it?"

"You should return it to Merrill, obviously, considering it's his. Seriously, Tristan—this is stupid."

"You know, Lawrence said something really good the other day." He tilts the cartridge in his hands. "He told me not to carry around any heavy baggage from being a kid. So that's my New Year's resolution: to not let that stuff hold me back. You know, about Merrill. He used to kick my ass at these games. This Stadium cartridge—we both put our best Pokémon teams in it—you know, imported from Red and Blue. The real deal. No matter how much I trained, he always beat me. And he loved that—his sense of nostalgia is 'remember how I used to always whoop your ass and how fun that was?' But I want to rewrite that memory now. Now, I'm the one with the game, and Merrill never saw it coming!"

He pauses. "Buffy—you said you saw him today, right? How did he react? Was he pissed?" He looks at you expectantly.

> Say, "Why do you want to tick off your best friend?"

> Or tell him what he wants to hear.

You nod. "And that Bubsy thing."

Tristan's face lights up and he laughs. "Yeah, Bubsy! I knew he'd get a kick out of that."

The laugh falls into silence.

You say, "So did it help? You know, that whole baggage thing?"

"What? Oh—oh yeah. Yeah, it helped. I just wish I could've seen his face. You know—when he's made so much fun of me. It would've been nice to see how he reacted when the joke was on him."

Up against the bookshelf, your boyfriend looks very thin and small—like a shadow, or a paper cutout. This is what you love about him: sometimes when you hold him, he feels so light that you could fold him up and carry him in your pocket.

You and Tristan are standing in his room. There are comic books on the floor and old *Nintendo Power* issues. On his nightstand, you see the gift you gave him for Christmas, still in its box. Between the two of you is an absurd distance. It's probably only a foot or so, but it feels suddenly overpowering, and you don't know what to do with it.

You walk across the room and embrace him. You open his mouth with yours and inhabit the warm space there that the two of you create. That warmth—you think—maybe it can save the both of you.

Hospital:
January 12, 2010

Your phone rings. Usually when your phone rings, you ignore it until later and call the person back. But right now, you know you should be working on your art portfolio and want some means of procrastination.

> Pick up the phone.

You hold the phone up to your ear but don't say anything—not even like a hello or something that any normal, civilized person would say.

"Buffy? You there? This is Chase. I don't know if you heard, but Sephora's in the hospital—"

"What?"

"She—well—I guess I'll let her tell you what happened, but I think she could use some company. Can you come by?"

"What happened—is she okay?"

"She's fine—she just had, well, a food issue."

"Like food poisoning?"

"Something like that."

"I'll head over now."

You hang up, and stand there, staring at the wall for a minute, waiting for Chase to call back and say this is a joke, just like that time he said he was stuck in a ditch. You reach for your phone, ready to call him back when you realize how tired and defeated Chase sounded. That he couldn't fake that, even if for some weird reason he wanted to.

> But...people I know don't get hurt.

YOU ARE IN THE FRONT lobby of the local hospital. Everything smells like it's been cleaned too many times. Exits are: up, out.

> Go to front desk.

You open your mouth to ask for Sephora, then remember that even you don't believe that's her real name.

The woman at the front desk has matted auburn curls and looks like she needs to escape life.

"Can I help you?" the woman asks, her eyes on the computer screen.

"Do you...you don't have anyone named Sephora, do you?"

You try to think back to old yearbooks, transcripts, graded school papers—anything that might've indicated her real identity.

"Sephora what?" the woman asks.

You realize you've known this girl for the past five years but still don't know her real name.

And as much as you dislike her, the thought saddens you.

"She's very pale," you say. "Has black hair, down her back. Skinny and no boobs."

The woman's eyebrows raise. "*No* breasts, ma'am?"

"No—I mean, she's just flat—"

"Oh. For a second I thought she'd had them removed. Not that I'd mind the surgery." She motions to her overly endowed chest. Breast-talk makes you uncomfortable.

"She went to high school with me," you say. "She had some food issue—food poisoning? Probably throwing up or something?"

"Oh gracious—you mean Mary Anne Jarvis?"

"Mary?" You expected something at least a little more spectacular.

"The poor thing. I hear the doctors think she's had this problem for years. How could no one notice the signs?"

> Years?

She shakes her head. "Jarvis is in room six twenty-three. Tell her we're all praying for her, all right?"

You nod and run down the hall to the nearest elevator.

THE ELEVATOR IS SLOW AND stops at every floor. When someone steps in the doorway, the doors keep closing. It almost devours this old man on the third floor. Maybe you don't have much hope in mankind, but you at least hoped that elevator doors would be known for their consistent grace.

You get to the sixth floor. When the doors open, Chase is standing there, his hands shaking.

"Chase!" you say, stepping out.

When he doesn't say anything, you ask, "Is she okay?"

He looks at you with bloodshot eyes. You wonder when was the last time that he slept. And though Chase is known for his invincibility, you wonder if even invincible people need sleep.

> Hugs.

You hug Chase. "Are *you* okay?" you ask, patting his shoulder.

"What?" He shakes his head as if waking from a long sleep. "I'm okay. Just tired is all. It's a long drive."

You nod.

"I've gotta go. But look—I'm glad you're visiting Sephora. You're the only one of us that's been nice to her and all. And I think she really needs that right now."

You think about the possibility that you're the closest thing to kindness in Sephora's life, and hope that Chase is wrong.

"I'm just glad you came, Chase. I'm sure that really encouraged her."

You notice his cheeks turn a little red but don't proceed to point it out. He nods and walks into the elevator.

YOU ARE AT ROOM 623. There is a closed door. It intimidates you.

> Knock on the door.

"Yeah?" You hear Sephora, her voice loud as usual but hoarse. "Come in?"

> Step in.

You open the door to find Sephora lying on a bed, her arm hanging over the side. You realize how thin it is in the fluorescent light, skeletal even.

"Buffy!" she says when she sees you. She's smiling like you're her fairy godmother or something. "I can't believe you came—you and Chase—in one day! It's incredible!"

"Are you...feeling okay?" you ask, sitting in a chair next to her bed.

She nods. "They made me eat shit, Buffy. Pudding, bread, a lump of cranberry sauce that obviously came out of a can."

You look at her wrist. Even though it's wrapped and cleaned, the wound makes you think of Christ's wrists. You can't look at it for too long.

"Is it gross?" Sephora asks, trying to lift her body. "You think it counts for a battle wound? They say it'll heal with time. Chase didn't seem too grossed out, which is a relief—"

"Sephora," you say. "What happened?"

She smiles, looking to the wall. "I was doing a good job—no one even suspected anything. I was doing fine."

There's something you're supposed to know, you realize. You bite your lip, afraid of asking a stupid question.

"It's okay, Buffy. I didn't want you to know."

"But why?"

"You know sometimes—how when you get sick and don't eat for a while, it sucks because you're hungry, but then you look in the mirror and see how good you look? That time I got food poisoning—you probably remember—I felt my stomach after throwing up. And it was so flat! You know how good that feels, to like what you see in the mirror. So I kept it up. I haven't kept down a full meal in eighteen months now." She smiles as if she's telling you she made honor roll or something.

You wish that people came with these kinds of bios. That Sephora wore a sign around her neck, telling this story. Then, you might not have despised her so much.

Though really, when you think about it, the signs were there: Sephora refusing pizza some nights, other nights eating all the cookies Merrill's mom brought down, taking forever in the bathroom while all of you joked she must be preening herself because she was such an attention whore.

> It was so obvious. And we're her friends.

You manage to say, "So what happened for you to get here?"

Sephora sighs. "Last night, I got a craving. The worst one I remember having. I went and bought a bunch of shit—cakes, ice cream, Nutella, donuts—it's embarrassing just thinking about it. It all happened so suddenly—I couldn't even realize what was going on. But I hated myself for it and, after I threw up, I cut myself in the bathroom. But I guess I don't cut often enough to know how to do it well, or how to hide it well, so when my mom found some blood on the sink, she got me in here. The funny thing is that she brought me in for the cutting, but what worried the doctors was my weight. They say I should be dead, that I'm lucky to be alive right now."

Your throat becomes dry and burning with regret.

"They're going to make me eat again, Buffy—and I'm gonna get fat again. This totally sucks." She looks up at you and bites her lip. "I don't know why I can't keep a boyfriend. But I need to keep my body the way I want it."

She looks so harmless like this, you think to yourself. Her hair's slicked back from natural grease, and her face clear of make-up is much more appealing and sincere, you think. She looks so normal and young. You feel like you could be friends with this version of Sephora.

"C'mon, say something!" She pouts. "I just like—spat my guts out at you."

"I'm—I'm sorry about everything, Sephora," you say, touching her shoulder. "I'm here for you, okay? Whatever I can do to help, I'm here."

She looks at you like she's not sure what to make of that. You're not sure exactly what it means, either.

Your Dorm Room: January 28, 2010

E VERY MORNING AQUITANE RETURNS FROM a party, she brings something home that isn't hers. It started with a gaudy pink bangle, but the accumulations have gotten larger. Now, her desk is scattered with stranger's memorabilia: pens, keychains, a T-shirt, some softcover book that looks like it's for an English class… Her favorite new addition is a pair of combat boots that you can hear from down the hall.

Right now, you're in your bed, where you've been for the past seven hours. It only took less than a week into school for your throat to start burning. You're pretty sure it's strep but don't want to jump to any conclusions. So instead of going to class, you've been lying in bed, playing *StarFox 64* on an emulator. Actually, it's not been half bad. Except for the whole throat-burning part.

Without looking up, you hear the combat boots coming toward the room. A key struggles in the keyhole, and the door opens. Aquitane's eyes are bloodshot, her short hair slicked over her forehead with sweat. She looks like she needs bed rest more than you do.

"Elizabeth," she huffs. "Wanna go to a party?"

On a Monday night? Really? You remember what happened the last time you went to a party, and how you mentally swore to never go to one again. You also think about how many things have been going wrong with your life, and wonder if it's time to start making some responsible, adult decisions.

> Find a decent excuse.

"I don't know, Aquitane—I've been sick all day, probably have strep—"

"I had strep once," Aquitane said. "That's what I got for kissing a dude." She looks up at the ceiling, like it might give her some better answer. "You aren't seriously missing out on a party just because you feel sick…"

"I don't wanna go anyway," you say. "I'm having fun on my own."

Aquitane looks at your computer and the 64-bit rendering. Your life must look so sad to the outside world.

> They just don't understand the importance of classic gaming—

Suddenly, she reaches over and grabs you by the shoulders. "Drink and be merry!" she shouts. "For at finals we die!"

She starts laughing, and you can't help but join in and laugh, too.

> Should I tell her about Jeremy?

You look up at her and ask, "Have you ever felt attracted to someone you know is absolutely no good for you, but maybe that's exactly why you like them? Because there's no inherent value to them?"

Aquitane studies you. Then she breaks out laughing again. "All the time, Elizabeth."

"So what do you do? How do you get yourself to just stay away from them?"

"I…don't?" She smiles and pats your head like you're a friend's pet. "You're in *college*, Elizabeth. It's time to lose the moral values. Have some *fun*. Fuck around a bit. Love will come and go, it's not like you're going to catch their bad traits. Unless those bad traits are STDs."

Aquitane steps into the closet and grabs a flat shimmering dress. The kind that's easy to pull on and off. "We're leaving at eight, so hurry and get ready."

Over on your screen, a new message appears. It's from Tristan.

He types: *hug*.

> Reply

You type: *hug*. *Miss you.*

Your conversations are so riveting.

> A party would certainly be more riveting than this.

"I'm not sure a party's what I need right now," you say at last.

Aquitane turns around, her shirt half off. "What do you need then?"

What do you need? Do you even know?

> SAVE SLOT 3.

You save over Tristan's house.

IT'S EIGHT-THIRTY AT NIGHT, AND you're standing outside a building that looks like it should be condemned. It's some Greek life fraternity with a name that consists of three characters of a language that you don't know. Above your heads, a power line is draped in brown and molding shoes. Your throat hurts and you want to fall over on the blacktop and die. Your mom says that without antibiotics, strep can get to your heart and kill you.

So explain to me, Buffy: how did you get here?

> I still don't know—what I need, exactly.

Is it this?

> I don't know. Aquitane had a valid question: what *do* I need?

Whatever it is, I doubt you'll find it here.

> Whatever it is? Do you even *know* what I need to beat this game? Do you know *anything*?

If I told you how to play the game, that would sort of defeat the purpose.

> The purpose of what? I thought—this was simple. Get Tristan, game over. But—

But Tristan isn't enough, is he?

You follow Aquitane inside.

YOU ARE AT THE PARTY. Aquitane has disappeared but has handed you a nameless beverage to keep you company. In this room, there is a piano and lots of vomit. The room is heavy with the smell of body odor and fermentation.

> Make it happen like the movies.

I'm sorry, I don't understand. Make what happen?

> You know. A girl goes somewhere and doesn't know anyone, then someone appears out of nowhere and talks to her and they become great friends. It happens all the time on TV shows and movies. You know.

Actually, I don't. Because, well, I hate to break it to you, Buffy, but this isn't a TV show or a movie.

> Then what was the point of—

"Hey, Buffy. Funny how we keep running into each other." It's Jeremy, of course, because at this point, there's some new rule of science that if you're with Aquitane and/or Alice, Jeremy must be within a hundred-yard radius.

"And it's good that I found you—" he says, "Because I wanted to talk to you about something. But how can anyone talk before having a drink?"

He holds his cup up to you, but you don't take it.

You smell the sharp alcohol stench in his breath. "Jeremy, you really don't look too good. Don't you think you should—"

"I'm *great*, Buffy. Like a god. Never felt this good since...since..."

He holds his cup up, his words slurred. "I always thought people were *stupid* for drinking this shit...but it does *miracles*. Let's drink our sorrows away, Buffy. You and me. Drink them down, right here."

You have no sorrows to drink away, except for maybe the fact that you are miserable despite your lack of sorrows.

> Wow. It's really sad, when you put it like that.

You're not that into alcohol. What little you've tried you've found unappealing. You can't imagine Jeremy actually likes the taste himself.

Remind me: why are you at these parties if you don't like alcohol?

> Take the cup.

You put your cup to your nose, smelling it. The scent comes back, biting and powerful. Something exciting in the danger of that smell. Something that might change you into a completely different person—maybe the person you've always wanted to be? Before thinking about drinking it though, you'd like to know what it is. Make sure there's no gasoline or battery acid or something in there.

He nudges you. "Have you ever wanted a replay, Buffy? A do-over?"

Around the room, you see people wild and uninhibited. That was one of the things you thought you'd enjoy in college: the freedom. No dress codes, no detentions for wearing too many bracelets or doodling during class. But in a way, you almost miss the predictability of those classrooms, how wonderfully mundane they were.

"I mean, it's not like this can literally go back in time, but it can make you feel like it. For a couple hours, you feel like you can change the world." Jeremy chuckles. "It burns at first, but you get used to it. If you know that, it's not that bad. Tomorrow, you won't even remember…"

All these people will wake up tomorrow and not remember any of this. For a moment, they might not even remember who they are. You never understood why someone might want to forget everything and feel sick in the morning, but suddenly the idea has new appeal to you.

> This is it. This is how I reset everything.

That's a terrible idea. I did not give you that idea. I don't know where you—

> No. That's exactly what it is.

> This is time travelling.

> This is what you don't want.

> So take that.

> Drink.

You drink. ꓲꓳꓴ ꓒꓤiiiiiꓵꓵꓵꓵꓘ

——ꓹꓬl—$@——ꓹ—ꓱꓴˣꟄꟄˣꞰˣˣꟄꟄˣ

ACROSS THE ROOM, AQUITANE COMES over, carrying two glass bottles: one in each hand.

"Whoa!" she says, looking at Jeremy. "What the fuck are you doing here?"

> Escape.

You grab Aquitane's arm, whispering in her ear, "Help me."

Aquitane's voice gets louder. "You'd better not mess with another girl in our pack. You understand? You're a creep, Jeremy."

With that, she stomps across the room, pulling you with her. Once you're both farther away, Aquitane looks down at your cup. "Elizabeth! Don't tell me you drank that!"

You look into the drink. Your mouth still burns. If someone lit a match in your mouth, you'd probably explode.

She shakes her head. "Man, Elizabeth—you don't know the *first thing* about partying."

You want to point out that she's the one that gave you the bizarre drink, but whatever. She hands you one of the bottles in her hand. "Don't worry. Try this—it's cherry-flavored."

> Drink.

You lift it up and drink half the bottle in one gulp.

> It's so sweet! For serious.

Then you start coughing.

Aquitane comes up behind you and rubs your back. In her mom-voice she says, "Feel better? Wanna sit down for a minute?"

You feel yourself separate from your body. The room tilts on its side, and you wait for everything on the table to fall over, bUt it doesn't.

≗¬ʟ—$@——≗—ɵu×&&×⅃

> ARE *you* OKAY? YOU sound a little off.

I'm sorry. I don't understand. You should be asking yourself that question.

"I don't feel well," you say. "I think I'm gonna text my boyfriend to pick me up."

Fumbling for your phone, you text: *hey tristan im at a party on campus at delta sigma phi can u come pick me up or maybe lol just hangggg*

Your finger gets stuck on the G key until you realize you need to let go.

"Are you sure?" Aquitane studies you. "The party just started—you don't wanna bail now!"

As you scroll through your contacts, Aquitane puts her hand on your arm. You click on the name you're pretty sure is Tristan's and hit send.

> Try to be vulnerable to your roommate.

"Does it sound weird to say that my life sometimes feels like a video game? And sometimes, I'm not even the one who's playing it?"

Aquitane laughs. "Nothing sounds weird with enough shots. But I feel that way, too. All the time. We're all under a system."

You nod, twisting the bottle in your hand. "I bet you don't have a text parser controlling your mind every second of the day."

"*Text parser?* Shit, Elizabeth. Sometimes you speak English but I still don't understand you."

"That's okay. I don't understand myself sometimes, either."

Maybe you should drink some water. Or, you know, leave.

> Leave? But where would I go?

Somewhere else. Anywhere else.

"I need some water," you say.

Aquitane frowns. "What's that?" She points to some vodka on a nearby table. Definitely not water.

YOU ARE IN **A** **P@RT4.** **TH3RE** **!!S————**

> Hey, you doing all right?

> FIND WATER.

> I run into the kitchen, looking for the sink, but it's filled with ice and bottles of various alcoholic beverages.

> Take an ice cube.

> I put an ice cube in my mouth. It's better than nothing, I guess.

> Without looking, I run into the bathroom and stick my head in the sink, running water over my mouth.

————

It's LUK3WarM. JUSt LiKE 4OU.
¬L-$@——⅜-ΘU

YOUR BOTTLE IS GONE, AND your eyes are full of fluorescent light.

> Morning?

It's thirty minutes later.

> !

You feel sickness surge from your stomach.

> Toilet!

You crawl on your knees to the toilet and throw your head inside. You do it with such vigor that you nearly get your hair wet with toilet water. Ew.

It doesn't take much urging for you to vomit. It all comes out at once, and your stomach suddenly feels incredibly empty.

> Is this what it feels like to be homeless?

I don't know. I don't have a body, let alone the presence or absence of a home.

> Oh. I never thought about it like that before.
My head hurts. And I feel horrible. Why did I drink
all that again?

I don't know. Why did you?

IN THE CORNER OF THE bathroom, you see the shower curtain rustle. You half expect a shirtless girl to tumble through from one side on the tile, or something equally unsettling, but the curtain becomes still again.

> Examine shower.

You're no voyeurist, but you're curious now. And something tells you this isn't a sex scene, that it's not sex related at all. When the light falls through the curtain, you can make out one silhouette, small and hunched over. There's a small sound, like a wounded animal.

You wipe your lip on your sleeve and approach the shower stall. The figure behind the curtain stiffens.

"Hello?" you say.

No answer. You see the movement of an arm over a face, as if trying to wipe away tears.

Slowly, you grip the edge of the curtain and pull slightly.

Behind the curtain is Jeremy in a backward T-shirt, the tag hanging out under his Adam's apple. His head and upper torso are wet and above him, you notice the shower head dripping slowly.

When you pull the curtain back, he gasps a little.

> Retreat. Retreat.

You can't leave now. He looks up at you expectantly, and you wonder what you're supposed to do.

> Hug.

Not knowing of any better alternative, you reach over the bathtub ledge and hug him. It's at an awkward angle, not to mention you smell like vomit and he smells like alcohol, so in the end the details aren't important.

To your surprise, he grabs onto you, the way lichen takes hold of a tree.

> I want some explanation for this.

As if reading your thoughts, he says, "It's Alice. I'm at the end with her, I'm at the end…when she drinks, it's like she's a different person. I've tried this drinking thing too but I just can't—I can't get into her world. Like, when she drinks, she gets violent. The other day, she tried to throw a chair at me. And it makes me wonder, why do I even bother? It's funny—I know I shouldn't want her, but I do. I think I even *love* her."

As much as you know you shouldn't, you feel your chest sink in disappointment.

It's then you hear a familiar voice at the door, screaming and laughing at some girl, "Stop being such a bitch!"

You realize you're still holding onto him and let go. There's something incredibly masculine about him: the bodily scent, the firmness of his torso. You blush, feeling a desire you wish you didn't have.

Jeremy's expression tightens, and he looks like a deer in the middle of a lawn, disoriented by civilization.

That's when Alice walks into the bathroom. And you feel your muscles clench.

> Hide.

There is nowhere to hide.

> There's a bathtub with a shower curtain.

Fine. You jump into the bathtub and lay flat to the floor. It's very slick and brown with dirt.

Alice looks over at you jumping in the bathtub and says, "Elizabeth? You need water?" It's then that she recognizes Jeremy and shouts, "Fuck!"

"Alice, don't make this into something it's not—" Jeremy begins.

Exits are: behind Alice, the toilet.

"You're such a dirty little slut!" she shouts at you. "You totally did this on purpose—and after I thought you were my *real* friend! You were one of *us!*"

> Explain it so she understands.

"We were just *talking*, Alice. I'm not trying to steal your man—I have a *boyfriend*, for Pete's sake!"

> Not that that stops some people, I guess.

In the background, you hear the party chatter quiet and see some people looking into the bathroom.

Alice laughs. It's one of those hysteric laughs that sounds like it was recorded, then sped up to sound like a chipmunk. "*No*, no. I won't hear your shit, Buffy—"

"It's not like he's even your *boyfriend!*" You feel your voice get louder as you try to stand up. "Alice—if you want him, just claim him! But you don't— what're you afraid of?"

And maybe it's because you're still drunk, but you definitely didn't expect her to punch you right in the nose.

A red drop hits your shirt. You just stare at it, unable to decide between screaming and fainting.

In the bathroom door, you see people stuffed in, taking pictures with their cell phones.

"Alice, no!" Jeremy reaches across the bathroom and holds down Alice's wrists. "What's *wrong* with you? Buffy didn't do anything. She's probably the nicest, most legit, honest person here tonight. And she's right—you can't keep playing around like this. If you don't want me, stop texting me. I promise I'll go away if that's what you really want."

Alice tries to fight his grip, but he holds her firm.

> Maybe this scene isn't real. Maybe I'll wake up now, and Aquitane will tell me I just got completely wasted, and it'll be funny five years from now.

Some people start to leave the doorway. In the background, you hear the conversation return.

Alice starts tearing up. "Maybe I don't know what I want," she says.

> Prepare for another vomit spree.

You get to your knees toward the shower drain, preparing for another round of vomit, but nothing comes out.

Jeremy embraces her. "I really care about you, Alice. I lo—"

"Don't say it!" Her voice becomes shrill and wild.

Your mouth becomes sour, but still nothing.

Jeremy turns around and sees you there bent over, and on instinct puts his hand on your shoulder. It's warm and if you weren't so sick you might reach over and touch it. He asks, "Are you okay?" but all you can think is, *Why do people always ask the wrong questions?*

You don't remember what happens after that.

YOU COME TO WITH AQUITANE hovering over you.

She holds a drink out to you, and even though you don't know what it is, you're thirsty and will go with anything at this point.

"Where's your boyfriend?" she asks. "Didn't you text him a while ago?"

You sit up to drink whatever it is Aquitane has. Your tonsils burn. "Yeah, but it's not like Tristan ever comes to anything anyway. He's just lame like that. Like one time, he came two hours late to a date of ours."

"Two hours?"

"Yeah." You take a swig. "Maybe that's what his condition is—it's that he can't *not* disappoint people!" For some reason, the idea is really funny to you and you start laughing. You start laughing so hard that you start choking.

Then you feel a hand on your shoulder.

Aquitane looks a little above your head and asks, "Is this your boyfriend?"

You turn around and see Merrill standing there, his hand still on you.

> Is this like a nightmare or something?

"Is this like a nightmare or something?" you say, then cover your mouth, whispering, "How did you know I was here?"

"It's nice to see you too, Buffy," Merrill says, not smiling. "And as to how I found you—you texted me. As Tristan."

You look at him confused. "I texted Tristan."

Merrill studies you, says, "Buffy, you don't look good. I'm bringing you home, okay?"

"What're you, her mom?" Aquitane takes a swig, nudging you. "She goes home whenever she wants. Or never."

"I'm drinking my sorrows away tonight, Merrill." You lean against his arm. "Wanna join us?"

"Is this what Tristan's made you into? Do you actually think you're happy like this? C'mon, Buffy. You don't wanna do something you'll regret."

> What don't I regret?

> Stay here.

> Go with Merrill.

> I want Tristan.

> ...What *do* I want?

You feel a wave of nausea surge through you. You put your hand over your mouth and lean into Merrill. He puts his arms around you firmly, and you become encapsulated by his warmth. You've hugged him before, but never have you felt or understood so deeply how tall and large he is against you, like a soft room that consumes you. Against his body, you feel small and childlike.

You feel your feet lift off the ground. Merrill is picking you up. You feel him swing your body horizontal to carry you as if you're a rag doll. Before you can process to argue or thank him, he tells Aquitane, "It's been a pleasure."

When you get into the car, Merrill hands you a plastic bag. "Just in case," he says. "How you feeling?"

He brought you a bottle of water—which you've already downed. In your hand, the empty bottle crinkles.

You nod. "A little better, I think."

Before he puts the car into drive, he leans toward you. "Listen, Buffy—I know you think Tristan's the best thing ever, but seriously—rethink that. And rethink this whole partying shit."

You frown. "How can you say that? He's like, your best *friend*—"

"*Was.*" He puts the car in reverse, and starts backing up. "Do you know why he's dating you, Buffy?"

"Because I'm a wonderful person, obviously."

A hint of a smile surfaces on Merrill's lips. "Yes, you are. It's just—it's not that Watson means to be horrible, he's just still a bit of a kid. Haven't you noticed that?"

You shake your head, even though you totally know what he means.

"If I were you, I'd look and see if he's really worth your time. I know you won't listen to me, but if dating Tristan makes you drink…"

You frown. "But you *encouraged* us to date."

"I did. If I'd known better, I wouldn't have."

Merrill pulls up in front of your dorm. In the dark, it looks oddly welcoming.

You begin, "How did you know where my—"

"I know my way around," he says, not looking at you.

"Thank you." You get out of the car. "I'm feeling better already. If I'd stayed there, I don't know what might've happened. You're like my guardian angel!"

He smiles, looking out the windshield, and drives away.

YOU ARE IN THE COMMUNAL shower on your floor, and there is a small pool of vomit by your hands. Your throat and mouth are dry and thick. Your stomach aches and you wonder for a minute if you might die again.

> Am I dying?

You pull out your phone, ready to call 9-1-1, your mom, or maybe even Tristan. You see another message from Tristan: *lemme know when you're free to talk. :hug:*

> It's like I can never get away from it—

> My phone! What if that's the problem all along—

You've heard that cell phone batteries can cause cancer, that holding your cell phone so close to your body all day could expose you to some sort of radioactive waves. Your mom bought you a cell phone case for this very reason—though it's leather and looks like something a seventy-year-old man might use.

> Maybe—is that what's causing this game to even happen in the first place?

> Flush cell phone down toilet.

You reach into your inventory and pull out your cell phone. Crawling across the bathroom, you drop it into the toilet. But when you drop it, it just floats at the top.

Some problems aren't so easy to fix.

> Drown it.

You push the phone into the water. It sinks.

Bed:
January 29, 2010

L AST NIGHT, IT FELT LIKE a good idea to drown your phone. You've heard your mother say it enough times by now: technology's doing something to all of our *brains*. It's making us think in a different way. If we don't step back for a little while, it's going to drive us all crazy, make us all like mini crack addicts. You wondered there in the bathroom, with everything going wrong, if you cut yourself out of the world, maybe the game in your head would stop. Maybe things would slow down just enough for you to regain a piece of your life back.

But in the morning, waking up with a heavy headache, you realized your parents would have no way to contact you. That they might not come to pick you up this weekend. When you borrowed Aquitane's phone to coordinate with them, you realized you'd have to explain to them what happened. And somehow, that story would have to censor out:

- The party
- The alcohol
- The toilet (it'd bring up more questions than answers)
- The game inside your head

In the car ride on the way home, they don't ask. And you won't tell.

When you get home, the first thing you do is make a beeline to the family landline. You haven't used one of these in ages, but it's the weekend and that means you can see your boyfriend again. You're not a huge phone chatter, and neither is Tristan, but you call him, your heart thudding in your chest. It's late, and your parents are going to bed, but you feel compelled to talk right now.

The phone rings several times, only to go to the answering machine. A recording says: "Hi, this is Tristan—I'm not home right now, but my answering machine is, so you can talk to it instead. Just remember, you do have the right to remain silent, as everything you say will be recorded and can be used against you."

> Leave a message.

"Hey, Tristan, this is Buffy... So you're probably wondering why I'm calling from a weird number. I flushed my phone down the toilet last night—long story—so I don't have a phone right now. I hope you're doing good. Did you get my text last night? About the party? I thought I texted you but it was a weird night so I might just be going crazy. I had some serious drama, though—my roommate saw me talking—I repeat, *talking*—to a guy she likes. She totally flipped and punched me in the nose. I think I've told you about Alice? I mean, I like her and all, but I don't understand her. I wish you could've been there, but Me—my friend—stood up for me and helped, which was really kind. Just seeing Alice and the guy she likes—they're both dysfunctional, really. I guess a lot of college couples are like that. Well, I'm glad we're not like that, that we're reasonable human beings that can talk things out and not freak out at each other."

"I miss you, Tristan. And I'm so pumped to see you again—Facebook me with when you're free, all right?"

> Hang up.

You ARE IN YOUR DAD's office. It's Sunday morning, and he's getting ready for church, but this can't wait. You know this conversation isn't going to be easy—nobody likes explaining that they lost their phone, but the fact that you intentionally drowned it will be hard to explain. However, it's clear to you that a phone is one of those unfortunate necessities in life. An unfortunate necessity that you can't afford.

Your dad is putting on his socks when you come in. He looks at you like you've interrupted a lab experiment.

> Tell him, "I 'lost' my phone."

He listens and shakes his head, bending over to put on a shoe. "I guess this is what happens in college—first your laptop, now your phone? How many more things are we going to need to replace?"

> My mind?

You scratch the back of your head. The scalp is dry and there's something satisfying about peeling the dead skin off. "I know."

"Did you try asking your friends? Where was it that you lost it? Maybe the school lost and found has it?"

You bite your lip.

"Maybe we could try calling it and seeing if someone nearby can—"

"It's gone, Dad. It's gone, and it's my fault. I thought it'd help to get away from a phone, but I realized that's really dumb now."

He examines you, with a look that you're not sure whether to read as disapproval or intrigue. He laces his shoes.

"Are you coming to church?" He doesn't look up, knowing the answer is always the same.

You shake your head. "Maybe next week."

He stands up, fixing his tie. "Well then. When we get back, I'll take you to Best Buy. Consider it a late Christmas present." With that, he leaves the office while you stare at the wall. Eventually, a "thank you" leaves your mouth, but by then he's down the hall and out the door.

An Optimistic Perception of Reality: February 14, 2010

I T'S VALENTINE'S DAY, AND YOU still haven't gotten a text from Tristan. Not that you need a text to know that he loves you or anything, it's just—you know—it'd be a nice gesture. Even just a *Happy Valentine's Day* or *glad ur my gf* ☺ or *love you* (even though you haven't let him use the L word yet) would make you feel better about the whole getting out of bed thing.

> Maybe he's waiting for me to text him.

You text: *Happy Valentine's day! <3 <3 <3 <3 <3 <3*

> How many hearts are okay before it gets weird?

You remove three hearts. That seems more normal. Ish.

A few minutes later, your phone vibrates. Your hands shake as you look to see how Tristan replied. But it's not Tristan. It's Merrill.

It reads: *hey wanna come over for some shooting and hanging out tonight?*

> For serious?

Without much thought, you say: *Today? Isn't it valentine's day????*

A few seconds later, you get the reply: *yes, I can read a calendar, buffy.*

Maybe you're still tired, or irritated that Tristan hasn't texted you, but you say, *Well, maybe you don't have anything important to do today but some of us have plans.*

Plans? Do you really have plans, though? You've set apart the day for hanging out with Tristan, but he's yet to put anything in writing.

You don't hear back from Merrill.

I$_T$'$_S$ A LITTLE AFTER LUNCHTIME when you hear the doorbell ring. Tristan is standing on the front step. You're still in your Pac-Man pajamas. Against the side of the house, there is a snow shovel. Exits are: inside.

He smiles, handing you a heart-shaped chocolate box. "Happy Valentine's Day," he says. "I bought you a gift online, but it hasn't come yet, and my mom said she'd kill me if I didn't give you a gift on Valentine's Day."

You examine the chocolate box, optimistic for a seal of vegan approval.

"It's vegan," he says. "Or at least that's what they told me at Shoppers."

You're not really into chocolate, but it's the thought that counts.

You expect him to say something—maybe asking you out to dinner, or a movie, even Chuck E. Cheese—anything, really.

Tristan continues to stand there. You see the hot air escaping the house in desperate waves.

"You wanna come in?" you ask.

"It's fine," he says.

"Did you see Merrill's text?" you ask, opening the door wide for him to step in. But he doesn't. The cold air blows in and you know your mom is totally going to kill you for wasting all sorts of electricity.

He frowns. "No. What text?"

"About tonight? Some shooting practice or something?"

"No." Tristan balances from foot to foot. "Didn't get that."

"Hm. Weird." Another gust of cold air hits your bare arms. You rub them, but Tristan still stands there, unmoving. "Well, he wants to go shooting and for some reason wants us to go with him."

You grab onto the doorknob. "Can you come inside?"

"I really should be going," he says. His body stiffens for a reason you can't figure out.

> Try to look sexy against the doorframe.

"Just for a second. We've got the heating system on." You lean against the doorframe with your heel up and stick your tongue out, because you think that's hot or something.

He laughs and steps inside, so you can finally close the door. Jeesh.

"Just—I don't know." He shakes his head. "I can't do the shooting thing anyway. Even if Merrill invited me. I don't want to. I don't want to be around him."

Something leaks inside you. Probably the valve that usually keeps your emotions in check.

> Recall all the times Merrill has made me angry.

- When he toilet papered your car because he thought it would be funny
- When he toilet papered your dad's car because he thought it would be funny
- When he made jokes about God (= ~4×10^{12} times)
- When he made jokes about Tristan (= ~5×10^{15} times)
- When he hired that computer hooker to come over, just to try to not look so lonely
- When he wanted to go out with you and you couldn't get yourself to say no
- When he brought you home from that college party where you were super drunk and wanted to stay—

You nod, your smile souring. "Who's he think he's kidding, anyway? On *Valentine's Day*? Like, why do we put up with him? I don't know if I wanna be around him either."

"He's just jealous. He's never been good at handling not getting his way."

"It's just weird—does he really think anyone will show up?"

Tristan snickers. "He's *Merrill*. Of course he thinks everyone will show up. He thinks he rules the world."

"And why shooting? What's there to shoot, out in the cold?"

"Why not? Probably just wants to shoot some clay pigeons, show off, feel awesome again." Tristan puts his hands in his pockets. "Maybe I should go tonight. Merrill needs a reality check."

"Are you sure that's a good idea?" It's never occurred to you to go to something you've not been invited to.

"I think it's a great idea, actually." His eyes light up. "Merrill thinks I'm too weak or scared to go shooting, but I'll prove him wrong. I'll show him he's not all that."

> But what about Valentine's Day? Aren't we going on a date?

You don't look him in the eye, hoping he'll read your thoughts.

"I've…never seen you shoot before," you say. Not that you've really gone to Merrill's shooting gigs much before. You hate being around all those guns. It goes against your vegan morals.

"My dad taught me a while ago—not my favorite thing to do, but I guess it's good to know how to do."

You nod. "Well—do you wanna hang out here until then?"

"Sorry, I've got some stuff to work on." Tristan opens the door. "I'll pick you up in a couple hours."

> What time is "a couple hours"?

> And what about—

Tristan's already out into the cold. You are in the foyer with a box of chocolates. Exits are: upstairs, self, the cold.

MERRILL IS OUT IN THE backyard alone, his clay pigeon shooter shooting orange pellets into the sky. Every time they fly, Merrill shoots them and they burst like a broken cookie. In front of him, the woods look endless and skeletal. He's wearing a short-sleeved T-shirt, no jacket.

"So you made it after all."

"You didn't really make it sound like it was optional," you say, rubbing your arms. "Where's Chase and Sephora?"

"Not joining us today," he says. "It'll just be the three of us. You think you can handle a gun, Tristan?"

"I've been practicing," he says, which you think is totally a lie. Or is it? You're not so sure anymore.

"Great." Merrill nods toward a gun on the ground. "Come take some shots with me."

You assume he means Tristan and not you—which you're okay with. You're used to being a spectator at this point, considering you're a girl, and it never occurs to anyone that you might actually want to participate or something.

Tristan picks up the rifle, and you see how large it looks in his hands. His arms shake a little as he thrusts it over his shoulder.

Merrill glances at him. "You sure you're up for this?"

Tristan snickers, eyeing a clay pigeon whizzing in the air. You watch him focus, almost as if you can feel the sweat drop running down his forehead.

He pulls the trigger but the kickback from the rifle jams his shoulder, making him fall backward.

"Tristan!" You run up to him, but he's regained his footing. The shot missed the target, skimming the tree line.

Tristan puts down the gun, rubbing his collarbone. Pulling back his collar to examine it, you see already the skin's begun to bruise.

"Maybe you should just stick to your books," Merrill says. "Let's go inside—it's getting cold out here." But before he moves, he shoots one last pigeon, and hits it in the center.

Inside, Merrill goes to the fridge room. In Merrill's fridge, you see cans of Budweiser have replaced the Jolt and Gamer Fuel. He grabs a Budweiser, and Tristan follows suit (though you've never known Tristan to actually drink alcohol) as you all sit down in the living room.

You consider asking Merrill about his new drink choices when Tristan leans over to you and kisses you full-on. You peck back and pull away, but he continues forward.

> Um...

You gently push him away and try to laugh it off. "Whoa, buddy," you say. "We're in public."

He looks over to Merrill and chuckles. "Yeah. I guess I get carried away sometimes."

You look between Merrill and Tristan, trying to understand what exactly's happening here. You open your mouth: "Tristan…"

"Aren't you two so cute," Merrill says, putting down his drink. "I can feel the incredible substance of this relationship."

You frown. "What's that supposed to mean—"

"Like Buffy, aren't you so glad Tristan's always there for you when you need him? That he never lets you down or anything?"

You study Merrill in disbelief.

Tristan shifts on the couch. "You've got a problem with something, Merrill?"

"Oh, you didn't hear?" Merrill gets up, his voice getting loud. "How your girlfriend needed you, and not only did you not come, but you didn't even know it was happening?"

He laughs. "I knew you'd come tonight, Tristan. Don't you get it? I know you don't care about Buffy. If you did, why the fuck would you be here right now, and not on some Valentine's Day date? That's the problem with you, Tristan—I'm still more important to you than Buffy is. You don't know how to man up—and if you don't have the balls to care about someone other than yourself, you need to do the right thing and break up with her, tonight." He leans back, taking a swig of Budweiser. Even from your seat on the couch, you see his eyes are a little red.

> Please rewind to stop this conversation from even happening.

You look at Tristan, waiting for a defense.

He leans back into the couch, eyeing Merrill. After a minute, he says, "It's not my fault you're jealous."

Wordlessly, Merrill stands up, putting the can on the table. Walking over to Tristan, he grabs him by the collar and punches him. Tristan's eyes go wide, and it's as if Merrill's fist has gone through his chest, out his back like a skewer.

The color drains from Tristan's face. You get up and hold onto him. "Tristan? Are you okay?"

And that's when he screams that animal scream that will continue to haunt you for the rest of your life.

Merrill's voice wavers. "I was aiming for his head. He was sitting down, but then he—oh shit, oh shit oh shit." He reaches for the phone in his pocket, hands shaking, dialing 9-1-1.

You feel like there's something you don't know, like you're listening to an inside joke. "How hard did you hit him, Merrill? Is a punch really nine-one-one-worthy?"

Tristan reaches for his chest, bending over. His breaths become short and quick, like drowning in his own body.

"Hello? Yes, my friend was hit in the chest—and he has that—shit—I don't remember what it's called—but I know it could kill him—something with his heart—yes, he's breathing now—"

"Kill?" Your fingers dig into Tristan's arms as you hold onto him. "Tristan? Tell me you're gonna be okay—please—"

He begins to sway and on instinct you wrap your arms around him to catch him. You look at where your fingers were a moment ago, and see the beginning colors of a bruise.

Hospital II:
February 18, 2010

YOU ARE IN THE HOSPITAL. Didn't expect to be here so many times this year, did you? Tristan has been here for the past several days, and though you've visited him at least twice already, your hands are still shaking as if something very different might happen with him at any second.

You hate to admit it, but part of you secretly wishes he'd stay in the hospital longer. That way, if something goes wrong, there are people here to save him, but also because of the way he looks at you. Every time you come, he lights up in a way you've never seen before but only imagined. It's like you're his world, and the two of you are one of those couples on TV. You wonder what will happen once he's released and goes home, how you can have a relationship after something like this. If you'll still be his world.

"Hi, Tristan." You walk over to his section of the hospital room: where the curtains are wide open, and Tristan's sitting up in bed, his finger glowing red from an attached pulse reader.

"Buffy!" he calls, sitting up, his eyes wide like a kid who's seen his mom for the first time in weeks.

You don't ask him about the surgery. You don't talk about what happened at Merrill's, about his condition, or anything. Instead, you motion to the Wii his mother brought in and ask if he wants to play.

"As long as you're up for losing." He grins.

"Hey now!" The title screen for *Super Smash Brothers Melee* lights up the screen. "I've been practicing. I've had a lot of time to do that sort of thing."

Tristan nods. You half-hope he'll say something, but he sits there silently, choosing his character.

> Pick Kirby.

You always pick Kirby.

If it's any consolation, Tristan always plays as StarFox. And as you play, you both have your go-to moves: you keep hitting down-B, and Tristan keeps trying to fire a ray gun at you.

> It's cathartic, in a way...

"Everyone says hi," you say. "They're worried and want to make sure you're okay."

Kirby falls off the edge of the stage. Tristan goes, "Aw yeah," and you wonder if everything's just a video game to some people.

"Is the pain going away?"

"A little."

Kirby slams into StarFox, shooting him up in the air. The announcer's voice from the television says, "Game set."

"You know, after I'm discharged, I'm still required to stay bedridden at home for the next few weeks."

"That's okay—I'll come visit you—"

"No, it's not that. Missing that many classes, it's pretty much impossible for me to make it up. I did some research, and I'd be pretty much guaranteed to fail at least two of my classes, which means I'd either have to take online classes over the summer or add another semester to my graduation date."

"So?"

"So! Don't you get it, Buffy?" His face goes red, the muscles in his neck showing as he strains to lean toward you. "I'd be ruined. My GPA would be ruined. I wouldn't get into the grad schools I want to. Any hope of keeping my scholarship, or graduating in the top of my class is gone."

"I'm sure they'd understand, if it's for a medical reason—"

"You're too nice, Buffy—you can't understand. There aren't any second chances, there's no one who's going to ask why I failed these courses. They only want the best, and I can never be the best. I'm damaged goods."

He looks away, so desperate, and you know you need to say something but have no idea what to say. You were never into school, you never cared what grades you got. You reasoned you were already committing academic suicide by doing art so it didn't really matter.

> What can I tell him?

You stare at him in the hospital bed. In his hospital gown, his body looks even more skeletal. His wrists remind you of Sephora's: like if they bend too far, they might just break off like a twig. That fragility makes you want to hold him even more.

Leaning over him, you kiss him.

"I'll always be here for you, Tristan," you say. "Even if things aren't perfect at school, I'll do whatever I can to help."

You think that's a reasonable thing to say.

"I was going to be Steve Jobs, Buffy. I was going to be Einstein. I get it now—I'll never be anyone like that. I'm just going to be…Tristan. You know… all that stuff they taught us in school, all that theology stuff, I used to believe it without a second thought. But now—I don't know what to believe. I don't think I believe anything, really. I just exist. What do you believe, Buffy? What keeps you going?"

Even though your schooling has taught you answers to these kinds of questions, you have never had to actually answer them yourself. Tristan looks up at you, and you know you can't lie to him or give him something vague.

He's looking at you the way kids look expectantly at parents or teachers for the absolute truth. And you know you have anything but that to offer.

You wish you had an answer, but your brain feels like it's floating somewhere high above your head. Time lapses, but Tristan doesn't complain or tell you to hurry up. He just watches you. Like he wants to believe anything you tell him.

> I want to tell him I believe in God.

> I want to tell him I believe in *us*.

> But...

"I don't know," you answer, your voice weak. "It's complicated, I guess. Right? We just...keep on living. It's the default setting."

Tristan nods. How can you know how much you'll replay this conversation in your mind, over and over, asking yourself why you didn't say something— anything else, if there was anything you could've said that would've made things different.

You try to smile and prepare for the next round, but for the rest of the games your fingers are too slow and you just never seem to be able to land a hit on StarFox.

Somewhere Not Yet Decided Upon: April 1, 2010

YOU HAVE A DREAM TWENTY years in the future. Tristan invites you to meet his wife and kids for dinner. It's been fifteen years since you two dated or hung out or did anything cool. Tristan now makes lots of money solving math problems that computers can't, and has a blonde wife that perpetually wears crystal necklaces and is a top-line fashion designer. You hate her for so many reasons.

When you drive up, you're intimidated by the size of the front door. The house itself looks like it should be in a catalogue or a dream, but you try to not think about it too much.

You ring the doorbell, and Tristan greets you in a brown robe. He embraces you and your body stiffens. You didn't realize you had to dress up. You're in your typical art smock, paint splattered on your jeans. Your hair's up in an artsy ponytail. You feel like the thirty thousand a year that you make.

Tristan's wife hugs you when you come in. Her teeth are so white and you want to ask her how she got them that way but you're afraid that might sound like a stupid question. She looks like the kind of person who can keep herself busy, who doesn't sit around waiting for Tristan to come home. Their kids all come around to see the new guest, and you're amazed by the perfection in their small features: the baby fat cheeks, spread-out freckles, pink lips, open blue eyes. They watch you like you're an alien and ask why your pants have paint stains. Tristan's wife blushes and sends them off to play. Tristan asks how you've been but you don't know where to start, or what's worth noting, really.

You think about everything you didn't do in college: calculus, campus jobs, those open calls for art submissions, *career prep*…. You think about how, every time you try to say something at the table, Tristan just takes a bite of something and nods, like anything in your experience is so greatly removed from his that there's nothing he can really say to make it into a conversation.

Once you tell Tristan and his wife that you have to go, you wake up and feel a finality heavy in your stomach.

YOU ARE IN A LOCAL Chuck E. Cheese. You haven't been in one of these since you were nine years old, but you've been secretly hoping for an excuse to visit one since you hit that cut-off age where Chuck E. Cheese is no longer socially acceptable. A few weeks ago, you walked down the street of the old part of town and showed Tristan where your favorite arcade used to be. Now, this is the closest thing you can find to an "arcade."

The person working the door is reading a copy of *Wuthering Heights*. You are the only one here. You tried to invite Tristan, but he just recently got home from the hospital, and his mom refuses to let him go anywhere. Even if he could go somewhere, you know Tristan would refuse, preferring to stay home and try to catch up on all the classes he missed while in the hospital. Because of that, you've only seen him once since he was released, and that was while he was studying on his computer, emailing professors for extensions. "They'll say no," he told you, "but it's always worth a shot, I guess."

It's not like Merrill or Chase would ever go to Chuck E. Cheese, and it's not like you'd ever voluntarily do something with Sephora. So you came alone. Why Chuck E. Cheese is something only you can understand.

The Chuck E. Cheese is smaller than you remember. Maybe everything felt larger in those plastic crawling tubes. It smells like some kid's diapers came off, and you're realizing only now just how stupid of an idea this was, but you've already bought ten dollars' worth of tokens, so you might as well at least try to have fun.

> Play whatever game gives the most tickets.

You go over to that bowling game you loved as a kid. You probably loved it then because you were small enough that you could walk on top of it, over to the buckets, and drop all the balls into the one-hundred point bin. Now you can't do that, so you try to play the game the way it was intended. Big mistake.

> This isn't as fun as I remember it.

> Why do things have to change?

It's called growing up, Buffy.

Out from the birthday party area, Chuck E. Cheese himself approaches. You remember how tall and big he used to seem, but now he looks like he's no taller than you.

Meanwhile a woman comes up to you and says, "Excuse me—but the basketball machine isn't feeding out tickets."

You stare at her for a while, trying to understand.

"The *tickets* for the *basketball* machine," she enunciates, like you don't speak English.

You frown at her. "I'm sorry, I don't work here," you say.

And she walks off. Since when did your jeans and T-shirt look like a uniform?

Chuck E. Cheese is in front of you now. He tries to get all friendly with you, opening his arms out for a hug. Exits are: ball pit, outside.

> Kick in groin.

Before you can move, he embraces you, but holds on for much longer than is socially appropriate. And though it's nice to be held, Chuck E. isn't exactly your dream boyfriend.

Your phone vibrates.

> Fend off Chuck E.

You successfully fend off Chuck E. He retreats to a children's party near the stage.

> Check text message.

It's a new text from Tristan. It reads: *Hey, Buffy, can you get everyone to come over to my place? I have something important to show everyone.*

When was the last time all of you stood together in Tristan's front yard? It must've been years, really.

You find yourself analyzing his text. Something about the tone throws you off. Can you say it's formal because everything's spelled and punctuated correctly?

> Ask Tristan if everything's okay.

You begin to text: *Is everything okay? Your text doesn't sound right.*

> No, that sounds weird.

> Backspace.

You have a blank message.

> Call Merrill.

You hate using phones. On the other end, you hear the phone ring a few times before Merrill picks it up. "What's up?" he says.

"Tristan just texted me, asking everyone to come over. He says it's important."

Merrill snickers. "Tristan says everything's important. He just wants to make a huge drama scene, probably to guilt trip me about Valentine's Day. Not to mention it's April Fool's, so any part of Tristan you were trying to take seriously becomes even less authoritative."

"I don't know…"

Your phone buzzes, and you see a new text is in. It says: *If Merrill tries to blow this off, tell him I know he's at home and has nothing better to do. If that doesn't work, use your powers to get him over here* ☺.

> How—

> "My powers"?

Merrill asks, "Seriously, Buffy—you're not actually worried about him, are you?"

> Well, uh, *yeah*.

"I'm his girlfriend," you say. "Of course I worry about him."

You expect Merrill to laugh, but instead you hear him cough.

"*Please*—it'd make me feel better if you were there."

There's a pause—a silence you're not sure how to translate.

"I'll be there in twenty," he says and hangs up.

ON YOUR WAY OVER TO his house, you realize it's been a while since you last saved. In the car, you feel like you're driving up to a boss battle, and you know that it's always better to save before a battle, just in case. Not sure if that logic fully translates over into your life…

> Save over slot two.

You save over your birthday.

ALL OF YOU ARE STANDING outside of Tristan's house. Yes—after some desperate persuading, you've convinced Merrill, Chase, and Sephora to come with you. Sephora didn't take much convincing, and Chase was agreeable—but even as Merrill gets out of the car, you see his shoulders tense after he slams the door closed.

As you walk to the front door, everyone follows. It's like you're in an RPG and this is your party.

> Ring doorbell.

Since no one else steps up to the plate, you ring the doorbell. Tristan's mother comes to the door, wearing her Botox smile. "Oh, Buffy!" she says. "I'm so glad to see you—what brings you here?"

"Tristan called," Merrill says, his hands in his pockets. "Told us we should come over."

Tristan's mother's expression drops. "Tristan? That's odd, he hasn't been home since this morning."

You frown. "Are you sure?"

"He's not in his room, and I haven't heard him around the house today."

"That's weird." You check the text Tristan sent. It was sent at exactly 4:00 p.m. Suspiciously precise, you think to yourself. It's now 4:21.

She opens the door. "Well, feel free to come in. Maybe he's just been working quietly somewhere and I didn't notice." She laughs so fast it sounds like hyperventilating, and heads off to another room.

Everyone splits up, looking for Tristan, calling his name. You reason it can't take long to find him that way, even if the house is pretty large. Sephora goes up the foyer staircase, and Chase heads toward the kitchen. Merrill stands by the door with his hands in his pockets.

> Demand his help.

"Merrill, where do you think Tristan is?" you ask.

He shrugs. "Probably just hiding in a closet crying somewhere."

You frown. "You know what? We wouldn't even have this problem if it wasn't for you."

"*Excuse* me?"

"You know you've made him upset, being a jackass to him and all. If you'd just try to be nice to him…"

Merrill leans close to you. His face is close to yours, and unlike in past situations, there's nothing romantic or sweet about his movement. You feel his breath on your face and it terrifies you. "Don't assume anything about me and Tristan. Got it?"

The foyer is quiet except for Sephora's voice above you somewhere, calling, "Tristan? Tristan, you there?"

> Stand up to Merrill.

You feel your heart race in outrage. Your body is shaking, but no words come out.

> Look for Tristan.

"*I'm* looking for Tristan. But I can't blame him for hating you so much. You really can be a dickwad when you want to be."

Before you turn to walk away, you see Merrill close his eyes and shake his head.

You've all looked everywhere in the house, but still no Tristan. Everyone meets in the foyer by the door, all quiet and wearing their own looks of concern.

"You think this is a joke or something?" Merrill says at last. "Maybe this is a prank or something. He's trying to screw around with us."

"Or maybe he wants us to wait here for him to come," Sephora suggests, pulling her sleeves past her wrists.

"Maybe I'll give him a call and see if we can figure this out..." you say, pulling out your phone.

> Call Tristan's phone.

You dial Tristan's number. It rings for him.

Through the wall, you hear a cell phone ringtone go off, Tristan's ringtone: the *Legend of Zelda* "opening chest" noise. Everyone is still for a moment, listening.

> Follow the sound.

You follow the wall toward the sound. Everyone follows behind you, even Merrill.

The tone stops. "Hello, the person you are trying to reach has a voice mailbox that hasn't been set up. Please try to call again later."

> Call again.

You call again, and the familiar ringtone returns. You all follow the wall until you reach the kitchen. In the kitchen, there is a stainless steel fridge, granite counters, and a door.

"The garage," Chase says. You run to the door.

"Tristan?" you shout, opening the door. "We're here—you okay?"

You hear everyone come up behind you. But it's like you've left your body once you hear the car engine idling, and Tristan's phone vibrating on the trunk of his old station wagon.

Merrill runs over to the driver's side, trying to open the door while Chase goes on the other side, pulling out old T-shirts that surround a steel hose on the window ledge.

"Fuck," Merrill shouts. "It's locked."

Chase throws the T-shirts on the floor, wrangling the pipe out. He reaches through the window and unlocks the car, while Merrill swings the door open, hitting the edge against the concrete wall. You hear him shout Tristan's name over and over, see the shadow of Tristan's shoulders shake limply in Merrill's grip.

You're still in the doorway, watching smoke rise from the end of the pipe. It starts collecting into a cloud.

> Open the garage door.

You press the button for the garage door, which opens gradually like it's just been woken up from a long sleep.

> Tristan isn't going to wake up.

You know you should be up there, trying to wake up your dead boyfriend. But that's just it—he's a body now, and if this game's taught you anything, it's that no matter how many times you go back and try to change things, everything will play out pretty much the same way.

Merrill holds his breath, trying not to cry. On the other side, you see Chase's sneakers hanging out over the seat, still. Sephora stands behind him, taking the T-shirts from the ground and folding them one by one, placing them in a pile to the side. Under her breath, she moans something that sounds like a prayer you all memorized in school.

> Examine T-shirts.

You walk over to Sephora and examine the shirts. You remember most of these: his high school Mathlete team shirt; an XKCD shirt with a math joke you don't understand; a worn, red shirt with the *pi* symbol in cracked painted letters. You remember him wearing these shirts to class, on dates, or to game nights at Merrill's.

> Take Mathlete shirt.

You take the Mathlete shirt and sniff it. It smells like exhaust and Tristan. You put it in your inventory. As you do, you accidentally catch a glimpse of Tristan: relaxed as if taking a nap, his skin cherry red. You imagine he just came back from a day at the beach, and that when he wakes up he'll complain to you about a sunburn that'll take a week to heal.

Chase gets out of the car, holding a crumpled piece of paper. "It was on the floor," he says. Flattened out, it reads: *Thanks, Buffy, for getting everyone here—I knew you could do it. Go find someone worthy of you, okay? And thanks, Merrill, for helping me realize I really can't be anything extraordinary. Saved me a lot of time and frustration. Also: I'm not afraid.*

You see the not crossed out in green ink, frantically, as if maybe that's the last thing he did, right when he realized he couldn't breathe anymore.

```
> I knew you could do it. What does that even mean?
> And "someone worthy"?
> What am I, Princess Peach?
```

Everyone looks at the ground. Chase's hand shakes, the paper flapping in the air. On the car trunk, the phone has finally stopped vibrating and goes silent.

A Religious Setting: April 5, 2010

Y OUR PARENTS TELL YOU YOU need to go back to school. "Sometimes you just have to get back on the horse," your mom says, only there are no horses, only a dead boyfriend, so the analogy really doesn't make any sense.

You keep thinking about Tristan's funeral, and seeing him laying in that coffin like he was asleep. Part of you wanted to crawl in there with him. Once you were six feet under, you could tell him that he fell asleep next to someone he loved, and that the night would last for a long time.

And even more than that, you think about Tristan in the hospital, telling you he couldn't keep up. Was that supposed to be a sign? Was it really that obvious, but you still missed it?

You are going to class. On the fields to your right, a shirtless boy plays volleyball, even though it's eight in the morning and probably forty degrees outside.

In front of you, a girl on a park bench looks up at the sky and smiles. She looks familiar, but you can't remember her name. Then you remember she's the girl from your ESOL class, which feels like ages ago. You try to not think about that class, and how little you did for them.

You want to go up to the girl, tap her shoulder, and apologize for not believing her and letting your bitterness get in the way. You wonder if she'd even remember that, or you in general.

YOU ARE IN FRONT OF the campus chapel. Not exactly a place you expected to ever find yourself voluntarily, but it's better than being in class.

```
> Hey. I don't dislike church that much. I just—
```

Was looking for somewhere to go? And it seemed like a good idea?

You are inside of the chapel. It is eerily empty, but that's because it's the middle of the afternoon on a school day. There are stained glass windows you never noticed from the outside. The stained glass portrays different angels—ones whose names are all familiar to you by now. And though you've seen different depictions of all these angels, there's something familiar in one of their faces, but from where you couldn't say.

> Take a seat.

You go up to one of the front-most pews and sit down. The seat is hard but you don't mind.

This is the part where you've been taught to offer some sort of sacrifice, or confession. It only seems appropriate. You think about everything that has happened and don't know where to start.

> What I can offer, in a place like this?

> And what can I really hope to get back?

You finger your cross necklace. You still haven't taken it off. When you lift it, there's a black imprint of it on your collarbone.

In high school, Tristan said it was cool, that you were devoted to that sort of thing.

You were devoted to that sort of thing.

> What's happened since then?

You put your head between your knees and moan. It's very quiet in here, and you feel like you could fall asleep, if you let yourself. This place feels safe, in a way you can't explain.

"Oh. Sorry." Behind you, the door opens, and it's that kid from ESOL. What was his name? Jake? "Buffy?" Jake walks up to you. "It's good to see you. I'm glad to see you're okay."

> I'm okay?

"I was worried when you just stopped coming to ESOL. I thought you had an emergency or something."

> I sort of did...

> ...

You think about telling him about Tristan but stop yourself. "Things just got really crazy," you manage. "I'm sorry, I should've said something."

"I get that," he says, looking over you. His hand slides a little on the bench toward you, just enough that it seems intentional.

> Break the silence.

"So...how's ESOL going?"

"Good. We still have the same gang coming each week. They ask where you are."

"Why?"

"What'd you mean, 'why'? You're part of the team, aren't you?"

> Am I?

You lower your head. It's a nice idea, to feel like you're a part of something. "I'm sorry I haven't done much of anything. I thought—maybe I'd become more outgoing, if I made myself lead something."

He shrugs. "Not everyone's outgoing. It happens. Don't let yourself feel bad over something like that."

You've never been in the campus chapel before. Being here in the silence, you wonder why you don't come more often. Maybe to do homework, or to just sit for a while.

"I come here sometimes too, to think," Jake says, then gets up. "I'll stop distracting you and give you some space."

> No, it's okay.

"But if you ever need to talk about anything, you've got my number, right?"

Do you? You mentally scroll through your phone contacts list. Yes, Jake's in there, though you always seem to skim over it. Maybe you should give him a call sometime.

"Will do," you say. "Thanks. It was good seeing you."

"It was good seeing you, too." He lingers in the doorway for a second. You want to stop him, keep him in here with you, so you don't have to be alone.

But by the time you open your mouth, he's gone.

Tristan's Room: April 10, 2010

Y OU ARE IN TRISTAN'S ROOM. It's weird to be in the room of someone who you know is dead. Every time you've been in Tristan's room before, it's made your heart race: thinking about the things you might do with each other. Now, there's no potential for anything in this room. Your stomach tangles with nausea.

Without Tristan in here, the room is much darker than you remember. Above his bed, the neon *NINTENDO* sign is the main source of light. You notice the sheets on the bed are made (clearly by his mom, probably after finding him—since when did Tristan ever make his bed?). On top of his nightstand, you still see the Christmas present you gave him, still in the box.

> Open nightstand drawer.

Inside, you find several photos from high school: some of his Mathlete team and Lawrence, prom, him and Merrill at a local gaming con next to some YouTube legend you've probably watched before but can't remember his name. Underneath, you find Merrill's old PlayStation memory card. How he found that in the trash—and why—is beyond you.

> Examine shelves.

You walk into the room toward the bookcase. In the process, you feel your feet sink into the wet carpet. You try to not think about whatever spilled here.

On the shelves, you see the games lined up by console generation. Typical Tristan games, harmless games: *Mario, Animal Crossing, Pokémon*. Nothing to signal what was going on in his head. But wait—before that, there's even a sizeable collection of CD-ROM games stretching from MS-DOS to Windows 7. The games include some of your favorites: *Oregon Trail, MYST, Zork*, and *Return to Zork*. You like to think that your life, that like the *Zork* series, will also upgrade from just text input to the authority of point-and-click movement.

> Since when has Tristan played text adventure games?

There are lots of things—you realize—that you didn't know about Tristan.

You find a large gap in the shelves, where there should be SNES and N64 games. Merrill's probably come before you and taken them. You also notice the *Pokémon Stadium* cartridge is gone.

You don't know what you're supposed to do. When you came over, Tristan's mom said you should take whatever you want. "Whatever is left we're taking to Goodwill," she said, her eyes red. "It's better that way, I think." She tried to laugh.

But it's weird, going through a dead person's things. You're afraid to touch anything, like death is contagious or something. But why are you afraid of death all of a sudden? You've died enough times by now that you shouldn't be worried about that.

> But this is different.

It is?

> Yes. Tristan's *gone*. He's not coming back. He doesn't have a restart button. Why do some people respawn and other people don't?

Do you really see a bunch of people "respawning" all over the place?

> No, but *I* do it.

That you do. Have you ever wondered why only you get to do that?

You reach on the shelves, past the games, and find piles of books and papers: award certificates from school, some ticket stubs from prom and old hall passes, an agenda book from 2008, a yearbook, some theoretical math textbooks, an Orson Scott Card omnibus, and an unlabeled file folder.

> Examine file folder.

Your curiosity gets the best of you. Inside, you see a series of medical reports, all labeled with the condition Marfan syndrome. At the top of each is a summary of the reason for the visit: trouble breathing at recess, chest pain, back pain from sitting too long in class, persistent headaches—the list goes on. You try to remember hearing about any of this, but all you remember is Tristan leaving school sometimes, telling you he was on vacation or that his grandparents got sick. And you believed him.

Underneath where the file folder sat, you see a journal with pages sticking out. They're all worn on the corners and stained with various drinks, like there was a time he carried them around wherever he went.

> Examine.

You pull out the papers and realize that they're all used character sheets, from the times when Merrill had enough of an attention span to play role-playing games. Flipping through them, you realize just how many characters Tristan's made, but how similar they all are. They're all the complete opposite of him: large, powerful (often Fighters, though sometimes Mages), charismatic— they're all the exact opposite of his real self. They all have the same name too: Irrational Vengeance. Maybe Tristan hoped he'd "respawn" into "Irrational Vengeance" when he died.

> He was probably disappointed with the end results.

The journal looks pretty ordinary. You flip through it casually, glancing at some entries:

Dad tried to get me to go out hunting with him again. I hate hunting. I try to tell him, but he doesn't get it. Says it'll toughen me up. He shot a buck today and brought it home. Showed me how to mount the head.

I know why Merrill hangs out with me. Lawrence told me, and it makes sense—he said when I joined Mathletes, my mom told all the moms about my condition. She asked them to tell their boys to be careful with me, otherwise I might die. I mean, I know my body's a little strange, but really? He says he bets

Merrill's just friends with me because his mom made him, and it'd make sense from the way he treats me. What a fucking asshole! Who does that? We're not in kindergarten or anything. I'm not someone that needs pity. I hope Merrill gets sick so then he can understand what it's like.

Merrill was a complete dick to me today. I don't like cursing, but fuck him. He thinks I'm his punching bag but one of these days I'm gonna punch back.

Today, my advisor asked to speak with me. I came in and she showed me my grades and talked about how at college there are so many options that we need to keep our minds open to. She didn't say my grades were bad, but she said she wasn't sure if I was fit for my program, and that I should think about switching majors. At first, I was pissed. I blamed Merrill. I thought about what Lawrence said. I wanted him dead, even—and then I realized: he's not the problem. I am.

I decided what I'm going to do. I'm gonna use Dad's gun. Then he can see I know how to use it. Merrill can see I'm not a scared pussy. If I chicken out, I can always use hanging instead.

At the bottom of the pages, you see spots where the page wrinkles a little, as if it got wet.

Looking at the journal, you realize that this is the most you ever have or ever will hear of Tristan's thoughts. Holding these is like holding his mental schemas in your hands. You hold it close to your body.

> Where am I? Where am I in this journal?

YOU ARE IN TRISTAN'S ROOM. Outside, a bird makes this cry that sounds like, "We're going, we're going, we're going." The light shifts through the window over the floor and you notice just how dusty everything is. How in just a few days, this room will be empty, and people will go back to their everyday lives.

> Burn.

I'm sorry, there's nothing in this room to burn with.

> Exit room.

You leave the room and enter the bathroom. There is a bathtub, sink, and an incredibly normal toilet. There are also some scented candles.

> Open drawer.

You raid the bathroom vanity. There is a lighter.

> Light journal on fire.

You hold the journal in your hands, and light the corner on fire. The flame travels fast.

> Wait—no.

You put it under the sink and run the water over it. The flame dies. You now have a half-charred wet journal.

> Keep journal.

You put the journal in your inventory.

Going back into Tristan's room, you look toward the bed and remember how Sephora insisted Tristan had a hidden gun. While you didn't really believe her then, you also wouldn't have believed that Tristan would do what he did. It doesn't really matter anymore whether he has a gun or not—does it? But your body shakes with curiosity.

> Examine under bed.

You get on the floor and make yourself parallel with the bed. Underneath, you find all sorts of trash down there. In the corner you see a plastic grocery bag.

> Grab plastic grocery bag.

You put it in your inventory. It might come in handy later.

As you continue to look around, you see the dark barrel of a rifle. It looks brand new and shines when your phone's light runs over it. Around it, a wall of dust bunnies.

> But why? How was this enough for him to do it? Why couldn't I help, why couldn't I stop him?

> Closet.

You turn to the closet, opening the doors fast and desperate, as if you're looking for something that's gone missing. You part through his hanging button-up shirts and folded pants, but there's nothing else. You put your face up to one of his shirts and inhale.

Downstairs you hear Tristan's mother walk around in her high heels. Under her breath, she keeps saying, "You can do it, Lisa. You can make it through this."

Like a flea market shopper, you begin to frantically grab pieces of Tristan: Photos of him at Mathletes. One of his old T-shirts. An old stained *Nintendo Power* issue.

Before you leave the room, you turn back to the bookshelf and take the *Zork* game. It might be a good way to pass the time.

Y OU HAVEN'T SLEPT WELL FOR the past couple weeks. Every time you almost fall asleep, Alice walks in and turns on the lights, or Aquitane stumbles in, muttering, "Shit! Fuck!" or crying. You open your eyes and watch her shadow hover across the room, until you feel sad and fall asleep. But by the time you fall asleep, Alice turns her desk lamp on and aims it at your bed, like she's interrogating you.

After that whole party incident, Alice's status read: *ELIZABETH IS A COMPLETE BITCH WHORE. NEVER TALK TO HER UNDER ANY CIRCUMSTANCES.*

> That seems a bit...extreme

Despite what she says, Alice is a very committed girl.

Sometimes, you have nightmares of arguing with her. In those nightmares, you walk up to Alice and ask her if everything's okay, and Alice screams, "You knew! You don't care about anyone but yourself, do you? Does it ever occur to you what's going on in other people's heads? Or their lives?"

You're not sure if she's talking about Jeremy or Tristan.

Every time you see Alice, she looks angry. And whenever she opens her mouth, you're afraid she's going to shout at you: "bitch-whore!" But when she walks into the same room as you, she actively looks the other way.

Have you thought about confronting her about this?

> The idea of talking to her makes me want to vomit.

Every weekend you can, you go home. But even there isn't particularly peaceful. Your mom keeps asking if you're okay (whatever that's supposed to mean), and if you're sleeping all right. She keeps trying to hand off miracle lotions and chamomile tea to you. "Your skin's breaking out," she says, "And chamomile should calm you down. That's what I drink when I can't sleep."

You appreciate the gifts but know that no matter how much chamomile you make, it's not going to solve the problem.

YOU ARE IN YOUR DORM room, and Alice is going in and out of the room, slamming the door. She's been doing this every night for a while now, as if in an active attempt to not let you fall asleep. Even when you do fall asleep, you wake up from dreams of Tristan: the two of you playing N64 games, and the controller wire wrapping around his neck into a noose; or of him and Merrill shooting clay pigeons when suddenly Tristan becomes a clay pigeon and shatters into irreparable pieces. You try carrying the pieces around in your inventory, hoping to glue them together, but your mom tells you to throw them out because some things just can't be fixed. While you know that you're unable to sleep when Alice turns on the lights or slams the door, you don't know if that's something to confront her about or if it's a personal problem, and you need to learn how to fall asleep despite having a dead boyfriend.

> It's just that—I don't like confrontation.

But tonight, you look up at the ceiling and start breathing fast. Your muscles tighten and you start convulsing in your bed. You don't remember when you became afraid of falling asleep, but as you lay there the sheets feel like bugs crawling over your skin and you have to bite your lip to not start screaming.

> It'll pass—I have to fall asleep at some point, don't I?

Several hours go by and your heart's still racing. You try everything: watching mindless YouTube videos, imagining yourself on an island getaway, drinking some of that chamomile your mom gave you. But none of it works.

In the dark, you can see Aquitane on her bed, and Alice at her desk, bent over a textbook. It's almost three in the morning and you don't have much hope of falling asleep.

At some point, you hear yourself crying. You have nothing else to give. And when you have nothing else to give, what do you do?

> Call Mom.

Your hand fumbles for your new phone and you call your mom. On the other end, your mom groans.

"They're so rude!" You start crying. "They keep coming and going but I can't sleep! I can't sleep!"

"Did you try the chamomile?" your mom asks.

"Yes, I tried everything!"

"Did you try eating something?"

Perhaps there are things you haven't tried.

"Did you eat something?" she repeats. "Find something to eat—some crackers, a banana, anything."

Across the room you see Aquitane shuffle in her bed. "Buffy?" she calls.

And it never occurs to you to answer her. While you keep crying, you bend over the bed to your bag and grab a pack of crackers. They're all crumbly from being in your inventory so long, but you eat them anyway. After crying a little longer, you fall asleep. Maybe all you needed to do was eat something after all.

THE NEXT MORNING, AQUITANE FINDS you in the bathroom. She puts her hands on your shoulders. "Girl. What's wrong? I heard you crying last night."

> Never accept defeat.

"It's no big deal," you say, wiping your eyes.

Aquitane shakes her head. "No, it *is*. And you'd better tell me before I beat it out of you!"

You try a laugh.

"You were crying last night."

You nod.

"Was it a boy issue? No, no. It's Alice, isn't it?"

You frown, trying to remember Aquitane at that party. You try to remember anything about that party, outside of Jeremy and Merrill.

"Alice can be a real bitch," Aquitane says, "And you know, I'm sick of dealing with her, too."

"It's not just that—" You begin. "I feel like I did something wrong to her. That I didn't explain everything. But I don't feel like I can explain things now."

Aquitane shakes her head. "Alice isn't great at listening."

"I just don't know—if I can stay here. I don't think I realized that there are certain things I need. Like right now, my hands are shaking. See?" You hold up your hand, and it wavers like a theremin.

"Have you seen a doctor?"

"It's not that big of a deal." You put your hands in your pockets. "It's just that—I guess I feel like I can tell you—but I think I'm gonna commute for the rest of the semester. Like with my parents, and maybe have my dad drop me off on his way to work."

She snickers. "Well, if it works, that's great. You're lucky you have that kind of option."

LATER THAT NIGHT, WHEN YOU come back to your room, you notice Aquitane has pinned up a towel around her desk, to minimize the light spreading through the room.

> Sleep.

You lay down in an attempt to fall asleep. You feel your body begin to drift as if floating, and as you try to think about your day it all becomes jumbled into dream-like thoughts.

> That means I'm falling asleep, right?

> I hope so.

> I'd really hate to not sleep again tonight.

You are at your desk, and you look up to your bunk bed to see Tristan sitting on top, waving to you.

You get up and climb toward him. It feels like it's been so long since you saw him smile like that. You ask him how he is, where he's been, how he found you on campus. You reach the top of the bed when your foot slips.

Your arm twitches and it feels like your body's fallen from the top bunk onto the floor. You wake up.

Without thinking, you reach for your cell phone to message Tristan. Then you remember.

If you can't talk to Tristan about them, then who can you talk to?

> Flip through contacts.

You look through your phone contacts: Adrian, Merrill, Tristan, Sephora, Aquitane, Alice, Jeremy, Tristan (something makes you reluctant to delete it—such a permanent thing to do), Chase, Jake, that girl from your art class who lets you copy off her notes when you miss class…

Jake. You stare at his name and feel your heart race.

> Why? It's not like I really know him that well.

You wonder what he'd say if you told him about everything going on. He'd probably listen, you reason.

> Text Jake.

Hey, Jake. I'm sorry I haven't been at ESOL—I've had a lot going on, and I try to talk to people about it, but it's like no one wants to listen. Everyone just wants me to move on with my life, like nothing's happened. But something has happened—and I don't know what I can do. Sorry if I'm being weird. I just thought it'd be cool to talk to you or something.

> Backspace

Hey, Jake. I'm sorry I haven't been at ESOL—I've had a lot going on. Can we talk sometime?

I T'S A SUNDAY, AND YOU'RE home from school. Your parents keep trying to ask how you're doing, what you've been up to, but all you want to do is sleep. You keep thinking about Tristan in the hospital bed, looking at you expectantly, as if you could know what he wanted—

> Why didn't I know what he wanted?

Your parents know about Tristan and, out of respect, try to leave you alone as much as possible. Even so, that doesn't stop your mom from whispering about you.

"I know I shouldn't be worried about Elizabeth...but I'm her *mother*. And just staying cooped up in her room all day can't be healthy for her..."

"We don't know what she saw when she found—him. It's best to give her some space for a while," your dad says.

> Thank you, Dad.

"I know, I know..." You hear your mom pacing on the other side of the wall then stop. "I've got it—what Elizabeth needs is a nice *surprise*. Something to cheer her up a bit."

Despite your dad making protesting noises, you hear the door close and your mom walk down the hall, toward the kitchen phone.

You get very afraid. Your mom's "surprises" have a tendency to be more horrific than pleasant.

Inside your room, it feels like the walls are going to fall over and bury you. You think about all the things you could do today but none of them sound appealing, not even playing emulator games on your computer. Every video game on your bookshelf has Tristan's face on it. Every game on your computer has characters who all make you think of Tristan.

> Check inventory.

You reach over the side of your bed and dig through your purse, hoping to find something to make you stop thinking about Tristan.

The first thing you touch is the necklace Sephora gave you. You think about her SOS note, and wonder if maybe Sephora understood something that you didn't. If she really did know something about Tristan that no one else did.

You hear a knock on your door.

"Elizabeth?" your mother calls, her voice sing-songy. "Someone's here to see you…"

The door opens and it's Merrill, who looks disproportionately large in your doorframe, against the yellow-and-white checkered curtains your mother refuses to change out.

"Merrill?" You get up. "What—"

"Your mom called me, said I had to come over because you were upset." He looks out the window. "I'm pretty sure she thinks we're still dating or something."

> Chuckle.

> Vomit.

"Yeah, my mom has trouble with transitions sometimes." You motion to your bed, the only sitting surface in the room. "Wanna sit down?"

Merrill against your girlish bed sheets. You try to not blush. "So…" you say.

"If it's any consolation," he says, eyes on the floor, "I think about him, too. A lot. I hope you know that he might've driven me crazy, but I would've never wanted him to do—that—"

You nod.

"Did you get anything from his place yet?"

"Yeah."

"Any good games?"

You feel your mouth start to taste sour. "It's funny—I never knew he had so many. He had some text adventures, too, which was cool."

"Yeah—I saw he left my Pokémon Stadium out front. Don't know why he wanted it so bad. I would've given it to him if he'd asked."

You look out the window. "He said something about you taking his stuff."

Merrill lets out a sigh. "It wasn't like that. Tristan's forgetful and would leave all sorts of shit over at my house, like game systems, beanbag chairs, lava lamps. I started putting them in the closet so he could get them when he came over, but he'd never remember and it was hilarious and pathetic—how could he not wonder where the heck his Xbox was? Then I started wondering if he would notice if I took stuff off him. It started as small things, like pens or Pokémon cards, but it got out of hand. It wasn't out of spite. I never wanted to keep any of the stuff or anything. I always planned to give it back."

You nod. You know this is the part where you're supposed to invite Merrill to play something with you—whether that's a board game, video game, or movie, anything really—but no words come out.

Merrill gets up. "I should probably get going."

You think about telling him you can get over Tristan. You think about this being a second chance. You know somewhere inside you you should stop him.

"Okay. I'll see you later."

YOU ARE IN YOUR ROOM. It's 2:00 a.m., and your body is shaking from exhaustion.

> Talk to Alice.

"Alice?" Your voice comes out muffled. She doesn't look up.

"Alice? Can we talk? About why you're upset and all?"

She looks up at your bunk bed and scowls. "I'm done with you, Elizabeth. I have no interest in fixing anything."

You want to tell her that you're the one that can't sleep and, hence, require something to be fixed.

> Be persistent.

"I'm sorry that the whole Jeremy thing caused confusion," you say. "I didn't mean—"

"Will you just *shut up*? It's not about that."

"It's not? Then what—"

Then she starts sobbing. Outright sobbing. You're scared of an RA knocking on the door and asking what's going on in here.

> Comfort her.

You get down from your bed and reach over to her. You pat her shoulder and say, "It's going to be okay—"

Her body jolts up and she looks at you with a terrifying combination of emotion. You notice just how red and bitter her eyes are, and how deep the purple bags are under her eyes.

> Retreat.

You take your hand away and exit your own room. Before you leave, though, you pull the blanket off your bed and carry it behind you, like a flag.

Yᴏᴜ ᴀʀᴇ ɪɴ ᴛʜᴇ ʟᴏʙʙʏ. On the floor in the corner, there is a boy in a cat suit with an empty bottle of scotch. There is a book on the table, as well as a box of stale candy. There is an empty loveseat, also. Exits are: hallway.

> Loveseat.

You lay on the loveseat, the wooden arm rests nudging the back of your head. It's probably the most uncomfortable position you've ever been in, but it's better than having to share a room with Alice right now. You lay there, but nothing happens.

Iᴛ's ᴛʜʀᴇᴇ ɪɴ ᴛʜᴇ ᴍᴏʀɴɪɴɢ, and Aquitane stumbles into the lobby with paper bags. Even in the dark, you can see the exhaustion in her eyes.

"Buffy!" she whispers. "You still up? Thought you had a strict bedtime!"

"Can't sleep," you say.

Aquitane laughs. "Want me to read you a bedtime story?"

You shake your head.

"What'cha doin' in the lounge?"

You don't know where to begin. "It seemed like a good idea."

Aquitane takes the empty seat next to you. "You're not the only one she's kicked out, you know." Aquitane pulls a bottle from the bag, long and slender like the neck of a bird.

"I'm not a horrible person," you say. "At least, not in the way Alice thinks."

"Ha!" She takes a swig. "She might try to be a rock, but inside Alice crumbles. Like, all the time. You don't have to be a horrible person for Alice to hate you, you just have to be in the right place at the wrong time.

"Sometimes I can't stand the bitch." Another swig. "I don't know why I even invite her to shit. She only screams a lot and sleeps with everyone."

"And what do you do?" you ask, drowsiness overtaking.

"Me? I watch the world fall to pieces." She laughs.

Aquitane offers you some of her drink, says it helps with falling asleep. And at this point, you'd kill a puppy for a good night's sleep.

> Take a sip.

You sip and lay there, curled on the love seat. As Aquitane stumbles away, you wonder what would've happened if Alice hadn't walked in at the party, if you'd been just a little more tipsy, what might've happened between you and Jeremy. And you can't tell when you think about it if it feels nice, thinking about him, or disturbing.

Within a few minutes, you fall into a deep, overwhelming sleep.

IT'S MORNING. THE LIGHT IS thick on you, but at least the cat boy's gone. On the floor, you see the paper bags from Aquitane's visit, as well as a bracelet you've never seen before.

> Take bracelet.

You take the bracelet. It's shiny.

Exits are: hallway.

You get up and your body shakes, and you notice a deep throbbing in the back of your neck. You don't want to go to your room. In your head, you can hear Alice shouting at you again, on loop. It's an hour before your first class, but the idea of going anywhere makes you want to curl up on the floor and cry. And that's when you decide you can't stay here anymore.

> Run.

A Distant Car Ride: April 30, 2010

IT'S TWO WEEKS BEFORE THE end of the semester, and you tell your mom you need rides from school.

"What do you mean you need rides from school? Isn't that why we're paying a thousand dollars a month, so you can live at school?"

You're in your mom's minivan, back from campus for the weekend. There is a stain on the floor, right next to your shoe, and as much as you stare at it, you still can't figure out what exactly it is.

> Justify this to yourself.

"I mean—look, it's only another week or two. That's not that much of a waste. I'm sick and tired, and just need to be at home for a little while."

You want to tell her how your roommates are violent drunkards in unhealthy romantic relationships, and how Alice keeps shining that light on you like it might eventually make you evaporate. You want to explain that you'd rather be on campus, really. You'd rather be far away from Merrill and the void of Tristan.

At a stop sign, she turns and examines you. "I'm just trying to understand," she says. "I thought things were good at school. Did something happen there?"

What didn't happen?

"I just need a place to sleep," you say. "And to not be afraid of myself."

For the next four days, your mom refuses to leave you alone in a room, or to let you anywhere near the kitchen knives.

EVERY TIME YOU TRY TO fall asleep, your heart starts racing, afraid you might see Tristan again tonight.

On your desk, your cell phone sits, untouched. Your cell phone still looks new, hardly different than the day you got it. You only use it in desperate circumstances, preferring the home phone whenever possible. The only contribution you've made to your phone is a piece of duct tape taped over the camera. When people ask, you say it's because there are guys in Russia who might hack your phone to watch you undress and record it. They laugh like it's a joke until you look at them and then they stop. If only they understood that you aren't afraid of Russia watching you, just the game inside your head.

> Save slot 2.

Sorry. Saving is not available at this time.

> What do you mean "saving isn't available at this time?"

Sorry. Saving is not available at this time.

Aquitane's Closet: May 3, 2010

SOMETIMES YOU GO TO YOUR old dorm, just during the day when you know Alice is gone.

The room looks much older than you remember it. Aquitane's bed is stripped, empty, and her walls are blank. Even her desk has no memorabilia. In the corner by her dresser, there is a neon blue shoe with spikes on the surface. But that's it. That's all that's left of Aquitane.

Alice has taken over the triple, slowly expanding over your and Aquitane's territory. Where she gets all the things, you can't imagine. Your desk is still there, though it's covered with papers that aren't your own.

> Move the papers.

At first you thought they were homework papers, but as you pick them up, you realize they're letters to and from Jeremy. Your fingers feel contaminated and you drop them. They fall on the floor.

> Put them back in place.

You bend over to pick them up and can't help but read in the process:

Alice, how are you?

Alice, I haven't heard from you in a few days.

If I don't hear back from you, I'm going to kill myself.

I mean it. Why won't you talk to me?

I'm sorry, I didn't mean it—can we get dinner tonight and talk?

Or are you afraid of something?

You think you can do this alone, but you can't.

You need help. We both need help. But that's what it means to be human, right?

You carry the papers away, unable to look at them anymore.

> Put them on Alice's desk.

You turn to Alice's desk and jump at the body in the chair. It's Alice, hunched over a book.

> Freeze.

"She's gone," you hear her mutter. "It's just me now."

You watch her, waiting for her to move, but she stays still.

> Examine your roommate.

You tiptoe up to Alice until you can see her face. Her eyes are closed and, from what you can tell, she's asleep. There's a scar on her cheek, a trail of dried blood riding to her chin. Her hair is tangled, coming out of her headband. The floor by her trashcan's littered with pieces from broken bottles. Her cell phone's still on her desk, with a new unopened message from Jeremy.

Alice mutters over the surface of her desk, "She's gone, and she won't come back." You wonder if she's talking about you, or Aquitane, or someone else entirely. "Why do I have to do everything myself?"

> Write her a note.

You go back to your desk and find an empty sheet of paper under the Jeremy letters. You want to write some last word to her, something inspiring that will bring about resolution, but you stand there for a few minutes and can't think of anything.

Looking back at Alice and all the broken glass, you wonder if she ever wishes she could start over. If she could load a different save slot.

Alice is asleep still—at least that's what you assume. Your room doesn't even feel like the same room you lived in before. Exits are: out.

> Examine Aquitane's closet.

A heavy despair falls over you. You step into Aquitane's closet, hoping for some forgotten alcohol bottles. It's dark in there, but you get on your hands and knees and feel for anything.

You really shouldn't ᑲᙓ ᑯᖇᓵᐢᏦᓵᐢᏳ Ƨᴑ ᗰᑘᏟᏥ.

> Load game.

Error. Loading not available at this time.

```
YOU aTe in AQUitane'S cLoSet.
tH3Te iS a bottle.
eH!!!tS: ???
---ⱯⱯS̈i£ ¨$$²*ß Ɐ^^@--
```

Y OUR MOM HAS BEEN WORRIED about your video game habits for some time now. She keeps telling you that the weather's great outside, that you should go see your friends. And for a while—thanks to your dad—she tolerates you staying in your room for long periods of time. But at some point, she hits that threshold and comes in, saying, "I'm tired of you playing those video games. When are you going to grow out of those things?"

It's 11:00 a.m. but you feel like you just woke up. You've been playing one of those Japanese dating simulators for the past three hours and it takes you a minute to remember that you're still in your bedroom at home.

"They're not something you *grow out of*," you say. "You think people grow out of books?"

"*Some* books." Your mom walks over to the bed and closes your laptop. Before you can protest she says, "I hate to say it, but I don't think these video games are helping you right now. It's an *addiction*, preventing you from moving on. Go outside, spend time with your friends, get some fresh air, *anything*."

As much as you don't want to pay attention to your mom, something about what she says hits you. Maybe this whole text adventure game would go away if you got away from your computer, your games, your technology—it's an idea you've been playing with for a while, but suddenly in that moment you feel your heart race, wondering if your room and things are bugged, if maybe that's how this game is happening, and if you went away for a while it might finally go away. But where to go?

```
> Print list of safe places:
```

- Old game stores.
- Tristan's room.
- My bedroom (kind of).

You feel the panic spasm through you, your muscles clenching and your breathing going fast. It's almost animal-like, your need to escape.

> Take a walk.

You're not sure how long you'll be out walking, so you add a few things into your inventory:

- PowerBars.
- Extra tampons.
- Two candles.

You never know what might happen, after all.

YOU ARE WALKING PAST TRISTAN'S house to the old side of town. Most everyone stopped going down there when you were in middle school, and since then your mom has actively avoided what she describes as "dangerous." But as you're walking, it doesn't seem dangerous, just quiet. It's late morning now, and the bright light makes everything look the way you remember it. The shops are mostly closed—some of them don't open until noon while others haven't been open for the past five years. Leaning against one of the windows, there's a man smoking a cigarette.

You walk faster, as if you know where you're going.

Ahead, a car slowly drives past. You remember coming here as a girl, before the new town center was built closer to the highway. Even though everything is disturbingly quiet here, and you feel your throat tighten just being here, there's something empowering about actively going against your mother.

Even though it's been so long, you still remember what the layout of stores used to be. As you walk forward, to your left was a shoe shop, then a café. Now they're both antique shops, currently closed. To your right, a dusty café has their sign turned to *open*. But there's a specific place you're going, that you hope is still there.

As you walk, you start getting nauseated.

YOU ARE IN FRONT OF an old arcade. When your mom used to get her hair done across the street, she'd let you come over here and play games. It feels so long ago since that happened, when a quarter felt like a serious responsibility, and you could walk away from games and sleep well at night.

> When I played the games, instead of the games playing me.

You brought Tristan here once, told him how you once had the high score for *Puzzle Fighter II*. He said that was really hot and the two of you started kissing in the middle of the sidewalk.

You half hope to see the familiar lights through the window, but instead everything is dark. You press your face up to the glass, but it's completely empty inside. Maybe if you saw an old cabinet or a familiar chair, it wouldn't be quite as bad: having something to hold on to. But the room is cleared, and you know that this is a representation of your life: that everything about you has been removed, leaving an empty space.

> Go into arcade.

The door's locked.

Pressing your face to the glass, you see a door at the back wall. Even the old glow-in-the-dark and blacklight stick-ons are gone from the walls.

> Examine building.

You walk around the building into a trashy ally way. Around the side, you find another door.

> Open door.

You jiggle the handle and with a push, the door opens.

> Wait, really?

You are in a dark room. There is lots of dust. In the corner, there is an old cabinet game, with a missing screen and cracked side.

You jiggle the joystick and look into the empty space where the screen was.

Against the wall, there's another door, probably leading into the store. You open the door and feel the light from the main windows flood in.

> Close door.

From your inventory, you pull out a PowerBar and a candle. You think about your phone at home. It must be ringing continuously right now. Maybe your mother thinks you're dead too, just like Tristan.

> I wouldn't do that.

You wouldn't?

> No. I don't want to die, in the way that you can't restart. It's all over when you're dead, and I don't know what to do with "all over."

It's dark and quiet, except for your one candle flickering. You've moved the arcade cabinet against the door to prevent someone from coming in. As if that'll prevent someone from coming in here, if they really wanted to.

But even in the quiet, your mind is racing.

> Did I used to do this? Was it that I was always constantly thinking before?

> Or was it just when you came along?

Outside, you can hear the wind rattle against the roof. There's always sound everywhere. It's impossible to completely escape it all.

Leaning against the wall, you fall asleep.

DURING THE NIGHT YOU WAKE up to a scratching on the outside door.

> Investigate.

Your mouth is sick with anxiety. Or maybe that's just from the mildew.

Grabbing a metal rod off the ground, you get up close to the cabinet and the door. There's a faint meow.

In your hands, the metal bar is cold.

Even after the scratching stops and you assume the cat is long gone, your arms are shaking, and you're still holding the metal rod. Your knuckles are white, gripping it so hard and long.

"Why won't you go away?" you shout. Your lips become hot, and you feel tears start running down your cheeks. "Don't you get it? I don't *want* you around. I don't want you to tell me what to do, and I've tried *everything* to make you go away. But you know what? Maybe I *will* die. Maybe that *is* better than having you in my head!"

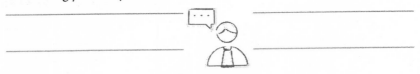

Everything goes silent. Truly, phenomenally silent. As if someone hit the mute button for the world.

"Hello?" Buffy says, eyes wide in the dark.

"Are—you actually gone?"

I<small>T'S MORNING,</small> I <small>GUESS.</small> N<small>OT</small> that there's any light in here, but I wake up, and look at the door toward the shop, and there's light under the door.

"Hello?"

No answer. No sound. Am I deaf?

I snap my fingers right next to my ear and there's sound. I'm not deaf.

I don't know why I'm here. I don't know why I ran away, or why staying in an abandoned arcade room makes any sense. What'd I hope for, anyway? Silence?

Well, I guess I *did* get that at least.

But what'd my mom tell me about abandoned places? Drugs and rape. It's a miracle I made it through the night, really. I've had a lot of miracles recently, haven't I?

It's quiet, and I've never been good at making decisions. What'm I supposed to do from here? I'm already gone. I don't have a phone. It's like I don't exist anymore. I'm like this arcade, these games that were popular for a little while but then forgotten about and shoved in a dark room.

What would going back at this point mean, anyway? Maybe I'm already dead, like Tristan, and there aren't any second chances. And even if not, will the voice come back again? Is it better to die or to slowly go insane?

I open the shop door and look into the room. There are pieces of broken glass on the floor, along with dusty clumps. As a girl, I remember always circling around the room, studying the floor, looking for dropped game tokens. Every time I came, I found at least two or three.

Now, I look at the glass and feel my body shake. I don't know what to do. I feel like I haven't known what to do for the past year, but at some point a voice would always come and tell me what to do. And what about now? Will that voice come once it's too late?

There's a distant sound in the silence, almost like footprints. I run out the back door and down the street.

But even when I'm running, I can still hear footprints. Is that true? Or am I just making it up?

The street's so empty that if someone is following me, it wouldn't be too hard for them to catch me, and no one would know. It's before anything's open, and it's not like people come down here unless they have to.

I keep running. My breaths get short. I need to tell someone, get someone's help.

While I'm running I see something. It's a phone booth. I go inside and stare at the phone stupidly. How do you use these things again? How do you use phones?

My stomach gurgles and groans. There aren't any more PowerBars. The blood in my head evacuatest.

The phone booth is covered in graffiti and pieces of torn flyers taped to the glass. Picking up the phone, I hold it to my ear and hear a dial tone. It's been a while since I've heard one of those.

What's my phone number? What is a phone number?

The dial tone changes to that alarm tone, the one that means "why's it taken you this long to plug in a number, you moron?"

And I start crying. The voice is gone, and I don't know what to do without a voice.

Treatment VII: August 30, 2010

I STILL HAVEN'T LEARNED HOW TO sleep the same again. I'm taking new pills now, and even though I am faithfully taking them every day, the only things that have changed are that I grow less body hair and cry all the time. My mom says this is good prep for birth control pills, and laughs—like there's anything funny about all of this.

I've been laying on my bed for the past two hours in silence. Is it possible to have a phobia of silence? Because now, without a game inside me, I feel like someone's removed my spinal cord. It's amazing how we get used to—and depend on—even the things that drive us insane.

It's been years since I last bothered praying. It was probably early high school when I kept praying that Tristan would notice me, praying that I wouldn't be so alone, but nothing happened. There wasn't a voice to tell me yes or no. And classmates in theology class would talk about their "experiences" with God, but that was just it—I didn't have any experiences. And while teachers kept saying that you don't necessarily experience God in an obvious way—it's called faith for a reason—it felt so fake. Of course it's easy to believe in God if you see him.

But right now, I want to pray again—probably because I don't have any better options. I've tried chamomile, melatonin, eating some crackers—I'm tired of going through the checklist of rituals that might help me fall asleep. So I pray what they do in the movies: "If you're there, come out where I can see you!"

Whether I'm talking to God, or the presence that I feel is watching me, I'm not sure.

But nothing happens. Go figure.

I close my eyes to try to fall asleep again when I feel a light coming from the window. The last time I woke up at two in the morning to light it was because the neighbors decided to host a wild bonfire for burning all their old furniture. But I look out the window and there's no bonfire. There's just light.

Is it morning already? No, it can't be. The light's coming from the side of the house, but the other side of the yard is still dark.

The light comes closer, and there's a figure standing outside the window. I rub my eyes but it's still there. It's coming closer, actually—through the window (is that even possible?).

I open my mouth to scream, but the figure puts a finger on my lips. I recognize him (I assume it's a him)—but I can't exactly describe where or how.

"You have completed POST-HIGH SCHOOL REALITY QUEST. You scored eighteen out of one hundred points," the figure says, biting his lip. "For someone who says she's good at games, you got a depressingly low score."

"You—you—"

"You are in your room. There is a figure that just came through the window. You can't help but think of the angels you've seen pictured in church…"

"I'm *not* crazy! You have been following me around—what I felt—it was real…What the *fuck*?"

"I'd appreciate if you watch your language."

"Right. Sorry. I never used to like to say things like that. I guess it just starts to *happen* at some point…"

"Buffy." The figure gets close to me. I reach out to touch it, but my hand goes through.

"Buffy, the game is over. I hoped that—well—it would make things easier, to frame things like this, but you haven't taken to it well."

"Frame *what* things?"

The figure smiles. "We exist to encourage and guide you. Not to do things for you, but to give you extended opportunities to choose what's right. If that makes sense."

"Okay then." I think about that for a moment. "So is this the part where you tell me what I'm going to do with my life?"

The figure laughs. "Well, I'm not sure about that. But I have come to tell you something: we've reached the end of *this* game. You have a choice now, Buffy. Would you like me to continue, or would you like to return to how things worked before graduation?"

He hovers in front of me watching, waiting. What am I supposed to tell him? It's been so long since my head was silent. Would I really rather be alone again?

"I guess it's too late to undo all the stuff I've done…"

A hand grips my shoulder. It's warm and glows against my skin. "I'm afraid you might've missed the entire point in all of this."

"What's that supposed to mean—"

"It wasn't about *undoing*, Buffy."

I pause, trying to understand. My eyebrows furrow. "I'm not sure I—wait!"

The figure's at the window, like he might just jump out and become part of the sky.

"I'm willing to keep playing," I say. "But if you won't tell me why, at least tell me this: if it's not about 'undoing' or 'redoing,' then what's the point of save slots? What was the point of any of this?"

The figure watches, waiting for me to continue. As if I have more to say.

So I make up more to say. "I guess I mean, they give this false hope that you can go back and retry something. And sometimes, I did get to retry stuff—though I didn't necessarily do any better. In the end, it's just like normal life, that I can't control anything."

Looking over at the figure, I notice one part of him that isn't glowing—in his chest, there's a dark slash like a wound. The dark slash almost looks pixelated, like one of those DVDs that gets scratched too much so when you try to play it, there are frames that get paused and distorted.

Even though he doesn't say anything about it, or make any suggestion toward anything, I know I'm the one that gave him that wound.

The figure smiles. "It sounds like you're beginning to understand."